M000199083

money
power
Respect

Money
Power
Respect

A novel by

ERICK S. GRAY

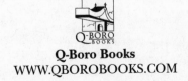

Q-Boro Books
WWW.QBOROBOOKS.COM

An Urban Entertainment Company

Published by Q-Boro Books
Copyright © 2005, 2008 by Erick S. Gray

ISBN-13: 978-1-933967-36-3
ISBN-10: 1-933967-36-6
LCCN: 2007923276

First Printing: February 2008

Printed in the United States of America

10 9 8 7 6 5 4 3 2 1

Cover Copyright © 2007 by Q-BORO BOOKS, all rights reserved.
Cover layout/design by Candace K. Cottrell
Cover photo by JLove; Models Akintola and Essence
Editors: Tee C. Royal, Candace K. Cottrell
Styling by Rowshana Jackson; Clothing by Crown Holder and
Heatherette

Q-BORO BOOKS
Jamaica, Queens NY 11434
WWW.QBOROBOOKS.COM

Dedication

Gone, but never forgotten.
Rest In Peace, Baby Brother.

Corey L. Gray

September 6, 1979 . . . May 14, 2005

We miss you so much.

PROLOGUE.

I once heard someone say that a king isn't always the strongest man, and he isn't always the smartest either. It's really just the people he keeps in his corner who make him a great king. When you have great people by your side, great things can happen. I thought about my situation. Me as a king? I laughed. The people I trusted to be by my side had betrayed me. We weren't kings anyway. We were fuckin' hoodlums. We killed. We robbed. We were true menaces to society. In our world, money was everything. I watched the rich get richer, and the poor didn't get a fuckin' thing.

Some of us have great people by our sides who can mold us to become great kings and leaders, but sometimes we're too ignorant to know it. We get tempted by things of this world, like money and cars. And we think success is having a huge bank account and owning lots of material things. I learned that money and fine things do not equal success. But, I learned that the hard way.

ONE.

Money, money, and more money is what makes the world go round and round every fuckin' day. There was nothing else I loved more than makin' dat paper and ballin' like a muthafucka.

They say that money and fame can change a person. Damn right it does. It changed my ass, dat's for sure. It changed my frame of thought. It changed the way I dressed and the way I saw life. At thirteen I saw how having money could affect people and change their lifestyles. See, when you're pulling in some serious cash, niggas and bitches look at you in a totally different way, especially when you're a young, black-ass lookin' nigga like me. They show you love and respect. But when your ass is broke, and you're down and out, muthafuckas show you no fuckin' respect and no fuckin' love. And dat's the truth. If you can't do for them, then they ain't gonna do for you.

But I loved the attention. I loved hustling, and I loved making money. I loved sex. I loved women. And a steady cash flow kept them around. You keep a dollar in a bitch's hand, and she on your dick like white on rice. I loved to dress in Gucci, Levis, thick gold rope chains, and three finger gold rings. To put it simply, I was a fuckin' showoff.

The niggas I idolized and respected in my hood were men like Fat Cat, Pappy Mason, Supreme, and so on. They had it all: cash, cars, women, and, most important, respect. Around the way, nobody fucked wit' them because of their notorious reputations. And I loved that shit. And I wanted that same status for myself.

So I started hustling for Fat Tony when I was thirteen out in Jamaica, Queens in the summer of 1990. First I was lookout on the block. Then I graduated to bottling the crack and dispensing packages to the dealers in the streets. I was only thirteen and clockin' eight hundred to nine hundred dollars a week. I rode around in BMWs, Mercedes, and Jeeps wit' other hustlers. I had the phat gold rope chain around my neck along wit' the monster three finger ring, Adidas on my feet like Run DMC, and my Lees and Levis around my waist. Yeah, I was dat young nigga doing me back in the day. Them old heads and hustlers out in Queens, they gave me respect because, for one, I was so young and already making dat paper. And two, because I was down wit' Fat Tony. Niggas in the hood knew dat Fat Tony was nobody to fuck wit'.

I was one of the hardest workers Fat Tony had working for him. During the summers of '90 and '91, I hustled from sunup to sundown. I was on the streets grinding—making money. One day Fat Tony took notice of my hard work and called me over.

"Yo, Ricky, c'mere, son . . . let me holla at you fo' a minute," he shouted out to me.

He was standing outside the bodega on Rockaway Boulevard wit' a few of his boys. He always wore t-shirts, shorts, and Nikes. He had a scruffy beard, and got a haircut like twice a month. But his pockets stayed lumped up. No matter how unkempt Fat Tony's appearance was, nobody dared to diss him. He had it like that.

"Yo, Ricky, you my little nigga, right?" Fat Tony put his arm around me.

"Yeah, Fat Tony," I replied.

"Walk wit' me."

I did. He led me down the block to where there were a few niggas crowded around. I had had no idea what was going on. I learned to mind my business when it came to Fat Tony's business.

"I'm gonna take care of you, Ricky, because you do good work for me. You like fourteen, right?"

"Yeah."

When we got to the crowd of men, everybody got quiet and looked at Fat Tony like he was the Messiah or sumthin'. I looked into the crowd and saw this one nigga lookin' terrified. He was surrounded by eight men, and they were all lookin' like they wanted to whip his ass.

"Yo, Ricky, slap dis nigga for me," Fat Tony told me.

"Huh?"

"Yo, slap dis faggot muthafucka!" Fat Tony shouted.

I was lookin' reluctant. The man he wanted me to slap was like six foot three, muscular, and clearly looked like he could whip my ass and Fat Tony's ass wit' one swing. But instead, he was pressed against the wall, looking like he was about to shit on himself.

Fat Tony looked at me and said, "Yo, Ricky, he ain't gonna do shit to you. He pussy! I want you to fuck dis nigga up for me."

He continued to egg me on, along wit' a few other niggas. I felt my heart beating like it was about to explode within me. I looked at the man Fat Tony wanted me to slap, and he stared back wit' this pitiful look on his face.

"He too tall," I said.

"Yo, get da fuck on your knees, nigga!" Fat Tony said to him.

Looking reluctant, the man got down on both his knees without an argument or fight. Fat Tony pushed me toward him. "Slap da shit outta him, Ricky."

Everybody's attention was on me. It was my moment. I knew I couldn't fuck this up. I respected Fat Tony too much to disappoint him. I stared my target in his eyes, and then raised my right hand in the air, and SLAP! I caught him wit' the hard right across his cheek, and that nigga face went red and shit. Fat Tony and his men started laughing.

"Yo, Rick, you hit dat nigga like a fuckin' truck, son," Black said, laughing his ass off. Black was Fat Tony's right hand man.

"Yo, hit dat nigga again," Fat Tony said.

I followed orders again and raised my right hand in the air and came down across the man's face even harder this time. Shit, I hit that nigga so hard, my damn hand started to sting.

Fat Tony, Black, and the rest of them were cracking up laughing. They began cheering me on and shit. They wanted me to do it again. And no lie, I began to get caught up in the moment. They all started slapping me five and telling me that I was the man. But what put the biggest grin on my face was when I heard Fat Tony say, "Yo, dat's my little nigga right there. I told y'all niggas Ricky got heart."

I became content and shit. I no longer cared about the feelings of the man I was slapping. It was about me that day. And I wanted to go out wit' a bang.

"Yo, give me dat bottle," I shouted, grabbing a forty ounce from someone's hand. I looked down at my victim and suddenly shattered the forty ounce across his head. He stumbled and then fell over, and I started to laugh.

"Oh shit, yo, he hit dat nigga wit' the bottle. Yo Ricky, you a wild boy, nigga," Black said to me.

Fat Tony came up to me, laughing. He put his arm around me again. "Dis nigga here, y'all better watch out for my nigga," Fat Tony said. He then looked down at the man I humiliated and said, "Yo, get da fuck up and get da fuck outta here, faggot. Bounce, nigga!"

The man said no words. I noticed that he was bleeding tremendously from his forehead. He looked like he was in pain. But that didn't stop him from jumping up and running across the street like a scared bitch.

"Yo, lets go for a walk," Fat Tony said.

He kept his arm around me while we crossed the street. We stopped in front of another bodega. Black stood behind us.

"Ricky, you know why I let you fuck up and humiliate that nigga like that?"

"Nah, why?"

"Because I can. Who gonna stop me, yo? I run dis shit out here, you hear me? And you know why I let you do it? Because I know you got heart. And you listen, nigga; I like dat. I say sumthin' to you, and you don't hesitate to do it, like some of these bitch-ass niggas I got workin' for me, you know what I'm sayin'? And you ain't even got to worry about homeboy coming back at you. Yo, you could bump into that nigga by yourself tomorrow, and I guarantee he ain't gonna touch you or lay one fuckin' finger on you. You know why? Because he know if he do, I'll come back on him even worse. Niggas fear me out this bitch, because they know I don't play," Fat Tony said.

Fat Tony reached into his pocket and pulled out a wad of bills, mostly hundreds. He continued wit', "You see dis shit, Ricky? Dis is what everybody respects out here: dat money, nigga! Without it, you ain't shit! Niggas don't give a fuck if you're broke, they care about being paid. Niggas will follow this." Fat Tony held up the wad of bills. "Niggas will chase this money till the fuckin' end. You hear me,

Ricky? Niggas live and die for this shit here, and you gotta keep your ends by any means possible. Niggas rob or steal from you, you hunt dat muthafucka down and take care of the situation. Never let any man fuck wit' your bread and butter, baby. Money is power, and power gives you respect. You keep doin' what you doin' out here on these streets, baby, and you gonna see plenty of dat money real soon." Fat Tony walked off wit' Black, and they both got into a silver Benz.

Yo, on da real, Fat Tony's words stuck to me like glue. I looked at a nigga like him and saw what he had, and I wanted the same thing for myself. He wasn't a handsome man, and he wasn't the best dressed man in the hood, but niggas envied and feared that muthafucka. He was definitely respected.

I looked at niggas like Fat Tony and other hustlers, and compared them to my father. My father had nothing in his name but overdue bills, a fucked up car, and was living paycheck to paycheck. I care for my pops, but I could never see myself living his way of life. It was too boring and too broke for me.

My money-making days wit' Fat Tony were good until the spring of '92. I was fifteen. It was a bright and sunny Friday afternoon, and everybody was outside in the hood, either getting wet in the Johnny pumps on the streets, playing ball on the basketball courts, riding their bikes up and down the streets, or trying to kick it to a female. Me, I was playing skelly on the streets and losing as usual. We would play for dollars, but when I lost, I never paid up. I didn't have to. Niggas already knew who I was at fifteen. I had a name for myself, and the older boys, they never fucked wit' me. In fact, some of the older boys would cling to me around the way because they knew my status wit' Fat Tony.

I was about to take my turn in the game when Fat Tony's silver Benz pulled up on the block. The game stopped when the Benz parked. Everybody knew the car. Black stepped out first, and then Fat Tony came from behind the passenger's side.

"Yo, Ricky, c'mere, son," Fat Tony called out to me.

He didn't have to tell me twice. I dropped what I was doing and ran over to Fat Tony.

"What up, Fat Tony?" I asked.

"Get in the car."

I glanced back at my friends, shrugged my shoulders, and jumped into the back seat. I knew not to ask any questions; I just did what I was told. Black jumped in on the driver's side, and Fat Tony rode shotgun.

It was the first time I ever rode in Fat Tony's Benz, and I treasured every moment in silence. It was roomy in the back, and the air conditioning cooled me off quickly from the afternoon sun.

It was about a fifteen-minute drive before we got to Hollis, Queens. Black stopped in front of this white and blue two-story house.

"C'mon, step out," Fat Tony said.

I got out the car and was a little nervous. Fat Tony came up to me and put his arm around me. "You're a soldier, Ricky. I like you. So as of today, I'm promoting you. You're going to be handling product going in and out of the 40 projects."

"Word?"

"You hold it down for me, nigga. Ayyite?"

"Of course."

I followed Black and Fat Tony into the house. When we walked in, the place was empty: no furniture, no pictures, and nothing that symbolized a home. I knew it had to be a front. I followed both men down into the basement. We met up wit' two more of Fat Tony's people. I knew the two men who waited in the basement. They were killers; their names definitely did ring out around the way: Prince and KT.

When Fat Tony came down, they nodded their heads and remained silent.

"Yo, where his bitch ass at?" Fat Tony asked.

"In da back room," Prince said.

"Bring his bitch ass out!" Fat Tony said.

Prince and KT went to the back room. I stood behind Fat Tony, being quiet as a mouse. The basement was concrete and bare. I also noticed stains on the floor. My heart began to beat faster and faster. I was fifteen, and I should have been outside playing basketball, causing mischief, or hollering at girls, but instead I was hanging wit' a drug kingpin, his right hand man, and two well-known killers.

Prince and KT dragged a man tied to a chair out from the back room. He was tied up wit' rope and had duct tape around his mouth. His eyes were swollen, blood trickled from his eyes, and he mumbled something under the duct tape as he squirmed in the chair.

Black walked up to him and hit him real hard. Fat Tony then turned to me and said, "You see this nigga here, Ricky? You taking over for him. Dis muthafucka been robbing from me, mixing my product with some cheap shit, and then hustling my shit on his own. You steal from me, muthafucka? You thought I wouldn't find out? And dat's not the worst. You snitching, Pete?"

Pete squirmed and mumbled something again. But it was incoherent.

"Yo, Pete, I'm gonna show you what happens to niggas that do me wrong," Fat Tony said. "Yo, y'all two niggas start handling y'all business on dis nigga."

Prince smiled, and then pulled out a huge knife. KT grabbed his head, and then Prince took the knife and began cutting away at his ear. Pete tried to fight, and fidgeted even harder, screaming out in pain from under the duct tape. I turned my head. I was wide-eyed and shit. But Fat Tony grabbed my head, making me look, and said, "Don't turn your head from this, Ricky. This is da game. This is what happens to niggas that fuck wit' me and think I'm stupid. You get butchered out dis bitch."

Prince cut off Pete's ear and held it in his hand. The blood that gushed out from Pete's wound was crazy.

"Cut off his next fuckin' ear!" Fat Tony ordered.

And Prince didn't hesitate. He went straight for Pete's other ear and cut that shit off too. Pete was in severe pain. He wiggled and twisted so hard, he fell over in the chair and landed on his side. Everybody laughed.

After Prince cut off Pete's ears, he went for the fingers next, slicing off his pinky and then his ring finger. I felt like I was about to throw up. There was so much blood, and after a while, Pete stopped fidgeting, and just lay there whimpering—Prince and KT were hacking off a piece of him one by one—gradually too. This was how ugly the game got. It was horrendous for me. I watched them slaughter a man in cold-blood. I was speechless.

"You saw enough?" Fat Tony asked me.

I nodded. I wanted to leave.

"Walk wit' me outside, Ricky."

He didn't have to tell me twice. We went to the back yard. It was only me and Fat Tony.

"I'm sorry you had to see dat, but, Ricky, dis is da game . . . dis shit is real life. I can't afford to fuck up, and you can't either. You do right by me, and I'll do right by you. Pete, he had it coming. He was too smart for his own good. And don't feel sorry for dat nigga; he dug his own fuckin' grave. I ain't running no daycare out here. I see my soldiers and workers as men, no matter how old you are. Everybody gets treated the same in my camp. You got his position now, Ricky, and I expect you to hold it down. Don't let me down. Don't fuck shit for me, or yourself. You hear me, nigga?"

I nodded.

Fat Tony then went into his pockets and pulled out a wad

of bills. He peeled off ten hundreds and put in my hand, a
G. One thousand dollars. I was excited.

"Dat's your first payment right there. Don't spend it all
on one bitch," he joked.

When he put that money into my hand, it made me forget about everything. I thought about the new Jordans I
wanted to buy, and I wanted to cop that new herringbone
chain I saw on Jamaica Avenue the other day. This is what it
was about for me—having a lump of cash in my hand and
being able to do whatever I wanted. I knew that I would
never put myself in Pete's position. Fat Tony was too good
to me to betray him.

"Go wait in the car. We'll be done shortly," Fat Tony said.

I walked over to the car, counting out my money on the
streets. I wasn't going to fuck up. I was confident in that.
Shit, I was making too much money to fuck up.

But I never got the chance to fuck up, because three days
later, Fat Tony caught a bullet in the back of his head by
rival competition for the drug trade in Queens. Black got
arrested a month later for possession, murder, attempted
murder, and conspiracy. The feds hit that nigga wit' thirty-
seven counts, and he got convicted on all thirty-seven
counts and is now doing twenty-five to life in a federal
prison. Fat Tony's crew was in chaos; niggas were either
dying or getting hit wit' football numbers.

The game was changing in the early nineties, and a lot of
niggas started dying, dropping like flies and shit. So I
stayed low for a minute and started going back to classes at
August Martin High School. I stopped going to school for a
moment because I was makin' too much money on the
streets. I knew I had to get back in school. I needed something to do in the mornings and afternoons. I did think
about getting myself an education like my parents always
told me, but the money and streets were more appealing.

But no matter how low a profile I tried to keep, I was still a showoff. I still wanted to be dat nigga, especially in high school where popularity meant everything.

I was a young nigga.

I got down wit' this nigga named Kinko when I was in the tenth grade. He had this connect so that we could sell marijuana, crack, and other minor things in the streets and in the schools. I had to be down. I had a rep to maintain. So Kinko and I established a clientele throughout Queens for our drug sales, and we were both clockin' like ten to fifteen thousand dollars in one month off the sale of marijuana and crack. Not a bad figure when you're only fifteen or sixteen. What can I say? Kinko and I were both good businessmen even at our young ages. We knew how to flip a dollar and make a hundred. We moved eight balls for $150. A gram from us went for $50 to $90, rocks went for $10 to $15, and an ounce from us went for $1,200.

Now, Kinko was a year older than me and a grimy-ass nigga. He was about five feet nine wit' a lean frame and braids. He looked like a thug, wit' the do-rags and jewelry. When I first met him, I heard he was kinda crazy. I heard stories that he committed his first murder when he was ten. He shot a fifteen-year-old kid in the head for snatching a pack of candy out of his hand. They said he only did three years in a juvenile detention center for that.

We met through this bitch I was fuckin' out in Hollis. He heard about my name from back in the day when I ran wit' Fat Tony and his crew, and he wanted to link up wit' me. He came through shorty's crib one afternoon looking for me. I never heard of Kinko until shorty put me on to him. She told me his name rang out in Hollis, and he was the type of nigga I needed to get down wit' if I wanted to get that money.

When we first met, he sized me up. We talked and I knew he was bout it. He was a thug from the moment he opened up his mouth. Kinko's street motto was, "Do unto them, before they do unto you." In this game you had to strike first before your enemies came at you.

He was definitely a bugged-out nigga, but he knew how to get his. He knew how to network and he knew how to put fear in niggas' hearts. And that was important in the game. You had to know how to put your product out there and have your clientele stick around. And you had to know how to handle a situation before it handled you. You had to protect your product and your clientele. If you ain't got clientele, then you ain't got product, because those were the two ingredients in getting money on the streets. And when you had both, then you had to have heat or muscle to protect what's yours from the wolves and scavengers in the game.

At the time, Kinko was sixteen—a year older than me—but the nigga had been around. He could move weed and yayo not in a month, but in a day. He got kicked out of three schools, so the nigga dropped out and became a full-time hustler.

One day in my history class, my history teacher, Mr. Richard Jenkins, asked his students, "What do you want out of life?"

Man, I knew the answer to that question right away. When Mr. Jenkins came around to ask me what I wanted out of life, I stood up and answered, "I want it all, Mr. Jenkins. I want to drive the finest cars that money can buy, live in the most extravagant homes, and have jewelry like these rappers in videos. I want the ladies. Word, Mr. Jenkins. I wanna be successful and do me lovely. You know what I'm sayin'? I always wanna have a pocket filled wit' cash, and spend as much as I wanna spend. Forget budgeting and dat layaway shit. I wanna be able to buy whatever I want, whenever I want. I feel dat if you gotta put stuff on layaway, then you can't afford it in the first place."

After my words, I smiled down at this fine honey dat was seated in front of me. Her name was Kiesha, and she had a big butt. I was kinda sweating her.

"So, you want to live like Donald Trump, I assume, Mr. Johnson?" Mr. Jenkins asked.

"Better."

"Seems like you're already living part of that life now, Mr. Johnson," Mr. Jenkins said, referring to my lifestyle and clothing. That day I had a phat, costly gold herringbone around my neck, a gold bracelet on my wrist, and a phat diamond ring on my pinky. I was sporting Karl Kani Jeans, fresh new beige Timberlands on the soles of my feet, diamond studded earrings, and a Cartier watch.

"You gotta live your life, Mr. Jenkins. I mean, bitches today ain't gonna love and respect a broke-ass nigga, right? Money makes da world go round. Wit'out it, we don't exist."

"Why we gotta be bitches?" this one girl chided.

I sighed and replied, "I'm sorry . . . I meant these hoes today . . ."

"No, nigga, you need to respect a sistah. What if I went and called your mama a bitch?" she returned.

"Hey, you da only one up in here get offended by my statement. If da shoe fits, then a ho's a ho."

"No nigga, you see. . . ."

"Hey, everybody settle down," Mr. Jenkins shouted. "Ricky, what I tell you about using that kind of language in my classroom? Act like a gentleman."

"I'm sorry, Mr. Jenkins."

Shorty who caught the attitude wit' me sighed and rolled her eyes at me. Fuck her anyway, she was just mad because I had her suck my dick last year, and I didn't want to get wit' her. I didn't even know her name.

"Money isn't everything, Mr. Johnson," Mr. Jenkins said, continuing wit' our topic.

"Yeah, well, tell dat to my girl," I joked, stirring up the class wit' a little laughter.

Mr. Jenkins smiled. "Well, do you believe money makes everyone happy? Do you believe that those without it always live a poor and problematic life? That the poor, or the ones who are not fortunate to live a lavish life, are constantly unhappy all the time? And the ones with money, do you believe they are always fortunate and continuously happy?"

"Man, listen. Where I'm from, if you ain't got it, you ain't living. Cause in my hood, those wit' dough like that, they get all the respect. While these bum-ass niggas out here, they get stepped all over and get played out."

"Before I start my lecture today," Mr. Jenkins said, "I have one piece of advice to you, Mr. Johnson. The more money you have, the more problems you gain. Not everyone is your friend when it comes to having a lot of money. Don't let greed and wealth destroy the world around you. Money is not everything. It doesn't have to control your life, and you do not have to wreck others' lives to maintain riches. The love for money can be the root to all evil."

I looked at him and replied, "Nah, I believe the lack of money is the root of all evil. Man, you just saying that because you broke and get paid a teacher's salary. It's all good, Mr. Jenkins. You're right, money ain't for everyone."

I had the entire class roaring wit' laughter from my humorous comment. Mr. Jenkins was a cool dude. He was in his late forties and a handsome man for his age. He had grayish hair and reminded me of Morgan Freeman. He actually held cool classes. You could talk to him about anything, even about sex, and he wouldn't get offended or coy about the subject. Sometimes Mr. Jenkins would deter from his scheduled class lecture and the class would end up discussing certain events, like drugs, sex, the streets, and even shit that was wrong wit' the school. Although he was a history teacher, the majority of the time we talked about the present or the future.

The bell for the next class went off, and everybody jumped from their seats to rush to their next class.

"Mr. Johnson, I want to have a word with you," Mr. Jenkins said.

"Now?"

"Yes. I'll write you a pass to your next class."

"Ayyite, whatever," I said, but I ain't need no pass, because I wasn't planning on going to my next class anyway.

I took a seat in front of the classroom. It was just the two of us. Mr. Jenkins took a seat behind his desk, looked at me and asked, "How's your father doing?"

"He ayyite, working everyday as usual."

"Tell him I said hi."

"Will do."

Mr. Jenkins then shuffled through some papers on his desk. He then looked up at me and said, "Mr. Johsnson, I've known you since the fifth grade when I used to teach at 223. You were a good kid back then ... bright and full of dreams. But your behavior has changed a lot."

"My behavior? I'm doin' ayyite in your class, right? You're passing me. You told me last week."

"It's not your grades; it's the way you act in my class: calling women hoes and bitches, flaunting money and jewelry in the hallways, and hanging with the wrong people outside of the school."

I sucked my teeth, because I wasn't trying to hear what he had to say to me. "What you getting at?"

"I want to see you have a goal. I want to see you accomplish something in your life. You cut class all the time, I barely saw you in school your freshmen year, you take your education like a joke. Where do you think you're gonna end up in a few years with the road you're taking now?"

"C'mon, Mr. Jenkins, we go to school to learn how to get

paid in the future, right? I mean after this, it's supposed to be college, and after college, then what? I'm living the American dream now; the streets taught me how to get paid. People respect me around my way because I get dat money. Without it, I would be a nobody."

"Mr. Johnson, there are no shortcuts in life. You need to understand that. What you put into life is what you get out. How long do you think your lifestyle is going to last? Answer me that. You're a young and smart kid. Don't waste your youth and your life with these streets. Everyday, I watch you get sucked in deeper and deeper, and it bothers me that you're foolish enough to jump into what you think these streets have to offer you."

"I can handle myself out in these streets."

Mr. Jenkins reached into his pocket and pulled out a card. "Take this. I want you to attend some youth meetings I have on Friday nights and Saturday morings. It's at the youth center on Merrick Blvd."

"Yeah, I know where it's at," I said, taking the card.

"Good, I want to see you there sometime in the future. You get to talk about your problems, and meet with young men your own age. It's a good program; I help young kids like you get their diploma and enroll them into colleges. And you can also bring your father along."

I stood up, looking nonchalant and shit, and replied, "Yeah, we'll see. Can I go now?"

Mr. Jenkins let out a low sigh then said, "Remember this: determination begins with being focused, becoming a man is your reward. Become a man, Mr. Johnson. Allow people to help you. Money is not the answer to all your problems. You need to learn that."

"It helped so far," I said. "You have a good afternoon, Mr. Jenkins. I'm out."

I walked out his classroom without a second thought to what he'd just told me. *Become a man. I'm already a man, and getting paid like one, too.* Mr. Jenkins was bugging. I wanted to chase that dollar until I couldn't chase it anymore. Mr. Jenkins was a cool teacher in the fifth grade. But now, he was all in my business—like he really cared for a nigga. He probably got a bonus for every student he helped to graduate.

I didn't give a fuck about some pass to my next class, I wasn't going anyway. I was on my way out them school doors to link up wit' Kinko for the day.

When I came down the bottom steps, this face caught my immediate attention. I knew that face. He had on a school safety uniform, and when he noticed me, he glared at me. *What da fuck?* I noticed a small scar running down the side of his face, by his left eye. I must have put that scar there. He continued to stare at me. *Fuck him.* I walked right by him. The last time I saw that face, I gave it two hard slaps because Fat Tony told me to, and then I had smashed a bottle over his head. Ironic now that he was in a school safety uniform. I figured he was a pussy then, and he was still a pussy.

TWO.

In the spring of '93 I was sixteen and I needed to step my reputation in school up even more. A nigga like me? Shit, I was the best dressed in the school. I stayed wit' proper gear and I was one of the most popular students in August Martin. I had these bitches ready to fuck a nigga. They were sweating a nigga like I was Michael Jordan. And I had these niggas out here dying to be like me. Everybody was sweating my style and taste. I was definitely that nigga, and I was going to continue to be dat popular nigga. I had the haters on my back too; they wanted me to fuck up.

So, to shut the fuckin' haters up and have them envy me even more, Kinko and I went out to this car dealership up on Hillside Avenue and I copped me a '91 Nissan Pathfinder. I got tired of footing it and decided to cop me something official, a sweet ride to profile in. The dealer was crooked. We showed him a ton of green, and he helped Kinko and me get around reporting the cash transaction. I put the truck in my mother's name.

The truck ran me twelve thousand dollars. We negotiated wit' the dealer since Kinko and I were both paying cash, and the dealer hooked us up wit' good prices. I paid another three thousand dollars on expensive luxury items that I added to the car. Everything was power, from the windows and locks, down to the steering. The seats and interior were all black leather, and I had a moon roof for those warm summer days. The truck was money green wit' tinted windows. Then, of course I had to add a phat music system to my ride. The entire system ran me five thousand dollars, which included a CD changer wit' cassette player. The speakers and amp in the back pushed up to 1,500 watts of power.

I got my truck that Friday afternoon, and that Monday after school I was parked in front of Martin blasting some Onyx. "Throw your guns in the air." I was sixteen-years old and had money and things like the rest of them old ballers around the way. I remembered the students coming out after their eighth period class and their eyes lit up when they saw me profiling hard in front of the school. I had the bass thumping and my jewelry was gleaming. I got the smiles and the hellos, and I also saw the envy and the hate. That same afternoon I bagged up this fine shorty named Tiffany. She lived out in Far Rockaway. I wasn't worried about my girl finding out because she lived in Brooklyn and she ain't rock wit' bitches around here like dat.

Tiffany, she was cool, and nothing but a quick fuck for a nigga like me.

When the end of May came around, word around the school was that I was hot. I had this faggot-ass security toy cop muthafucka on my ass. Michael Stone was his name; I called him scarface, mocking him. He hated me. I mean, I couldn't blame him; I did give him his small scar. But he was starting to interfere wit' my business in the school. I didn't stress him, or tried not to. In my mind, I was making too much money to stop hustling, and I thought I was too smart to get caught out there like dat. The only time I brought a large amount of drugs into the school was once a week when I had to re-up certain muthafuckas I had pushing for me. I would move mostly ounces, and once in a while bring a pound or two of that hash. I would stash the shit in my gym locker during homeroom and hit niggas off at the end of the day. I had eight niggas in the school working for me.

"Ricky, don't you have class, nigga? I'm gonna write you up," Stone said to me.

"Nigga, why you sweating me for?" I asked him.

"Because I can, and it's my job to fuck wit' you, nigga. You ain't ill."

"Ayyite, faggot, fuck you and your mother!" I replied.

"Nigga, what you say to me?" Stone shouted, walking up to me. He grabbed me by my shirt and pushed me against the wall. There was no one around but him, me, and a few of his buddies.

"Yo, get da fuck off me!" I shouted.

"Nigga, I know what you about in this school, don't forget that shit. You ain't here for no muthafuckin' education . . . you a hustler, nigga, and still a bum nigga!"

"Whatever, scarface. Get da fuck off me before I have you lose your petty fuckin' job, nigga," I said and then gave him a smirk.

He let me go and took two steps back. I continued wit', "You can never be like me, nigga. Remember dat shit. Just because Fat Tony ain't around no more, don't think you can run up on me. I'll still get you fucked up, nigga."

"Fuck you, Ricky. You gonna get yours, nigga. I'm watching you, yo. When you fuck up, I'm on dat ass," he threatened.

I chuckled and walked away, taking his threats lightly.

I met up wit' Kinko two days later and I told him about my situation wit' Stone. It was the first time in months that

I was actually getting nervous about selling drugs in the school. I never had any previous problems until Michael Stone came into the school. Now, I was watching over my shoulder constantly, thinking security was going to run up on me at any given time. Kinko told me he was going to take care of it. He knew about the nigga, and how much of an asshole he was. But he said we had bigger problems.

"Like what?" I asked.

"We need to take out our competition," he said.

"Fuck you talking about, Kinko?" I asked. "We got this shit on lock."

"Nigga, you need to keep your ears to the streets and fuckin' listen to what it got to say. You're too comfortable, Ricky. But word is these niggas from Far Rockaway wanna move in on our shit."

We both were parked in back of the school by the football field. His '92 Blazer was parked behind my Pathfinder, gleaming in the afternoon sun, looking like it was still fresh off the lot.

"Far Rock niggas?" I said. "Like who?"

"I keep hearing about some nigga named Heavy. You know about him?" Kinko asked.

I shook my head. "Nah, never heard of the nigga before."

"One of my niggas from out there keep informing me dat our names be constantly coming out of this nigga's mouth. He a hating-ass nigga, talking shit, saying to his boys that we too young to be clockin' money like dat."

I sighed.

"I don't like dat shit, Ricky," Kinko added. He pulled out a cigarette and placed it between his lips while he searched in his pockets for a light. "I'm ready to murk dis nigga, son!"

I can't say that Kinko was a nervous nigga constantly, but sometimes I felt he be stressing about little shit. I never heard of a Heavy, so it was obvious to me that he was a nobody. He was probably just some cornball nigga who saw what we had and wished he could be us. I felt that the nigga wasn't worth me stressing over.

"Yo, if I was you, I wouldn't even be stressing dat shit. I ain't never heard of the nigga, and you ain't never heard of the nigga until now," I told him.

He took a pull from his cigarette, exhaled a cloud of smoke, and replied, "Fuck you talking about, Ricky? We gotta take care of this shit."

"Like how, nigga?" I asked.

"There's only one way to handle the competition," Kinko said. "Money is too good out here for us to have some whack-ass nigga trying to come along and fuck up our shit."

"Yeah, well, I told you about that faggot nigga Stone. Dat nigga clockin' me hard, Kinko. Plus I'm hearing that they gonna install metal detectors in the school next year. You know, ever since they had that shooting in Thomas Jefferson like two years ago, schools be trying to tighten up and crack down on certain shit."

"Ricky, don't even worry about Stone. I told you I'm gonna handle that. And as for the metal detectors, nigga, all you gotta do is wait till third period and bring your shit in around the back. Have some nigga you know open the door up for you every day . . . simple as that."

"Yeah, ayyite."

I glanced at the time. It was five in the afternoon. I told Kinko to page me later. I gave him dap and bounced. My shorty, Des, had been blowing up my pager for a minute now. I knew she was gonna be heated if I didn't call her ass right back. She probably assumed I was out fuckin' another bitch.

I jumped into my truck, made a quick U-turn, and drove to Rockaway Boulevard.

I lived near the school. It was about a five or ten minute

walk. All I had to do was cross Baisely Pond Park, and August Martin was right across the street. But I would rather drive my truck everyday and show the school what I was working wit'. Why have it, if you couldn't push it and floss?

I lived in these low rise project buildings that are located on Rockaway and Sutphin Boulevard. The buildings had been around for a few years. The city built them in the early eighties, and ever since, major drug activity had been prevalent in the area.

My parents moved into Jamaica, Queens in '86 when I was nine-years-old, and I've rested my head in this neighborhood ever since. I've seen a lot of niggas come and go, but I hung around the big dawgs during my younger years and made good money—illegally, of course.

I pulled up into the housing parking lot, parking my ride in my official spot. I got out and activated my alarm, but it ain't like I was worried about niggas stealing my shit, 'cause everyone knew me around there. And they knew my ride.

I saw that my pops was home. His blue Cutlass Ciera was parked in his usual spot. I headed to my apartment, greeting a few of my neighbors as I walked through the low risers.

I walked into my crib and my pops was sitting on the couch. He was watching TV wit' a beer in one hand and the remote in the other.

"What up, Pop?" I greeted, standing behind him.

"Hey," my pops greeted back in a dry and slow voice.

"Everything good?" I was worried about him lately. Ever since Moms left, he had never been the same.

My moms left Pops and me three years ago. I was thirteen when she bounced. She took off wit' some rich Jamaican man who promised her the world. She had no problem leaving her family behind for that promise. I hated her for what she put my pops through. That man loved my moms. He worked his ass off his whole life to try and please her and buy her the things she wanted. But that wasn't good enough for her. She wanted more out of life. She eventually found what she wanted wit' another man.

The day she left, my father was crushed. He could never comprehend how his wife of twelve years could leave him so easily. He thought they had love. Obviously, their love wasn't that strong. Well, hers wasn't anyway.

I remember when I was young and I would hear my parents arguing in the kitchen from my bedroom. My moms would be beefing about how she needed a better place to live. She hated the projects. Her main excuse to my father was, "It's not safe for Ricky here." But it's funny because when she left, she left her son behind. My moms stayed bitching about bills, a better car, and money. Face it, she was a materialistic woman. My grandparents, my mother's parents, had money. I met them once. They lived upstate, had a four bedroom crib wit' a swimming pool and acres of land. And my father, he was from the Bronx and worked hard all his life. I never met my father's parents.

My pops was a mechanic, and he knew everything there was to know about cars. To this day, I'll never understand how the two of 'em hooked up, coming from such different worlds.

But you see me. That's why I did what I did. And I was gonna continue to do what I did 'cause these women don't want a broke nigga. It ain't about love. It's about who's in control and who's banking what. Females respect your wallet more than they respect the heart.

I left my pops moping in his chair and went into my bedroom. It looked like he had a hard day, so I didn't want to disturb him.

I gave Des a call back since she paged me like six fuckin' times.

"Damn, Ricky, why you wait so long to call me back?" Des barked over the phone.

"I was taking care of business," I said calmly to her.

"Business? I'm supposed to be your girl, and you ain't got the respect to call me back? What if I had an emergency?"

"Then you woulda put 911 in my pager."

"Whatever! Where were you?"

"Des, I told you, I was taking care of business. C'mon, don't be coming at me wit' dat bullshit. I ain't gotta fuckin' explain myself to you all the time."

"Why you gotta get loud for?"

"'Cause you getting on my nerves right now. What da fuck you page me for?"

I didn't mean to get so hostile, but this bitch could be so insecure sometimes, it be driving a nigga crazy.

"I forgot," she uttered. "So, you coming over? 'Cause my moms leaving for work tonight."

"Word?"

"Yeah. I ain't seen you in like three days. I miss you, boo," she said.

"Yeah, I'll be out there. Give me an hour."

"Ayyite, boo. Call me before you leave."

"Yeah, whatever!" I said and then hung up.

I met Des a year ago at some house party in Brooklyn that Kinko and I went to. It was cool—ghetto hood style. Des was fourteen at the time. She turned fifteen three months after we met.

But on the real, Des' priorities were fucked up. She lived at home wit' her moms, who worked mostly nights. Des was a bitch who cared about materialistic shit more than anything else. She was always concerned about the way she looked and dressed. If you was a nigga who was bank-ing—you could fuck her. I got to knock them boots a week after we met. And the only reason I ain't get to fuck sooner was because her moms was on vacation when we first met.

Des was a bad bitch though to be only fifteen. Her body was like—Whoa! She had the phattest ass, the smallest waistline, and titties like you wouldn't believe. The bitch was fine. She had that caramel complexion going on, wit' brown eyes, thick firm thighs, and long jet black hair reaching down her back.

I was wit' her because she was definitely a prize to have under your arm. A nigga wit' money needs a fine-ass wifey to sport around. Even though she was a young bitch, Des could pull off being older. She was looking like she could be in her early twenties, fuckin' wit' niggas' heads and shit.

And the pussy—shiiiittt—off da hook, son. She was having a nigga's toes curling whenever I was deep inside her. Her shit was dat fuckin' good. I'd trick on the bitch, give her money to splurge, get her hair and nails done, and have her shop at the mall, where she'd spend about six hundred dollars in an hour—all because her head game was so tight.

Around seven that evening, I started to head out to go and check Des. My pops was still on the couch watching TV.

"Yo, Pop, I'm heading out. You want me to bring you something back to eat?" I asked.

He shook his head no. "I'm okay, son. Be safe out there."

"Always," I replied and walked out the front door.

I jumped into my truck and headed out to East New York, where Des stayed wit' her moms. She was the only child.

I got to her crib around seven-thirty and called the bitch from a payphone on the corner of her block. Sometimes I be thinking that I need to get myself a cell phone and save myself time and quarters.

After the third ring, Des finally picked up.

"Hello," she answered.

"Yeah, it's me. I'm outside. Everything cool?" I asked.

"Yeah, my moms left for work an hour ago. I'm gonna leave the door open."

"Ayyite."

I hung up and walked down the block. I got to her crib and saw the front door slightly opened and I walked right in. I didn't give a fuck about her neighbors seeing me 'cause they didn't know me. And whatever they said, that was on Des.

I walked into her crib and Des was standing in the middle of her living room smiling, wearing just a white t-shirt. She had her black hair pulled up in two long pigtails, and I knew she ain't have no bra on cause I could see her large breasts protruding through her shirt.

I was instantly turned on. Des was looking so fuckin' sexy, wit' her thick legs glistening wit' baby oil.

"What?" She playfully asked, taunting me, twirling one of her pigtails around her index finger.

"You know what's up, coming downstairs looking all good," I said, smiling. I felt the bulge in my jeans rising already.

I closed her front door, stepped to her, pulled her into my arms, and started to kiss and grope around her fine figure.

"Damn, you sure you're only fifteen?" I taunted, feeling up her body, my hands grasping her phat ass. We started to tongue kiss. I just got so fuckin' horny that I said to myself, *fuck upstairs*, and I tossed Des down on her mother's leather sofa. Wit' her on her back, I began to pull up her shirt, exposing the fact dat she wasn't wearing any panties. Des bent her knees back and cocked her legs wide in the air. I loved it. My dick got so hard that it felt like it was about to rip through my jeans. Her pussy was phat and moist and not overcome wit' ugly pubic hairs, but looking nicely trimmed. Shit, if I ate pussy I woulda went down on her, but that wasn't my thang.

I quickly began to unbuckle my pants. Still positioned in between my shorty's thighs, I pulled my pants and boxers down to my ankles and leaned toward Des, pushing my dick into her. She gasped out, clutching my back as I started to thrust my erection deeply inside her.

We grunted, moaned, and got deep into our sexual bliss for about five minutes until I felt myself about to cum. I gave it three more thrusts and then I quickly pulled out and busted off on her stomach. I was done.

"Oh, shit," I muttered.

"You okay?" she asked.

"Yeah, I'm cool." Damn, she got some good ass pussy. A nigga like me couldn't even last five minutes. She had that young, wet, and tight pussy.

I got back on my feet and pulled up my pants.

"Damn, Ricky. You can't go get me some tissue or something to wipe your babies off my stomach?" she said. She looked down at her belly, seeing the huge nut I just let off on her.

"Yeah, hold on." I went into the kitchen and got some paper towels for her.

"Look at my hair. You stay fuckin' my shit up," she complained. "I'm gonna need some money to get my shit right again."

I looked at her sideways. "Yeah, ayyite."

"I'm serious, Ricky. I can't be going outside with my shit looking all wild."

"Your hair is fine. Don't front, you just want money."

She sucked her teeth. "I'm sayin' though, I'm supposed to be your shorty, right? I thought that we were going out this weekend. You were gonna to take me to Red Lobster and the movies."

"Yeah, we still down."

I was 'bout ready to leave her place 'cause there wasn't a

reason for me to stay any longer. I already got what I wanted. I know it sounds fucked up, but that's how it be sometimes.

"Yo, I'm about to be out, Des."

She looked at me. "Why you leaving so soon? My moms ain't gonna be home till four. We got time to chill."

"I got things to take care of."

"Well, before you leave, can I at least get two hundred dollars from you?" she asked, wit' her hand already out.

"For what?" I shouted.

She sighed. "I told you. I need to get my hair done, along wit' a few other things."

"Yeah, whatever," I said, reaching into my pocket to pull out my knot of hundreds I had rolled together wit' a rubber-band. I peeled off three hundred dollars to give to her. I gave her the extra hundred because the sex was tight.

A broad smile appeared on her face as she waited for my money.

"Here," I said. "Try not to spend it all in one place."

"Thank you, boo," she said as she planted one long kiss on me. "So dis weekend we gonna do our thang, right?"

"It's about us, you feel me?" I said.

"I wish you could stay longer, baby. But I understand, you gotta go make dat money and do you," she said.

"I'm glad you understand dat."

"And you're not cheating on me, right?"

I sucked my teeth, "You better go somewhere wit' that insecurity shit, Des. What I told you about dat already? I'm about money, I ain't got time to cheat," I said.

"I know, but I just be getting jealous sometimes. You come over, fuck me, and then leave like dat. You know what I'm sayin'? I know you care for me and all . . . I just wanna see my man more often."

"Come here and give me another kiss before I leave," I

said, pulling her close to me. I embraced her in my arms, shoved my tongue down her throat, and slobbed her down for a good five minutes.

"I'll call you tomorrow," I told her.

I swear, the one advantage wit' fuckin' a young bitch, is you fuckin' wit' a dumb bitch. Des was fine and sexy as fuck. But up top? I guess God didn't give her all her change back. The bitch actually believed I was being faithful to her. Shit, I looked too good to be faithful to one lady. I had about half a dozen hoes holding me down throughout Queens and Brooklyn. I tricked on a few bitches here and there. I wasn't tight wit' money. It came fast in my hands and went out just as fast. If I spent a hundred, I'd see $500 the next day. Cash was not a problem for me.

When I walked out her crib, my pager went off. It was Kinko. I called him back from a corner payphone.

"What up, you page me right?" I said.

"Where you at now, nigga?"

"I just left my girl's crib. Why?" I said.

"Yo, niggas from Far Rock got Corely," he said.

"What?"

"Dey shot Corely, and robbed him for five large, son. He in da hospital right now."

Corely was Kinko's first cousin. He was older than Kinko by three years. He was a little slow. He couldn't read for shit, but he knew how to count money. And when it came to the streets, Corely was no joke; he put the murder game down like it was free to kill a nigga.

"Where he at?" I asked.

"Jamaica Hospital. He got shot three times. These niggas disrespected me, son, you hear me?" I knew Kinko was upset. Corely was like the only family he had.

"I'm on my way, yo," I told him.

I jumped into my Pathfinder and did 60 to Queens.

THREE.

The next day at school, Kinko was blowing up my pager again, putting in 911. Corely was in stable condition at Jamacia Hospital. One bullet grazed his head. The other two struck him in the abdomen and right side of his chest. It was fucked up. Like he needed more damage done to his brain.

I left school to go use a payphone outside by the corner. I called his cell phone.

"Yo, who this?" he shouted.

"You paged me, right?"

"Yo, Ricky, where you at now?" he asked, sounding like shit was urgent.

"School, why?"

"I need to link up wit' you soon," Kinko said.

"Now?"

"Yeah now, nigga."

"Ayyite, yo. Meet me in back of the football field in half an hour. Dat's cool wit' you?"

"I'm on my way now."

I hung up the phone and stood there for a minute, thinking some shit musta really went down. I didn't wanna go back into school. It didn't make any sense going back in when I was coming back out to meet up wit' Kinko. I parked my Pathfinder behind the football field and waited for Kinko.

Fifteen minutes later, Kinko pulled his Blazer up in front of my ride. He quickly got out, walked toward my truck, and hopped into the passenger side. His whole demeanor was edgy.

"Yo, what up?" I asked.

"I think you got a snitch in your crew," Kinko told me.

"Snitch. Who, nigga?" I could've sworn I was tight wit' my niggas I had hustling for me.

"You know this nigga named Terrance? I think he da one running your fuckin' business to that toy cop up in da school."

"Terrance? Nah, nigga. He making money. I'm looking out for that nigga lovely. Why would he be hating like dat?"

"I'm telling you, Ricky. I got word on dat nigga. He hating on you, son. Plus I heard dat nigga Heavy be making promises to dat nigga. He from Far Rock, ain't he?" Kinko asked, locking eyes wit' me.

"Yeah, but . . ."

"So what da fuck you think, Ricky? You think y'all buddy-buddy because you putting paper in his pockets? I'm telling you, son, he da nigga running his mouth off to Heavy, having this nigga in our business like dat. He da one dat probably set up my cousin and got him shot."

"Who told you about this shit?"

"Yo, don't worry about dat. We need to start worrying about this nigga. You know what he look like, so when he come out dat school, I want you to point the nigga out to me."

"You mean today?"

"Yeah, nigga, today! This shit gotta be dealt wit'."

I sighed.

Kinko looked at me. "What, you acting pussy now, Ricky? This is business, and niggas dat snitch and run they mouth too much, they gotta get da business done to them. Dis is how we gotta hold shit down. We gotta put fear in these niggas' hearts. They thinking because we some young niggas, dat they can just easily come up on us and take money out our pockets. It ain't happening, Ricky, and we gonna show these niggas we ain't playing. You feel me, nigga?"

"Yeah, I feel you."

"So when dis nigga, Terrance, comes out dat school, you point da nigga out to me. I'll take care of it, and then we'll take care of Heavy and dat bitch ass Stone."

I sat back in my seat thinking about the situation. It was a sun-drenched Friday afternoon and quiet around the school. Kinko remained seated in my truck and smoked a cigarette. Terrance was a junior I put on a year ago. I saw how the kids in school were constantly teasing and ragging him about his gear. He was a bum nigga. He'd wear the same old funky worn out jeans twice or more in the same week, and he looked like he got a haircut once a year.

So one day I had a talk wit' the nigga. I told him he could make some money by fuckin' wit' me, and a month later I had this nigga pushing 600 grams for me. He knew how to take risks. He had to eat. So I really didn't fuck wit' him about getting caught. When a nigga's desperate, starving, and hungry, he'll do anything for a buck.

Since Terrance had been down wit' me, his popularity jumped from a 0 to being a 360 degree playa. Them same bitches who dissed him a year ago and gave the brotha no kind of play and always ridiculed his ass, were the ones who were on his dick and bout ready to have his baby today.

We sat in my truck till two-thirty that afternoon.

"Yo, jump in my shit," Kinko said.

I didn't argue. I locked my truck and hopped into his Blazer. We pulled around to the front of the school and parked across the street, waiting for eighth period to get out. I knew Terrance had eighth period gym, and would be coming out the front exit.

"What you gonna do to this nigga?" I asked.

"Fuck his ass up. Don't worry, Ricky, I ain't gonna kill him. I'm just gonna let his ass know don't fuck wit' you or me."

I was nervous. I tried not to be seen so easily in Kinko's Blazer by slouching down in the passenger seat and peering out the window looking for Terrance to come out. Kinko told me not to get involved. He was going to handle Terrance himself. Kinko didn't go to Martin, so he could beat down a nigga in front of the school and get away wit' it. But me, I made money in that school, and everyone knew that Terrance was affiliated wit' me.

Two-forty came, and that's when all the students started pouring out into the streets.

"You see dis nigga?" Kinko asked.

"Nah," I said.

I continued to look, trying to be discreet.

"There he go right there!" I pointed out, spotting Terrance exiting the school. "He right there, got on the white polo outfit and the baseball cap."

"Dat tall, dark-skinned nigga right there?"

"Yeah, dat's T."

"Ayyite."

Kinko reached under his seat and pulled out a black .45 handgun.

"Yo, I thought you wasn't gonna kill him," I said.

"I ain't," he said wit' a straight face.

He got out the truck and tried to conceal the handgun by keeping it close to his side. Kinko casually walked across the street, heading toward Terrance. Terrance was wit' some thin light-skinned bitch. He didn't even see Kinko coming.

When Kinko was right up on Terrance, he said something to Terrance, and Terrance looked up. That's when Kinko suddenly started striking Terrance across the face wit' the gun. He started pistol whipping him in front of hundreds of students. The girl Terrance was wit' started screaming. Terrance dropped to the ground, and Kinko pounded all over him, beating him severely wit' the gun and kicking him wit' his Timberland booted feet. The students who lingered around the scene didn't know what to do. They all looked helpless as they watched a fellow student get hammered by Kinko.

I looked over by the school entrance and I saw security rushing out of the school. School safety ran to the scene while yelling in their hand radios. I guess Kinko noticed them too 'cause he stopped whipping Terrance's ass and hightailed it back over to his ride.

He peeled off, busting a quick left by the school, and leaving Terrance to lay in his own puddle of blood.

My heart pounded rapidly. *God, I hope nobody saw me.*

Kinko dropped me off by my parked truck in the back of the school, and sped away when he heard sirens.

I quickly jumped into my Pathfinder and headed home. I couldn't be seen. It was too much of a risk.

That night I was chilling in my room when Kinko paged me. I hesitated to call back, but I picked up the phone and dialed his cell.

"What up?" I asked.

"Yo, be ready tonight," he said.

"Ready for what?" I asked.

"Yo, we going after that nigga Heavy tonight. I know where he stay at."

"Heavy? Tonight? Yo, we never even seen the dude before. How we gonna go after him?"

"I got this bitch out there. She know where he be at. So you down or what, nigga?"

I sighed. "Yeah, I'm down."

"Good. I'll scoop you up around eight."

It was exactly 8:02 PM when Kinko swung by my crib. We got out to Far Rock around eight-twenty and ended up in the projects called Edgemere. Heavy was staying in this building known around there as Vietnam. That's what shorty put us on to. She informed us that Heavy was popular around her way. He was in his early twenties and you couldn't miss him. I was assuming he must be really fat— some overweight nigga who probably couldn't see his feet or his fuckin' dick.

Kinko handed me a silver .357 and he had the .45 he used earlier to pistol whip Terrance. We chilled up in this shorty's apartment for a minute. Sherry was a thin, unattractive, short bitch wit' curly hair. She was running us down wit' information about Heavy. Seems they went to school together and they used to be cool, but he shitted on her when she used to hustle for him back in the day, and now they didn't fuck wit' each other. But there was more to her story. I knew the bitch was cracked out and shit. She was probably smoking the same product she was supposed to be selling.

She mapped out this nigga's apartment for us and told us where he kept his stash because he was too stupid to move it. He knew everybody and their mama knew where he kept his goods, but he believed that no nigga out there was gonna test him and get at him like that. He was wrong.

Heavy lived on the fourth floor. Sherry told us that niggas were in and out of his place 24/7. Obviously she was in the plot for a free hit. She easily volunteered information, because we'd promised her free crack for her to smoke up.

"You promise to hit me off, right? I'm lookin' out for you, Kinko," she said.

"I got you, Sherry. Don't worry, you gonna get yours," Kinko said.

Around ten that night, Kinko, Sherry, and I headed down to Heavy's apartment. Sherry described him as a stout, 250-pound nigga who had a big burn on his face.

"You nervous?" Kinko asked me.

"A little," I lied. I was extremely scared. I ain't never been in a situation like this. Back in the days when I was running for Fat Tony, he kept me out of the beef and the violence that came along wit' being in the game. He had his trigger men for that. I did my job, and his hit men did theirs.

We came to Heavy's apartment door. The hallway was narrow, quiet, dirty, and vandalized wit' graffiti. I wanted to make this quick.

"Relax, Ricky. We gotta take care of dis nigga now before he becomes even more of a headache for us. Remember, nigga, do unto others before they do unto you," Kinko stated.

I locked eyes wit' him for a minute as we waited in the hallway. I thought, *has he done this before*? I never asked because really it wasn't none of my business. We made money together, but didn't kill muthafuckas together, and I preferred for it to remain like that. But Kinko seemed too cool and nonchalant not to have done this before.

We stood outside Heavy's apartment door like we were the police or something. Kinko had Sherry knock twice on the door. Anyone would have known we were rookies because we went by some bitch's mouth. We weren't even sure that this was the right apartment. And if it was, we ain't map no plan out. Our stupid asses just assumed that these niggas were going to open the door for Sherry.

We got lucky. We began to hear someone moving behind the door, fuckin' wit' locks. "Yo, dat's you Trey?" a husky voice asked behind the thick brown door. Kinko looked over at me, and I shrugged my shoulders.

"Jay, open the door, it's Sherry," she said.

"Bitch, what you want?"

"What you think, nigga? I'm tryin' to get my high on, nigga," she said,

Kinko and I stood off to the side, out of sight from the peephole.

"Sherry, you know Heavy don't want you up in this crib, you steal too fuckin' much."

"Jay, stop playin', nigga. I'll suck your dick," Sherry said.
"Word?"

"Jay, you know how good I can suck a dick. C'mon, let me in," she teased.

"Yeah, I've heard stories about you, Sherry," he said.

"I know you did," Sherry said.

Kinko and I remained still and out of sight wit' our guns out and waiting for Jay to make that mistake. And he did.

The apartment door began to open, and the nigga dat was opening the door continued to talk. "Yo, Sherry, I hope you ain't fuckin' playin' around on a nigga. You know how . . ."

When he saw the barrel of Kinko's .45 aimed at his head, the nigga paused and looked stunned. Kinko and I rushed into the apartment. Kinko grabbed Jay and violently beat him wit' the butt of his gun. When we got into the living room, there was another man seated on the couch, engaged in a phone conversation. When he saw us coming in, guns drawn and running up in the place, he shouted, "Oh shit!" and that's when he tried to reach for his gun that was on the coffee table.

Kinko fired a quick round at him, striking homeboy in his chest and dropping him dead on the couch.

"Where da fuck Heavy at?" Kinko yelled at Jay.

"He ain't here," Jay spat back, wit' blood trickling down his face.

"What da fuck you lying for? Where Heavy at? And don't have me ask you again," Kinko threatened. He pressed the barrel of the gun to homeboy's head.

"Nigga, I said he ain't . . ."

Kinko blew the nigga's brains out and dropped him before he could even finish his sentence.

"Yo, nigga, what da fuck?" I shouted.

"Ohmigod!" Sherry shrieked.

"Bitch, shut da fuck up!" Kinko yelled.

Kinko had this sadistic look on his face. I mean da nigga was looking pure fuckin' evil.

"Fuck dat nigga. We'll find Heavy our goddamned selves!" he shouted.

I panicked. I knew nearby neighbors had heard the shots.

"Yo, I'm out. I ain't wit' this shit, Kinko," I said, backing toward the door.

"Nah, nigga. You gonna help me look for this muthafuckin' money Heavy got in here," he said.

"Yo, we ain't got time."

"Yeah, we do. Now hurry up, nigga. You too, Sherry. You check dat bedroom and I'll check the other," he said.

"C'mon y'all, hurry up. I know his peoples is gonna be rollin' up in here soon," Sherry said. "Let's get his shit and bounce."

I mumbled, "Shit," and did what he said. I ran into one of the two bedrooms and looked everywhere for the money where Sherry said he be stashing, but I found nothing.

"Bingo, nigga," I heard Kinko shout out from the second bedroom.

"You got it?"

"Yup!" He held up a brown tattered duffle bag.

"We out then," I said.

"You got his shit, thank you," Sherry said wit' a smile.

"Yeah, but we forgot one more thing," Kinko said.

"Like what?" Sherry asked.

Kinko raised his weapon to her head and fired point blank into her face. Sherry dropped to the floor like a sack of potatoes.

"Like I'm gonna ever share money or drugs wit' a fuckin' crackhead," he said. "Fuck dat bitch! Dat's for my cousin."

"Yo nigga, what da fuck?" I shouted.

I hurried out the apartment, fearing that a neighbor might have called the cops on us. Kinko was right behind me. We headed for the stairs, fleeing down four flights of steps. I was scared. In all my years of hustling, I'd never been in a situation like that. The other day was the first time I ever heard of this Heavy character. Kinko assumed that we had to strike first, living by his street motto. Then the following night, I was in this nigga's apartment wit' Kinko, 'bout ready to murder and rob this nigga, all so I could keep what's mine in the game.

It was funny because as I was fleeing down the grungy project staircase, I remembered what Mr. Jenkins said to me about not letting money control your life and causing havoc or some shit like dat.

When Kinko and I made it out of the lobby, we saw these two men walking toward the building. One was holding Chinese food in his hand. They glared at us, then one peeped the bag and he said, "Yo, ain't dat Heavy's duffle bag?"

Oh shit, I thought.

Kinko quickly raised his gun and fired at the two men. I did the same, firing off my .357. They dropped the food and began firing back. Shots echoed out and bullets ricocheted everywhere. I panicked because I wasn't really aiming. I was just shooting my gun off and trying to protect myself. Next thing I knew, I was sprinting toward the car wit' my gun still in hand, and Kinko was right behind me. We were being chased. I thought I was about to shit on myself.

I reached Kinko's Blazer and yelled for him to hurry the fuck up. Kinko hit one of the men in the shoulder, but his boy was coming at us, firing off rapid shots. I was sweating, my heart was pounding vigorously, and I still felt like I was about to shit on myself.

When Kinko got to the driver's door, dawg was almost on him. I took quick action and fired my .357 at him. The shooter ducked for the concrete, giving Kinko and me time to get in the Blazer and start the shit up. Kinko sped off without even giving me a chance to close my door. He made a hard right at the next corner and damn near flipped his truck over. We were doing like 60 mph for six blocks, and then Kinko slowed down when we heard sirens. We noticed a blue and white squad car speeding toward us wit' its overhead blue and red light flashing. I got scared. But when the cop car sped past us and kept going, I exhaled.

When we got back to Jamaica, Kinko warned me to chill and stay low for a minute. He said shit might be hot now. I told him I left the re-up in my gym locker. I couldn't risk going back into school the same day Kinko fucked up Terrance, so I left the drugs in my locker for the weekend.

"Yo, definitely go get dat Monday," he told me. He gave me dap and then said, "Thanks for having my back, Ricky. You good peoples."

I nodded. I just wanted to leave and forget about this whole day.

I had the weekend to chill and get my head right. I even thought about still taking Des out the next night to get my mind off what happened. What went on that night was sloppy, really fuckin' sloppy. Kinko and I were lucky we both didn't get our asses locked up or even killed. If shit had to get done, then we both needed to plan and implement the shit. What we did that night was too much of a risk for the both of us.

FOUR.

I'd spent my entire weekend fuckin' Des. I needed to forget about the murders that happened, and I did that by being in some pussy. Monday morning I got to school early. My first priority was to head to the gym to retrieve the two pounds of weed I had stashed in a black book bag inside my locker. I also had to get rid of the few grams of crack I had in there. I was just going to get my shit and quickly leave the school. I was too hot right now. I parked my truck in the school parking lot across from the school.

When I got into the school, I instantly got dirty looks from these toy cop security guards. The vibes were definitely bad. I tried to remain nonchalant and go about my business like everything was okay.

I got to the gym lockers and headed for my locker located near the back exit of the school. A couple of students were still getting dressed for gym nearby, so I lingered around my locker until they were completely gone. I didn't need any troubles from no one.

The plan was to get my shit and meet up wit' Kinko over in the shopping center in Rochdale and pass him my stash so he could take care of it. Kinko called me that Sunday night and informed me that he counted fifty-five thousand dollars from the duffle bag we stole from Heavy. I was cool wit' that split.

When everyone left, I went into my locker, grabbed the book bag containing the goods, and replaced it wit' a same color book bag that actually contained books and shit. I was going to exit out the back of the locker room because it was too risky for me to leave out the front. As soon as I closed my locker door, I peeped this security guard standing a few lockers down from me. We locked eyes for a minute, and then he said something over his radio. I tried not to panic.

I slung one strap over my shoulder and prepared to quickly leave out the back door, hoping this nigga wouldn't say anything to me. Maybe he was just back there doing a routine check, making sure everything was good in the locker room. But as I took two steps, that's when the toy cop shouted out, "Hey, hold right there for a minute!" and then he said something into his radio again.

Now I was starting to panic. I was thinking about bolting out the door. I knew this toy cop was too out of shape to catch me. I was too fast for him. He had a gut, and looked like all he did was stuff Twinkies in his mouth all day.

I ignored his demand and continued to walk toward the exit.

"Hey, I said hold it right there. Don't move!" he ordered, striding toward me.

I started to take off for the nearest exit. I tried to push the door open, but to my surprise the shit was fuckin' locked. I turned around and ran for the locker room door. Toy cop almost grabbed me by my bag, but I broke his grip and sprinted. As soon as I escaped into the school hallways, I was met by three more toy cops and two uniformed officers. They suddenly sprang at me and I tried to fight 'em off, but I was only five eight and 156 pounds, and all these muthafuckas' weights combined was like seven hundred pounds. I was quickly overpowered and pressed to the floor. They took my book bag, and one of the officers pressed his knee against my back while I lay on my stomach. Then he twisted my arms around my back and threw the cuffs on me.

"Yo, I ain't do shit!" I yelled out. "Why da fuck y'all messing wit' me?"

The cop stood me up on my feet. "You're under arrest," he proclaimed.

"For what? I ain't do shit!" I shouted. I tried to hold my gangsta attitude, if there was any, cause on the real, I felt like I was about to break down.

I was read my rights.

The principal came over and he stared at me, shaking his head like he was disgusted wit' me. I didn't give a fuck.

"He had this on him," one of the toy cops said. He clutched my book bag.

The principal took my bag and slowly unzipped it while the cop still had a strong grip on my arm.

It was over for me.

The principal pulled out my two pounds of weed and the grams of crack I had stashed in my book bag.

"This yours, right?" Principal Palmer asked me. I knew it was a rhetorical question, so why bother to answer.

"I ain't saying shit!" I said.

"You deal drugs in my school? How dare you!" Principal Palmer angrily stated, while glaring at me.

"Yo, fuck you! Where's my fuckin' lawyer?"

"Get him out of this school!" he yelled. "I want this piece of trash in jail and charged today."

Both cops hauled me off through the school in handcuffs. Students and teachers started to come out their classroom, staring at me. I noticed a few heads smirking at me, and some looking smug when they saw Ricky Johnson, the popular playboy/that nigga/baller being escorted out of the school in handcuffs wit' a stout cop handling each arm.

Before I got to the school exit, I looked over to my right and saw Mr. Jenkins staring at me. I couldn't read his expression. He just stared, and then he shook his head and muttered, "Damn, he was a smart kid, too."

I threw my head down and closed my eyes. I had to admit I was a little embarrassed. Mr. Jenkins be looking out for niggas, and it felt bad that he had to see me like this. It almost made me want to cry, but I held my own. The one thing that surprised me was that faggot Michael Stone wasn't around for my arrest. But it wasn't like I was looking for him. He always claimed he would be there when I got caught. He'd be the one to put the handcuffs on me. But he wasn't around, and knowing he'd missed out on my arrest put a quick smile on my face.

I got shoved into the back of a squad car and accepted my fate. I was going to jail. But for how long, only a judge and jury could tell.

FIVE.

It was crazy for me Monday night. Me and six other inmates were transferred in a van from the 113th Precinct in Queens to central booking on Queens Boulevard in Kew Gardens. I was handcuffed to two other inmates, as I sat in back of the vehicle staring out the window, thinking about my fate. I swallowed real hard and tried to tell myself that I was going to be okay. But the truth was, I was fucked. I tried calling my pops from the precinct, but he wasn't home. My situation went from fucked-up, to fuckin' critical when two homicide detectives came into the interrogation room and started questioning me about the murder of Michael Stone. It happened Saturday night. He was shot to death in front of a bodega two blocks from his home. I was shocked when they told me he was murdered. I thought about Kinko and knew he had had a hand in Stone's death. They tried to hit me wit' some drug conspiracy charges and tried to pin that bitch-ass nigga's death on me.

"Make it easy on yourself, Ricky, and confess about something," the detective told me, which meant he wanted me to snitch on someone. "You do us that favor, and your black ass will be back out on the streets within three years maybe."

I wasn't feeling that. I knew they were playing me. And I wasn't the type to snitch. I saw what Fat Tony and other niggas did to snitches: they got more than stitches. And I wasn't trying to be on no nigga's shit list, because I planned on coming back home in peace, and if I did do time, I didn't want to be labeled as a snitch in prison.

"I don't know nuthin' about no murder," I told them.

"Word on the streets is, you the one that gave Stone his small scar," one of the detectives said.

"Dat was years ago," I said.

"Whatever, muthafucka! You don't want to cooperate with us? Fine. You can rot your black ass in jail for twenty years."

They questioned me for about three hours. They wanted to know about Terrance. Kinko put him in a coma. They wanted to know about the drugs. They wanted to know who murdered Michael Stone. They wanted to know all the business. But I held my ground.

I was scared, but I didn't give up anyone. I could have given up Kinko. I mean, the nigga was linked to half dozen murders. But nah, that nigga was my man, and I knew he was going to hold it down for me. The detectives promised to make it easier for me if I snitched and told them something, but the truth was, I was too scared to snitch on anyone. I had a reputation, and being a snitch was not going to be on my resume. So the detectives got frustrated and promised to make shit for me a living hell. These mutha-fuckas knew I was a first-time felon, and they tried to fuck wit' me, break me down like I was some bitch. But the streets taught me better.

Fat Tony said to me one time, "If the cops don't indict or

charge you wit' a crime within the first 24 hours, then they ain't got shit on you. They gonna question you, fuck wit' you, and see if they can break you down. If you show weakness, then they gonna continue to fuck wit' you even more . . . shout out threats, say that you're fucked, and throw numbers at you. That's what the police do—they fuck wit' niggas they know are weak, and them the niggas that become snitches. But once you show the police you ain't breaking, you hard as rock, and you ain't intimidated by no badge and no gun, they ain't gonna know what to do wit' you. They either gonna respect you, or let you go. But either way, never show weakness to police."

And I didn't. I held my ground. I had too much respect for myself.

The van pulled into the back of central booking at 10 PM that Monday night. One by one, we stepped out the van and lined up single file, still handcuffed by our wrists and waiting to be processed. We were then escorted inside, and contained in a grimy holding cell where the handcuffs still stayed on. It was uncomfortable for me. Some niggas were stank and dirty and looked like they hadn't bathed in weeks. The odors of prisoners who came and went before us still lingered in the cell, and it was making me sick. I remained standing, until my name was called.

"Ricky Johnson," the officer shouted.

"Yeah?"

"Step forward," he said.

I did it without saying another word. He took off the cuffs and led me to an area where I had to empty out my pockets again, and then my picture was taken about four times. After that, I was led into another holding cell. Now this holding cell was crazy. It was the size of a small ghetto bedroom, and they had the nerve to jam about fifty to sixty muthafuckin' inmates into this tight-ass cell. I was in there wit' bums, killers, rapists, and all other types of criminals. They sorted you out from that particular holding cell. The toilet was overflowing and soiled, and the hard wooden benches were already taken, leaving me to stand.

It was 5 AM when I heard my name being called again.

"Ricky Johnson," a female called out.

"Yeah, right here," I shouted. I was crammed in the back of the cell, and damn near had to push niggas out my way to get to the front.

"Yo, move nigga . . . move . . . yo, I'm coming," I shouted.

I made it to the front and saw this white lady dressed in a gray skirt and white blouse, holding a clipboard. She glanced at me, and then her eyes went down to the clipboard as she jotted something down.

"How old are you?" she asked.

"Sixteen."

"Your address?"

I quickly told her, and then she asked, "Who do you stay with?"

"My pops," I answered.

"Is he employed?"

"Yeah. Why?"

"And your mother?"

"I don't know. She left, don't stay wit' us anymore."

She asked me for my phone number and a few other questions I thought were irrelevant. The information she asked for, I already gave at the 113th Precinct.

"Okay," she said, and started to walk off.

But I shouted, "Yo, how long am I gonna be up in here?"

"I can't tell. The courts are backed up today," she said, without even turning to look at me. It looked like the information on her clipboard was more important than answering my questions.

She walked off; her attitude toward my situation was nonchalant. To her, I was just another young black man behind bars. She didn't ask about my crime or my plea. I sighed and leaned against the wall.

In central booking, nobody cared about you. The correction officers constantly moved prisoners back and forth from one cell to another like we were cattle. They didn't care about your problems or your case. They were constantly shouting and clowning some prisoners, and some looked at you as if you were already guilty. I guess in their eyes we weren't even citizens anymore—just fuckin' criminals who got caught.

When lunchtime came, we all got served a piece of thick bologna between two pieces of bread and a small apple juice that came in a container you had to peel back the foil to drink. I didn't have an appetite, and gave my lunch to a bum who gulped his first sandwhich down in a matter of seconds.

Thursday morning, I was finally called to be arraigned. I sat quietly in the filthy bullpen beneath the Queens Courthouse and awaited my fate. I hadn't had outside contact in two days. My clothes were wrinkled and dirty from sleeping on hard benches and floors. I was out of it. I kept calling home to my pops, but there was no answer, which had me a little worried.

I met wit' my public defender a few hours before my arraignment, and he read the charges they had against me, which was criminal possession of a controlled substance in the second degree, wit' intent to sell. A Class A2 felony. I asked him about any murder charges against me, and he had no idea to what I was talking about. He told me if the charge he read wasn't in front of him, then there were no other indictments.

Now, I wanted to plead not guilty and take my chances, but my public defender, whose name was Andrew James, a middle-aged black male, said to me that if I pled not guilty and the case went to trial, and we lost, I could end up doing ten to fifteen years. But the D.A. was willing to have me take a plea to a lesser charge, and I could do no more than five years since I was a first-time felon. There was no community service, no probation; the D.A. wanted my ass locked the fuck up for a few years.

During my arraignment, when the court officer called my docket number, I was escorted into the courtroom wit' my hands shackled behind me.

"The People of New York versus Ricky Johnson," the court official called out.

As I stood in the courtroom, I had noticed Mr. Jenkins seated in the back, and he was alone. I couldn't even look at him, so I looked straight ahead and acted as if he wasn't even there. At this point in my life, Mr. Jenkins wasn't a concern to me. I didn't even understand why he was in the courtroom at my arraignment.

The D.A. spoke first, stating his deposition about my case to the judge, and so on and so on. Then my attorney said something, and blah, blah, blah, blah. I just stood there wit' my head lowered, and listened to these muthafuckas speak a different language—that courtroom shit.

The judge looked at me and asked, "Young man, how do you plead to the charges against you?"

I looked up at him and said, "Guilty, your honor."

The judge then asked, "Are you under the influence of any drugs, medication, or anything else at this moment?"

"No, your honor," I said.

"Very well. We shall converge in this courtroom three weeks from today for sentencing," he said.

Seconds later I was escorted back into lockup and back into the bullpens beneath the courthouse like a slave. I wanted to cry, but I didn't want to look weak. That's when realization hit home. Shit. I was going to do some time. It was inevitable.

They didn't want to waste the money and the time in taking my case to trial, so like every other low-level black male being pushed through the system, they offer you a plea bargain, see if you take it, and when you do, they quickly push you behind bars, and move on wit' the next nigga/case. Day in and day out, it's the same shit.

When I took a plea to felony possession of crack cocaine, my public defender looked over at me, smiling like he did me a fuckin' favor. If I had money like that, it'd probably be a different story. But the fact was, when I got arrested, I only had three thousand dollars cash to my name.

I was doing all that hustling and I didn't have enough cash to get a decent fuckin' lawyer to represent me correctly. On the streets I hardly saved a dime. I was too caught up in Polo, Guess, Timberlands, jewelry, bitches, and pimping out my ride. The money came and went, wit' nothing saved.

I got five years, serving the mandatory minimum sentence for possession of the amount of crack cocaine they found in my book bag.

I started my time on Rikers Island, aka the "Rock," where every incarcerated Black and Hispanic male in New York City starts out. A hop and skip to La Guardia Airport, Riker's Island is one of the largest prisons in the world.

I was processed wit' ten other inmates, and out of all of us, only one was white. We all were young, and the majority of us were scared shitless. On the streets, you heard stories about Rikers Island. I'd heard stories about niggas getting raped, extorted, tortured, and sometimes murdered. I remembered a friend of mines was supposed to do two weeks in Rikers, but he caught a murder charge and got twenty years. *Damn.* My heart was beating fast as we were being processed. I had my game face on, trying not to look scared, but on the real, on the inside, I felt like putty and shit. They made us strip down naked before they put us through searches and talked to us like shit.

"Y'all young niggas can forget about family and your mothers and fathers, because in here, I'm your daddy, and you do what I say. Y'all understand that?" this tall, beefy, scary-looking corrections officer shouted.

"Yes," we all shouted.

"I know some of y'all think y'all some bad asses, but I can look at some of y'all and know who's gonna be somebody's housewife by tomorrow morning," the same C.O. said, mocking us.

I was determined to go home the way I came in: untouched, unmarked, and still respected.

Since I was only sixteen, they had me up in the Adolescence Retention Detention Center—C74, where they keep you until you're nineteen. The medical examiner gave us our shots and made sure we ain't have any sicknesses or diseases and that we weren't crazy. They asked us a bunch of questions to see how mentally stable we were. Then they issued us a bedroll, a small green army cover, some old shabby sheets, a pillowcase, and a roll of toilet paper, and escorted us into our new homes.

When I first got into Rikers, it was crazy. My first week at Rikers, this fifteen-year-old kid got raped and sodomized wit' a stick of deodorant by three inmates one night. It happened at two in the morning, and I remembered hearing these cries, but they were mostly muffled, like niggas had a rag or shirt gagged over his mouth. They were three bunks away from me, and when I got up and looked over, all I saw was this young looking nigga bent over his bunk by three inmates wit' his pants pulled down to his ankles. They raped that kid something terrible. I couldn't help but to feel sorry for the nigga. He cried all night.

The next morning, he didn't even tell the C.O. what had happened to him. I guess he was too scared and the niggas who raped him had him shook like that. The rapes continued for a couple more nights, until he was finally transferred out of that unit.

As for myself, I had slight beef wit' niggas. My first month in, this dude stepped to me and said he wanted my Nikes. I paid $120 for them, and this nigga from Brooklyn tried to shop for my shits. That's what they do when you're a new inmate and you first come into Rikers wit' new shit, especially in the general population. When your shit's lookin' proper, niggas is gonna try to herb you for your gear or whatever they find valuable on you. Then either they gonna wear your shit, or sell it.

But dude, he came at me like he had some serious beef wit' me. Fortunately, someone stepped in and pointed out, "Yo, Mace, chill nigga. I know dawg. Fuck off, nigga!"

"Ayyite, yo, he got dis one," Mace said and walked off.

I looked at the man who claimed he knew me and asked, "Yo, where you know me from, son?"

He let out a faint smile and said, "You don't remember me, right?"

"Nah!" I admitted. He was thin, about my height, and his face had scars. One particular scar ran down from his forehead to his chin. From his demeanor, I knew he had some juice in the unit.

"You used to run wit' Fat Tony back in the day," he said. "You from Jamaica, Queens, right?"

"Yeah, and?"

"Little Ricky!" he proclaimed. "Damn, nigga, you changed. I heard you were doing your thang out there, making dat paper."

"Yo, who you?"

"Kirkland, nigga. I used to go by Dirty Rat."

"Oh shit, Rat! What up, nigga!" I gave him dap and a hug.

"Damn, you ain't even recognized a brotha. I changed that much?"

"How long you been up in here?" I asked.

"A year now. I'm supposed to get sentenced in three months. You know, they got me on some assault and drug charges. It ain't no thang."

Dirty Rat. Damn, that's what we used to call him. The nigga was a notorious stick-up kid in the hood. He ain't give a fuck about shit. He was a few years older than me, and the last time I saw Rat, they were throwing him in the back of a police car for some gun charge he caught back in '89. I was cool wit' him, but we ain't really rock like that wit' each other around the way. I did my thang, and he did his. But he knew me through Fat Tony, and sometimes that's all you need to get by inside—affiliation.

"So, what's good, nigga?" Rat asked.

"I'm doing five years, son, on some bullshit," I told him. "What's the deal in here?" I was a fresh nigga, knew nuthin' about being on the Island.

"Wild-ass dumb niggas in here dat be thinking they rock like that. You know some of these niggas be shouting Queens, Harlem, and Brooklyn. Dat's what most niggas be wilding about, claiming they hood like they be running shit like dat.

"But you good little Ricky. You tight wit' me, son. Ain't no nigga gonna fuck wit' you like dat. If you got a problem, come to me, nigga."

"Ayyite, good lookin' on dat, son," I said, giving him dap. I noticed while we were chatting a few heads were clockin' us. Or shall I say, they were clockin' me, and kinda hard too, trying to size up a nigga.

Up in there, if you didn't have juice in your house, or you didn't know someone wit' juice like dat, you would get extorted—simple as that. When I was in Rikers, I saw many niggas get the worst of it—niggas who thought they were too hard, and they weren't trying to run their shit like that. Them the niggas who got fucked up.

I'm not gonna front, before Rat got sentenced and transferred upstate, he made my time in Rikers easy. The nigga had juice almost everywhere, along wit' a little clout. Rat was only twenty, but the nigga had been around. He done things to earn his rep like that.

Because of him, I got my phone time constantly and ain't had to worry about niggas taking from my commissary. I had a few incidents, but they were quickly taken care of.

Rat definitely looked out.

When he got transferred upstate, I was good. I still had beef wit' niggas here and there, but I turned out all right. I was holding my own in my house.

I tried to do my time easy by mostly keeping to myself and trying not to get myself into any shit or beef wit' niggas in my house or any other house. I avoided getting myself thrown into the Bing (solitary confinement) or adding any more time on to my bid. These niggas in here were wilding out, beefing wit' other houses and trying to give rival muthafuckas Buck 50s across they grill.

I had my shank for protection, too. But it never went that far for me to have to use it.

Five months in Rikers, and I finally got my first visitor. You believe that shit? Five fuckin' months, and not one muthafucka came to see a nigga. My pops, man he was in his own fuckin' world. When I told him that I was locked up on some drug possession, he ain't know what to say. He got quiet over the phone. I spoke to my pops twice while I was locked down.

Des, well that bitch don't know how to write a nigga. Fuck her! I called her crib collect a few times, and mostly her moms be picking up, and she don't like a nigga anyway. She be screaming on a nigga, talking about, "Don't call here anymore asking for my daughter!" when she the one accepting my calls. I know Des can still come see a nigga. Yeah, I know she young, but other inmates up in here, they shorties be like fifteen and sixteen. And either they get a fake I.D., dress grown and come see they man, or get their older cousin or sister to bring 'em. Fuck that bitch. I guess I ain't got the riches anymore so now she dissin' a nigga—out of sight, out of mind.

And as for my other niggas I used to hang wit', and my fam that I left out there on them streets, they dead to me. Fuck 'em. Everybody got they fuckin' hand out when you on top, wanna be your friend, claiming they got your back. But when you're locked down, your collect calls get denied, no visits and not a fuckin' letter from no one. You're dead to the fuckin' world.

And as for Kinko, that nigga's been out of pocket for a minute since I got locked up. I was hearing about him and Heavy going to war wit' each other. Niggas were beefing hard and shit over some blocks and corners in Queens. But being up in Rikers, Kinko's beef wit' Heavy was the least of my problems.

The day of my first visit I got escorted along wit' four other inmates to the visitors' room. I was wondering who had come to see me. I was curious and at the same time excited. But I kept my composure.

I was the last to enter the visitors' room as we came in single file. My eyes started to dance around the room searching for a familiar face. I was praying it was Des.

A C.O. nudged me and pointed out my visitor. I looked near the back, and I saw Mr. Jenkins.

"What da fuck?" I mumbled.

Now I was dumbfounded. I knew he cared about his students, but damn, did he actually care about a nigga dat much to come see a nigga?

I started to walk over by the table where he was seated. He stood up when he saw me coming. He smiled. I didn't return it.

In the visitors' room, inmates sat one way, facing the C.O.s, and the visitors sat wit' they backs toward the C.O.s. It was like assigned seats.

"Hey, Mr. Johnson," Mr. Jenkins spoke. "It's been a long time."

"You ain't had to come see a nigga, Mr. Jenkins," I told him. "I'm good."

We didn't embrace, shake hands or anything. I just took my seat in front of him, and he did the same.

"So how's it going in here?" he asked. "You okay? I've been worried about you, Mr. Johnson."

"Mr. Jenkins, do me a favor. Don't call me Mr. Johnson anymore. Call me Ricky. We ain't in high school anymore."

"Okay Ricky. I'm sorry."

"You ain't gotta apologize."

There was an awkward silence between us. I glanced around the room and noticed a few honeys up in there I wouldn't mind getting wit' even if they were wit' they man.

"Yo, on the real, why you here, Mr. Jenkins? This ain't no school."

"You're better than this, Ricky. I'm here to help you with a new start."

"What? New start? Look around you, man. I'm in prison. There ain't no new start for me."

"Five years, Ricky. The state only took away five years of your life. You can still achieve something when you get out. You can do something. You're only sixteen."

I sucked my teeth, becoming annoyed and shit.

"Fuck dat! Fuck da state and those bitch-ass niggas dat put me up in here!" I cursed. "I'm a first-time felon, and they give me five years for trying to make money, you know what I'm sayin'? Them niggas be hating. I know murderers that got less time than me."

Mr. Jenkins placed his elbows up on the table and clasped his fingers together. He leaned toward me and said, "Ricky, I want to see you get out of this right. I want to see you have a future."

"Future. What fuckin' future?"

"You can still attain your diploma. I want to get you started with getting your GED."

"GED? Yeah, whatever! I ain't graduating. You and me both know that ain't ever happening."

"Listen, Ricky, there's always a chance. You gotta believe in yourself. I'm going to be here to help you get started, help you get through this."

"Started? I ain't even say yes yet," I said to him.

Mr. Jenkins smiled.

"What you smiling for?" I asked.

"You said, 'Yet.' That means you're interested."

I let out a heavy sigh. "Man, Mr. Jenkins, you crazy."

"You'll always have a friend in me, Ricky. I'm here to help you get through this the best way you can. You're a smart kid. I know that. You were one of the few students who aced my history exams. I want you to get your GED, and then after that, I know some programs that will help you get started in some city colleges. Maybe we can reduce your time."

"College?" I laughed. "You think a nigga like me ready for college? You think some college is gonna accept a nigga like me? Let's be for real, Mr. Jenkins. I'm a con, a hustler. I sold drugs. All I know is the street. That's my background."

"Ricky, I knew plenty of men who were in your situation, some much worse, and you know what happened to them?"

"Nah, what? They still locked up?"

"They made something out of their lives, Ricky. No matter how negative and bleak their situation or condition was. No matter what society thought about them, constantly labeling them as ex-cons and crooks, these men refused to let negativity and cynicism bring them down. And one of these men was my brother. He served ten years in a federal prison for drug trafficking and assault. And when he got out, you know how old he was?"

"Nah. What, your age?"

"He was thirty-eight. Much older than you're going to be when you get out. And you know what he's doing with his life today? He's got his own business in construction. He's a carpenter, and a damn good one. He's constantly being referred to throughout the neighborhood, and he makes good, honest money doing what he loves to do.

"Now you, when you finish your time, you'll be what twenty or twenty-one. You still got a long life ahead of you to make something right come out of your life. And if you need a slight shove, I'm there for you. And if you need someone to knock you upside your head when you're beginning to mess up, I'm gonna be the man to do that, too. I'm gonna push you, Ricky. Now it's up to you. I can only do so much to help you, and it starts with you being willing to help yourself. I can't help you if you won't help yourself. Set your life right. You made a mistake. We all make mistakes, but the ones who learn from their mistakes—those are the ones who come out on top. So are you with me, Ricky?"

I leaned back in my chair, contemplating shit. What did I have to lose? Mr. Jenkins, he was a good man to trust and he was well liked. He used to throw fundraisers in the school and put together scholarships for students who needed them. He did a lot for students in and out of the school. I couldn't sit in front of this man and tell him no, that I didn't need his help. It would be suicide. And honestly, if Mr. Jenkins was willing to pay me a visit and keep in contact wit' a brotha, I was down for that. Because on the real, I was getting lonely not having any outside contact. When you don't have any visitors coming to see you, it's the worst. It makes you feel like shit. I needed cash in my commissary. I needed things like clothes, and even company. If Mr. Jenkins was able to hook that up for a brotha, then I was down. So I locked eyes wit' Mr. Jenkins and said, "I'm down."

"You sure? Ricky, don't just say you need help because I'm sitting here in front of you and you feel pressured. I want you to be for real with this. I don't want you lagging behind."

"Mr. Jenkins, this is all I got. I've been in here five months, and not one soul bothered to pay me a visit, or even write me a letter. All them heads I knew out there and showed mad love to, now the niggas can't even come check on me to see how I'm doing. Fuck 'em! I'm willing to do whatever it takes. You got my word, Mr. Jenkins."

"Okay then, Ricky." He smiled. "I'm glad to hear that."

"Mr. Jenkins, before you leave, can you do me a solid?" I asked him.

"Like what?"

"I'm a little, you know, broke right now. It's hard up in here. I was wondering if you can drop a little cash off into my commissary. I mean, I'll pay you back when I get right, you got my word."

"I'll put $150 in for you."

"Yo, good lookin' out. I got you back on dat."

"No. The only way you got me is when you get out. You get your life right. Stay out of those streets, keep your head in the books, and get your degree. You do that, and then your debt is paid. Okay?"

"Okay. Thanks Mr. Jenkins."

We both stood up and shook hands. But then he pulled me toward him and embraced me wit' a hug.

"I know you'll be okay, Ricky," he whispered.

I went back to my unit and chilled on my bed for the remainder of the day, thinking about Mr. Jenkins' words.

As promised, I started going to school on the regular and hitting the books, trying to study for my GED. I tried to stay out of trouble and do me. I wanted my GED. Mr. Jenkins and me, we joked about it sometimes, calling it "Good Enough Diploma."

Mr. Jenkins kept in contact wit' me on the regular. He'd visit me like four times a month and even accepted my collect calls at his home. I even spoke to his wife a few times, and she seemed so cool.

Everything was going smoothly until three days after Christmas. I finally got transferred to a state jail upstate. That shit sucked.

But no matter what, and no matter how far away I was incarcerated, Mr. Jenkins promised he'd be there for me.

My first month upstate in Fishkill Correctional Facility in Beacon, New York, Mr. Jenkins came to visit me and he brought his wife along. It was a long drive, but he still came. We talked and socialized all afternoon, and he told me that he was so proud of me. But the best news was when I informed him that I'd passed my GED exam. Mr. Jenkins gave me a hug and told me he was so proud of me in so many ways.

I finally felt that I was on my way.

I had a strong positive role model in my life who was supporting me and had my back all the way. For the first time in my life I knew what it felt like not to want to let someone down. I had to succeed. Mr. Jenkins even got me set up into a city college after I did my time. He was part of this program to help get incarcerated young men, especially black men, enrolled into a city college wit' financial help for tuition.

Finally I had some clear vision of my life wit' the help of Mr. Jenkins. He had definitely looked out.

SIX.

January 1997

I was finally a free man after doing a four year bid. It was hell, but I got through it. I was twenty years old, and I felt that I had a new start on life. The minute I stepped out of the jail, I kissed the ground. Ah man, you don't know—not being able to do what you want to do for four fuckin' years was hell. You got C.O.s on your back constantly giving you orders and telling you when to shit, shower, eat, talk on the phone, and when to sleep. People take little shit like that for granted, on the real.

I got on the bus heading to the Port Authority station in Manhattan wit' only the clothes on my back and a large blue duffle bag that contained my personal things slung over my shoulder.

It was cold outside, but I didn't care. I was free. To me it felt like heaven, and that was the truth.

The bus pulled into the Port Authority station around noon that Thursday afternoon. I hadn't seen the city in so long I looked like a tourist peering out the bus window, smiling and showing all my teeth.

I couldn't take my eyes off the city. It seemed more alive than when I had left for upstate. I was finally home. But I knew that I had missed so much, and so much had changed since I left. I was going to need to make a lot of adjustments. I exited the Port Authority and got on the E train heading to Jamaica, Queens.

After about four stops, these three young ladies got on the train. They kept staring at me and laughing. I mean they were laughing at me. No one had ever laughed at me before, especially not while making fun of me. I was always that fly nigga. I was that nigga who bitches and wannabe niggas wanted to be around all the time. Muthafuckas emulated me. I was always on point wit' everything from clothes and jewelry, to women and the fine cars I was pushing.

But as I sat across from these young ladies, I couldn't look 'em in the eyes. I was embarrassed by the way I was dressed. My outerwear was fucked up. I had on these gray and slightly tattered sweat pants and an old blue coat wit' patches, fuckin' feathers damn near coming out my coat. I ain't had a haircut in months, so my shit was jacked up. And my shoes were some run down, fucked up dirty Timberlands.

Damn, I wished these same bitches woulda saw me back in my days, back in my prime. They woulda been begging to have my fuckin' baby.

I tried to let it be.

When they came to their stop at Roosevelt, one of 'em looked at me and uttered, "Damn nigga, times that hard? You need change or something? You lookin' fucked up." Then her and her girlfriends all laughed at my expense.

I felt fucked up. But I ate the mockery and thought about being home.

Stank bitch!

Before I knew it, I was at the Jamaica station stop, and I quickly got off, high-tailed it up the steps, and entered the streets of Queens. Soon as I was out of the subway, I glanced around at the scenery, taking everything in and trying to see what had changed and what was still the same. In my eyes, everything was still the same.

I got into a dollar cab, going down Sutphin Boulevard. I sat in the back wit' two other passengers, having my duffle bag crammed against my lap while the African driver drove and tried to pick up dollar fare after dollar fare.

People must have speculated that I just got out of jail because they kept glancing at me from time to time. But I paid them no mind.

"Driver, I'm getting off at Rockaway Boulevard," I announced.

He nodded his head and continued to drive.

When I got out the cab on the corner of Rockaway and Sutphin, a huge smile bloomed across my face. I was looking at my home. Home, baby!

I gave the cab driver his dollar fare, thanked him, and proceeded into the projects. It was cold, so hardly anybody was outside. I guess people were either at work or in school.

The first person I ran into on my way to my father's apartment was Ms. Nelson. She lived three doors down from me. I was walking down the hallway and she was coming my way. When we were close, she stared in my face and then uttered, "Ricky?"

I smiled. "Yeah. Hey, Ms. Nelson."

"Ohmigod. You're home, huh?"

"Finally."

"Well, this time I hope you stay out of trouble and stay home."

"Don't worry. I ain't trying to get locked up again."

"That's good to hear. I'm glad to see you home again, Ricky," she said, smiling.

"Thanks."

"Well, I got some errands to take care of. I know your father is going to be happy to see you. Bye bye."

She continued off down the hall.

I got to my apartment door and exhaled. I hoped my pops was home because I didn't have my set of keys, and I ain't had anywhere to go from here if Pops wasn't there. I knocked twice on the door, but no one answered. I gave the door another hard three knocks, but still no one answered. I glanced at the time and it was two forty-five. Damn, if my pops wasn't home, then I knew he was at work, and usually the man didn't get home from work until six in the evening.

I let out a stressful sigh and took a seat in front of the door, peering out at the projects. *Ain't shit change*, I thought. *Same ol', same ol'.* The buildings were quiet though. It hadn't been this quiet since I didn't know when—maybe because it was January.

I remained seated in front of the apartment door for a little over an hour. I didn't mind waiting. It was peaceful for me. I just sat there taking in the reality that I was finally home. I thought about my pops and wondered how he had been doing. I hoped he was holding up okay. I knew he was going to be thrilled to finally see his son home again.

I glanced at the time again, and it was three fifity. I leaned my head against the door, let out another sigh, and tried to keep warm.

Suddenly I heard the sounds of locks turning from inside the apartment. I quickly stood up. The door opened and there was my pops.

"Hey Pops, I'm home!" I cheerfully greeted.

"Ricky? Hey son," My pops greeted. He was not looking as cheerful as I was. "When you get out?"

"Today. You ain't heard me knocking earlier? I musta knocked like six times."

"No. I musta been sleeping," he replied.

"Well, anyway, I'm back home. How you been?" By his appearance alone, I knew he wasn't doing so well. He had aged more over the past four years. His face was lined wit' more wrinkles than before and he looked completely out of it. He was dressed in his regular work uniform and he had his lunch box gripped in his hand.

"You off to work?" I asked.

"Yeah, they changed my hours now. I work nights."

"Oh."

"It's good having you home, Ricky."

"Good to be home."

"Well, I gotta go. I don't wanna be late for work. Go on in and make yourself at home, son."

It wasn't the kind of greeting I thought it would be, but it was all good. My pops headed for the stairs, but then he stopped, came back up to me, and embraced me in a surprising hug.

"I missed you, son," he whispered in my ear.

"I missed you too, Pops."

And then as quickly as he hugged me, he let go and went on his way.

I didn't know what to do in the apartment. My room looked the same. In fact, everything in the apartment looked the same. Pops wasn't much of a decorator anyway. He was always a simple man. I raided the fridge. There wasn't much in there besides a few beers, some leftover pizza, bread, and something that looked like soup.

My pops also needed to clean up a little. It was looking kinda sloppy in there. There were clothes all over the place, food was left on the kitchen table, the carpet looked worn out, and a rancid smell lingered around in the apartment.

It was good to be home, right?

Later that evening, I couldn't take being inside anymore, so I decided to go out, get something fresh to eat, and maybe take a walk. I wanted to see what was up around the way. I had thirty-five dollars in my pocket. I never would have thought that I would become that broke-ass nigga. But now I was officially that broke-ass nigga.

I strolled down to the nearest Chinese store. I was starving. It was good to see that Great Wall was still in business. They made some good fried rice and egg rolls. I gave them my order and went outside to chill for a minute. I thought that maybe I might run into someone from back in the day and get the rundown on who's who now, who's locked up, and who's probably dead.

I walked to the corner store, copped me two loosies, and then stood on the corner, smoking and just looking around. I took a few more pulls, tossed my cigarette off into the street, and was about to head back into Great Wall to see if my food was ready. My hands were fuckin' freezing.

As I was walking back, I noticed this sleek black BMW moving down Rockaway. *Nice car,* I thought. *Really nice car.* Shit had chromed rims and it looked like the new '97 840ci.

I had a little hate in me, I'll admit. But I shook it off and thought about some other shit.

I got my order, paid the man, and walked out only to notice that the BMW was now parked in front of the Chinese place. Shit, seeing the car up that close brought out the envy in me again. I couldn't see the driver because the windows were tinted.

I tried not to stare too hard. I didn't want to give the driver that much satisfaction. I didn't want him to think I was sweating his ride so hard I couldn't take my eyes off it.

I began to walk off, but then I heard the sound of a car horn blowing. I turned around and saw that it was coming from the BMW. *Nah, he ain't honking at me,* I thought. I began to walk off again, and the horn sounded loudly again, causing me to turn back around.

"What da fuck!" I cursed. *Do I know this person?* I began to stare at the car, trying to see if I could recognize the driver.

"Yo Ricky!" I heard the driver shout.

I got curious and I walked slowly and cautiously to the driver's side. Just as I got a few steps from the car door, Kinko stepped out. He was dressed in a denim jean suit, and shining wit' gold like Mr. T. He was all smiles.

"Ricky, what's good, nigga? When the fuck you get out?" he asked, coming up to me and giving me dap and a hug.

"This morning, yo. What's good, Kinko?" I asked half-heartedly.

"You know, a nigga trying to do him. You see what I'm pushing right? Copped it yesterday. First Beamer off the lot," he boasted. "You like it, right? I'm holding it down around here now, Ricky. Niggas ain't fuckin' wit' me."

"That's good, Kinko."

"Yo, what's up, Ricky? You act like you ain't happy to see a nigga. What, we don't rock like that anymore, huh?"

"Nah, it ain't like that. I just got home and I'm trying to chill, you know."

"Man, you out, nigga. We need to fuckin' celebrate. Yo, come take a ride wit' me," he suggested.

"Yo, later, Kinko. I got things to do," I told him.

"You sure, nigga?"

"Yeah."

Kinko gave me a bizarre look as we locked eyes. "Ayyite, Ricky. I'll see you around. You be good, son. If you need anything, come check me."

"Ayyite, yo."

Kinko quickly got back in his Beamer and drove off, making a U-turn on Rockaway Boulevard and heading toward the Van Wyck.

Fuckin' Kinko. I was locked up damn near four years and this nigga didn't bother to throw me a line not once. And when I was in Rikers, I kept hearing this nigga's name. Kinko this and Kinko that. Kinko got shit on lock. I ain't forget that the nigga owed me that money we snatched up from Heavy. I really needed that money. And the last I heard about Heavy, he was gunned down on the streets two years ago. I knew who had a hand in that.

On the real though, I began to envy Kinko. He was pushing a brand new BMW, and he had riches, something I truly needed right now. But I had made a promise to Mr. Jenkins, and I planned on keeping that promise, because during my time in jail, he was the only person who looked out for a brotha.

Mr. Jenkins helped get me enrolled into a city college; one out in Brooklyn called New York City Technical College. I started at the end of January. I didn't know how he did it, but he did it. The man had clout like that.

I met up wit' Mr. Jenkins a week after my release. He was jubilant about my release and took me out to eat at Friendly's in Green Acres Mall.

"So, how does it feel?" Mr. Jenkins asked.

"How does what feel?" I asked, chomping down on my juicy cheeseburger and fries.

"To be a free man and finally have some vision and direction in your life?" he asked, staring at me, smiling.

"I feel good, Mr. Jenkins. You know I didn't get to eat like this inside. Food tastes like shit up in there, and my pops don't cook. I get tired of eating Chinese and pizza everyday."

Mr. Jenkins laughed.

"You nervous about college next week?" he asked.

"Yeah, a little. I mean, what am I supposed to do? College is for brainiacs, you know, smart people like Bill Gates or sumthin'."

"First all, Ricky, stop doubting yourself. You're a smart kid. I know first hand. And you'll be fine. Keep your head in your books, study hard, stay out of trouble, and next thing you know, you'll be graduating."

"I hope so," I said.

"No, don't say hope. Say you know."

"Ayyite. I know."

"Stop doubting yourself, Ricky. Those who doubt will never know because they're too scared to try."

I continued to gobble down my fries and shake. I never met anyone who had so much faith in me until Mr. Jenkins. I was a kid coming off the streets and he always treated and talked to me like an adult. He never judged me. He always claimed that he saw the potential in me.

"And Ricky, in order for you to succeed, you must stay away from your past and those friends of yours you used to hang with. Where were they when you were locked down? Nowhere to be found, right? They are not your friends. They never were. It's time for you to start over, Ricky, okay? I'm always going to be here for you."

"Damn, Mr. Jenkins, why do you care so much?" I asked. "I mean, I'm not your son, but you treat me like one."

He looked at me.

"I mean, it's not like I mind, but I just sometimes wonder wit' you." I said without meaning any harm.

He stared at me for a moment, then he closed his eyes and rested back in his seat.

"I had a son, Ricky," he responded.

"You did?"

"He was about your age at the time. His name was Jimmy and you kind of remind me of him—your attitude and demeanor."

"What happened?"

"Just like you, he wanted to be out in the streets, hanging with the wrong crowds. He wanted to spend all his time chilling on the corners and probably selling drugs. He would come in the house at all kinds of crazy hours. Lora and I, we tried with that boy. But I guess we didn't try our best. I had just begun teaching at August Martin, and Lora was constantly working at her job in Manhattan, so we didn't spend much time with our son. We wanted to, but our hours were crazy.

"One night, I got a call, and it's the police. They were telling me. . . ." He suddenly became quiet, and he looked like he was about to start crying. I just sat there, waiting for him to finish telling his story about his son. "They're telling me that my son was shot," Mr. Jenkins continued. "And I needed to come down to the hospital immediately. So I called my wife and then rushed down to the hospital. When I got there, he was already dead."

"Damn, I'm sorry to hear that."

"Jimmy was shot three times by some gun-toting fools who decided to do a drive-by shooting near the corner where he was standing because of some beef over money by a friend of his. He just got caught in the crossfire. My son was shot because of a dispute over twenty dollars. I couldn't believe it for a long time. My son died over a dispute for a mere twenty dollars."

"Niggas don't be thinking," I said.

"That's right, Jimmy—I mean, Ricky," Mr. Jenkins said.

I couldn't help but to think *damn* when he called me Jimmy. I knew he had his son deep in his mind.

"Y'all young boys are ready to kill each other over a dollar. But, why?" His expression looked hurt as he emphasized *Why?* He pulled out a ten dollar bill from his wallet.

"You see this, Ricky? This will always come and go, but a life will never come back, no matter what. Money is not everything, yet you kids will quickly shed blood over it like it's a god. It's paper. This is not something worth killing a soul, or losing your own soul over. Yes, it's good to have, but let's not kill each other just to maintain it. Remember this," he said as he pointed at the ten dollar bill again, "is nothing." Then he tore the bill in half. "I'll see it again, today or the next day, no problem. But y'all young kids today remain hardheaded about it. I pray that one day our youth will see that we're killing each other over foolishness."

I had no words. I was kinda moved by his speech. And I felt sorry for him about his son. It shouldn't have went down like that.

"I want to see you achieve, Ricky, and it's not going to be easy," Mr. Jenkins said after a while. "You have to struggle and constantly believe in yourself. And stay away from negative energy and negative people. You don't need that in your life. You made a mistake and I want you to learn from your mistake. You're young, and you still have your whole life ahead of you."

"I hear you, Mr. Jenkins."

"Okay now, I'm here for you. You begin messing up, and I'm going to be on your ass. You came this far. I don't want to see you looking back, you hear me?"

"Yeah, I hear you, Mr. Jenkins."

We both continued to talk and laugh as we ate. I admit, I was nervous. College? Shit, four, five years ago, my mind wasn't even remotely on college. It was on making that constant dollar and maintaining my reputation, name, and image. Things or people change, huh?

Well, we'd see.

SEVEN.

It was my first day at City Tech and I felt like a salt water fish thrown into some fresh water. Mr. Jenkins helped me register for morning classes. I decided to take up business management, you know, something to deal wit' money since I knew how to make it.

My first class started at 8 AM, which meant I had to leave my house around seven in the morning to catch the #7 bus and the A train to Jay Street.

My first day of college, I arrived late to my math class. It was eight twenty when I walked in, but the professor let me slide that once because it was my first day and all.

But the thing that was fuckin' wit' me was my gear. I had on some black Boss jeans, which were played out by now, a plain white t-shirt, and a pair of Nikes that were pretty decent on my feet. I looked around and noticed the other college students, a few anyway, rocking Polo, Nautica, Timberland, and Guess, and here I was looking like the average Joe, dressed the average way. I wondered if I could get used to this shit, this life. Was this shit really me?

My schedule consisted of five classes for the semester—

math, English 101, a business management class, AC101, which was computers, and some lab class I had to take once a week.

I had the math class and my computer class early in the morning. Math was a bitch. I hadn't studied or did math in so long, I had to start from the fundamentals. I did my math on the streets. You gotta keep up wit' that to make sure your money and count was right. But this other shit, like X3+X6-X4, when did letters get involved wit' numbers?

My English professor, now that nigga was a trip. His name was Professor Russo, and he was a middle-aged, jacket-and-tie-wearing muthafucka. Hard as a rock, and a fuckin' asshole too. First day of class he gave us fuckin' homework and assignments to do, and he gave this long-ass speech.

"When you come to my class, you come early and arrive before me," Professor Russo began.

"I don't accept any tardiness. I don't care what your excuse is. You give me respect, and I sure will give you the same. I am a man of honor, dignity, respect, and integrity, and I expect my students to be of the same. I want assignments and homework done on time. There will be no late papers or assignments handed in to me. Also, I hate private conversations during my class time. If you have something to say to another student speak to him or her before or after my class, not during my lecture time.

"I expect the best from my class and I will give the best. If you have a problem with me, there is no one holding any guns to your head. This is a free country, so feel free to drop my course at any given time. There is no sleeping during my class, and no eating. So do not bring any food or any kind of beverages into my classroom on my time. I don't care if it's a quart of water.

"I expect everyone to have my book by this week. If you cannot afford the prices, then I suggest you borrow from someone. Just get the book. It is important for you to pass this class. There is also no lagging behind in my class. If you feel you can't keep up with the lessons, then I suggest you go and hire yourself a tutor. Just know my work. If you put in the best, then you will receive the best. If you put fifty percent into my course, then you will receive fifty percent of a grade. Put in one hundred percent and you will get out one hundred percent. So, are there any questions?"

Within the first month, six students dropped Professor Russo's class.

The first day of his class I was seated in the back corner, as was routine in all my classes, wit' my baseball cap cocked right on my head and damn near feeling like I was 'bout ready to walk out already. Funny thing though, as much as I wanted to leave, my ass stayed.

Professor Russo was fifteen minutes into his lecture when a female student entered the classroom late, and distracted his lesson.

"Excuse me, young lady. Do you know what time it is and do you know what time this class starts?" Russo barked.

"I'm sorry," shorty softly replied, looking kinda embarrassed. "I got lost."

Russo glared at her. "You got lost. Everyone in here managed to get to my class early, but you were my only student who got lost. I just hope you don't get lost in this course. Take a seat somewhere, young lady."

Oh shit, I thought, *now that was some foul shit he did to her—blowing her up in front of the class like that. Now that was so wrong.*

I couldn't take my eyes off shorty. She took a seat in the front of the classroom, trying to get involved wit' the lesson. My eyes were fixated on her beautiful aura. She was light-skinned, wit' a slight tan, long black hair that was placed in a simple ponytail, and she had to be about five feet, five inches. She was cute and simply dressed in a pair of nicely fitted blue jeans, white sneakers and a white T-shirt.

I continued to gawk at shorty during the entire ninety-minute class. I ain't give a fuck about nothing else at the time except for noticing her, and I wasn't the only one in class who was checking her out. I saw a few other niggas up in class gazing at her. She was definitely the best looking female in the room, and I wanted to get to know her—real soon, too.

When English was over, mostly everyone rushed to leave except for me. I waited around, paying attention to shorty. When she left, I would leave. She was still seated in her chair, taking down the lesson off the blackboard. I fronted, still sitting in the back and acting like I was still jotting down today's lesson.

Russo packed up his belongings, and before he walked out the classroom, he said to shorty up front, "Next time, Miss, arrive to my class on time, and do yourself a favor, have a fellow student brief you about my policies that I gave out today. The ones you missed."

She nodded her head and Russo walked out the door. Shorty glanced around the classroom and peeped me sitting in the back. I smiled, but she didn't smile back.

I found out that shorty and me had the same business management class. I was kinda excited about that. I entered the classroom after her, and we were both on time. The professor hadn't arrived yet. I took my routine seat in the back of the class and shorty took her seat up front. By her demeanor, I could tell that she was into college and into her classwork. She was serious about an education.

I didn't step to her that day, but I definitely planned to. There was something about her that I loved, and it wasn't just because she was cute. She had an aura about her that just drew me to her.

Also, I wasn't yet ready to talk to her since I was kinda looking busted that day. My gear wasn't right, and my first impression had to be on point. I wasn't gonna fuck this up.

I got home around eight that evening only to see Kinko's appealing Beamer parked in front of the buildings. He was posted up on his ride, hollering at some young chick. When he saw me coming, he gestured for me to come over.

"What's good, Kinko?" I asked.

"You, nigga. You been back home for a month now, and you ain't checking a nigga. What's up, Ricky? You wanna make that money again, right? I'm hearing you in college. Damn boy, what's good wit' that? You a changed man now?"

"I'm on parole for one year, yo. I'm trying to keep a low profile. You feel me? I ain't trying to get locked up again."

"Yeah, whatever. Yo, come ride with me, Ricky," he said.

"Yo, Kinko, I got homework."

"Homework!" he shouted. Then he let out a slight chuckle. "Yo, just ride wit' me for a minute. You can play Steve Urkel later."

"Yo, Kinko . . ." I began to say, but the way he turned around and cut his eyes at me, I decided to roll.

I got in and he drove off down Sutphin.

I was quiet. The interior in the Beamer was nice, wit' the gray leather that had that brand new smell. The car also had a CD player, moon roof, and phone—fully loaded. He had the bass thumping in the car wit' the windows down in early February. Had a nigga freezing his ass off.

"What da fuck is on your mind, Ricky?"

"Nothing much, yo."

"You got beef with me, huh?"

"Nah."

"So why you avoiding me, Ricky? I thought we were cool."

"I'm just staying low right now, Kinko. I just got home."

"Yeah, I understand. Parole officers can be a bitch. What, they got you on a curfew?"

"Nine o'clock."

He sighed. "Fucked up. They don't let you live. Don't stress that, Ricky."

He continued down Sutphin till he hit South Road, and then he made a right. I felt awkward in the car wit' him. I knew Mr. Jenkins would be totally against it right now. He wanted me to stay away from him. He kept telling me that Kinko was bad news.

"Yo, Kinko, let me ask you a question," I said.

"What nigga?"

"What happened to my share of the money we stole from Heavy?"

"Nigga, I used that dough to start up what I got going on today," he said. "My empire. I'm big time, baby."

"Yeah, but that was my half, too."

"And? Yo, Ricky, you still my nigga, and that's why I want you down wit' me, be my right hand man. What I got today, it belongs to you too, nigga. We started this shit. And to be honest, you acting like a bitch about things. Look at you, dressed down like a broke-ass nigga. No money in your pockets, struggling. Nigga, you wanna continue to keep living like that, going to school and worrying about your next dollar? C'mon Ricky, you better than that. I know you wanna live like a king. Making this money is in your blood, nigga."

"I'm trying to pop off wit' some shit before the summer," Kinko continued. "My uncle, he got this spot on the low that he's trying to get rid of. He's offering it to me for forty grand. You know, I'll put in at least thirty, and you put up ten large, and we can get something jumping. You know, get them hoes popping off up in there, and the little sales. We can make at least a hundred easy off of it."

"I don't know, Kinko," I said, looking out the window. "I gotta think about it."

"Yo, you do that, Ricky. I want you down wit' me again. You hear?"

He ended up driving down Guy R. Brewer. I got curious and asked, "Yo, where you going?"

"Niggas owe me money around here. I'm gonna pick up," he stated. I saw the butt of a gun peek out from his shirt. I got nervous. "Yo, Kinko, let me out right here, I'll walk back."

"What? Nigga, I'll take you back home. Let me just handle some business real quick."

"Nah, Kinko, let me get out!" I stated firmly, staring at him. He stared back while he still had one hand gripped around the steering wheel.

"You sure?"

"Yeah."

"Fuck it then, get out, nigga." He pulled to the side, and I quickly got out. "Holla, Ricky!" he shouted, and then peeled off.

I didn't need to get into any shit right now wit' this nigga. Kinko had a temper. If he was going to pick up money wit' a gun tucked in his waist, it was gonna be problems, and I didn't want to be any part of that.

Wit' the twenty dollars I had in my pocket, I caught a dollar van down the Boulevard and walked the rest of the way home.

That same evening, I got to chill in the living room wit' my pops and watch some television. It was just him and me, like when I was young. My pops was sick, though. He'd been having this chronic cough for weeks now. And along wit' his diabetes, I come to find out that my pops was also sick wit' prostate cancer. And his fuckin' heart hadn't been doing so good either. He had not been to work in days, and he was scaring me more every day.

"Pop, you want me to get you some water?" I asked. He was bent over on the couch, out of breath, gasping for air.

"I'm, I'm. . . . okay. . . . Ricky," he said, panting.

"You sure, Pop? You ain't looking too good. You want me to call a doctor?"

He breathed a little more and then answered, "I'm fine . . . Ricky . . . it . . . it . . . ain't . . . nothing.   Stop . . . worrying about . . . me."

He began to cough intensely again.

"I'm getting you some water." I got up and poured him a glass of cold water from the fridge. "Here Pop, drink this."

He took the glass from me and took slow gulps.

"We're seeing a doctor this weekend," I told him.

He nodded his head.

I was scared about his health. His condition had me losing sleep at nights.

A few weeks passed, and so far I was doing all right in school. I was getting used to attending classes on a regular and not hustling drugs for extra credit. I'd been seeing my parole officer every Wednesday morning around ten, and he was ayyite. His name was Grey, and he didn't stress me on dumb shit like most parole officers did with they parolees. Officer Grey knew I was in school, that I stayed wit' my pops, and he even talked to Mr. Jenkins. Of course, Mr. Jenkins put in a good word for me. In everyone's eyes, I was living a straight life and staying out of trouble.

As for my crush, I was getting there wit' her. I found out that her name was Danielle Washington, and I was not the only guy in school who was interested in shorty. Niggas was trying to holla at that hard and fast. But she was shutting niggas down left and right.

I felt a little insecure about myself. I was a broke nigga, struggling wit' cash. I didn't have the clothes, car and jewelry anymore like back in the day. And if I did ask her out, and she happened to say yes, where the fuck was I going to take her?

I was used to taking females who had my generous attention to the most exquisite and expensive restaurants and spending hundreds of dollars on shorties just to show off my riches and my lifestyle, and Danielle seemed to be just the kind of high quality shorty I'd be willing to spend money on. Word, she looked like she could be wifey material for real.

Finally, I got my chance to get wit' Danielle in the school library. It was quiet and I was studying for English and math exams that were coming up. She took a seat next to my study booth, and being the book worm that she was, she immediately crammed her head into her books without once looking up.

I glanced over at her a few times, hesitating to speak out. But she was only inches away from me, so this was my opportunity. It was either now or never.

"Hey," I whispered, catching her attention. "Your name is Danielle, right?"

She stared at me wit' this blank look on her face. "Yes."

"Hi. I'm Ricky." I extended my hand. "We're in the same English class together. You know, we got that asshole Russo for a professor." I joked. She let out a small laugh. That was a good sign.

"I've seen you around," she admitted.

"Um, are you studying for his exam?" I asked.

"Yeah, unfortunately."

"Well, I was thinking. Since we're both in the same class, maybe we can study for his exam together. I mean, I'm not trying to impose on you or anything. It was just an idea. You know what they say, two heads are always better than one."

She smiled, staring at me. "I'm cool with that."

I smiled. *Yes.* "Ayyite, let's get started then." I pulled my chair closer to hers, and we started studying together. We were definitely vibing, making each other laugh. We stayed in that library for three straight hours studying. She even helped me wit' my math. Now that's a woman for you.

I noticed how the fellows in the school were approaching her, stepping up to her like they were Mack Daddy, on some suavé pimping shit, and she would shut 'em down quick. Me, I took the subtle approach and it worked. For the first time in my life, I didn't have to flash cash, cars, or jewelry to get a woman's attention. It was my mannerly approach that worked.

Weeks went by and Danielle and I became closer, almost approaching a serious relationship. She even got me to sit wit' her in the front of the class. I saw my fellow students watching and hating! Fuck 'em! We both were feeling each other. We would study together, eat lunch together, and sometimes I would ride wit' her on the train to Brooklyn, making sure she got home safe. She rented a two bedroom apartment wit' her cousin out in Bushwick. We would give each other a call every night, sometimes only to say good night to one another, or maybe to talk about school, or our personal problems. We confided wit' each other about everything—well, almost everything. I left out telling her about my past—about me being in prison and selling drugs.

I even told Mr. Jenkins about Danielle. He teased me about her, saying I had found myself a college girlfriend. He asked if I could handle a woman wit' intelligence. He wanted to meet her, and I told him in due time.

On our first official date, I got Pops' '85 Cutlass Ciera and took Danielle to see a movie. Afterwards, we ate dinner at some local IHOP on Hillside Avenue. I was trying to budget, which was awkward for me. I was used to having a serious bankroll of fifties and hundreds, and spending money like it was water. But that night I had to get used to the fact that I wasn't balling like that anymore. I was now a struggling college student—ain't that some shit?

Danielle was looking so fine. She finally let her hair down, instead of the way she regularly had it pinned up in a bun or ponytail. She was rocking a pair of tight fitted Guess jeans, which exposed her curvaceous figure, a denim jacket, heels, and a pair of hoop earrings. She didn't need to wear any make-up because her beauty was natural. The most make-up she put on was lip liner or lipstick.

I was dressed simple—jeans, shirt, Timberlands, and a leather jacket I had from back in the day. I found it in the back of my closet and it still looked new. I probably had only worn it twice.

"You like the movie?" I asked.

"Yeah, it was cool."

We saw *The Fifth Element* starring Chris Tucker and Bruce Willis. It was a pretty cool flick. I enjoyed it.

I began to stare at her. "You got a lovely smile," I said, causing her to blush.

"You need to quit it, Ricky," she giggled.

"Why? You're beautiful. I wouldn't be lying about it."

"Yeah, whatever, you probably say that to all the ladies."

"Nah. I haven't met anyone quite as exceptional as you. I mean, on the real, Danielle, you got a nigga open. I love being around you."

"That's good to hear. And to be honest, I feel the same way about you. You're just different. You keep to yourself mostly."

"Yeah . . . well. . . ."

"Nah, I like that about you. You're not like other men, flashy and all talk, full of bullshit trying to get a woman's attention. You're more the coy type. You're simple, like me. Stay that way, Ricky."

I smiled and returned wit', "I'll try."

The waitress came over wit' our food. I had ordered the

lumberjack meal, which consisted of a huge T-bone steak, scrambled eggs, and sausages. Danielle had the shrimp and salad. As I ate I thought about being honest wit' Danielle and telling her about my past. But I second-guessed myself and decided against it.

She thought I was coy—now that was funny. I had to laugh at that one. If she only knew.

Later that evening I pulled up in front of her crib in the old Cutlass. I looked over at her.

"Get out," I joked.

"You know you love my company." She smiled.

We both stepped out and I began walking her to the front door. It was pretty pleasant outside, wit' spring just around the corner. We both stopped at her front door and gazed at each other.

"I wrote you a small poem," I said, feeling somewhat romantic, which was definitely a first for me.

"Ah, you did?" Danielle asked. "That's so sweet, Ricky."

"Ayyite, don't laugh. It goes like this."

"I promise not to."

I took a deep breath and exhaled wit', "Goodnight is what she told me. She called me to tell me goodnight. All that night I had dreams of that call. I had dreams of her, both of us together forever. I had this good feeling inside of me after she hung up. I felt as if I was needed. I felt as if I was wanted. I felt that I was loved. She made me feel that way. Goodnight is all she said."

I got nervous after I read my poem to her. She continued to look at me. I couldn't tell what she thought. She started to lean toward me, and then I felt her lips press against mine. We started to share a passionate and long kiss. I pulled her into my arms and held her petite figure.

When we finally broke loose from each other, I said, "Okay, now I'm definitely feeling that."

She laughed. "You're crazy." And then she began to stare

into my eyes. It was at that moment that something lovely sparked between us. We couldn't stop staring at each other.

"I loved your poem. It was nice. You got skills with the pen."

"Thanks."

"You want to come in for a minute?" she asked.

I shrugged my shoulders. "Hey, whatever."

She searched for her keys in her small handbag, and then unlocked the front door. We walked up one flight of steps to the second floor and entered a dark apartment. She searched for the light switch against the wall and turned on the living room lights.

Her place was spacious wit' parquet floors, leather furniture, a ceiling fan, full-size windows, and a giant screen TV near the kitchen entrance. I thought, *Brooklyn be having places like this?* From the outside you wouldn't think it would be this nice of an apartment. The front of the building looked dilapidated and shit.

"Do you want anything to drink?" she asked.

"Nah. I'm cool." I took a seat on the sofa and glanced around. I noticed the time. It was ten fifteen. I thought about my 9 PM curfew, and became slightly nervous about my P.O. I hoped he didn't call or come by the crib. I damn sure didn't want to violate my parole over some dumb shit.

When Danielle came back out from the kitchen, those disturbing thoughts disappeared quickly.

"You sure you don't want anything?" she asked again.

"Nah. I'm cool."

She went over to the stereo and started browsing through her lengthy collection of CDs.

"Damn, you sure love music," I said. There were about six different sized speakers placed around the room.

"Nah, most of this belongs to my cousin. She loves to dance," she said.

Danielle put on some Sade and her soft and serene voice

traveled throughout the apartment, causing a tranquil sensation. Danielle then stood up and said, "I'll be back, Ricky. I'm gonna go change."

"Ayyite. You know I ain't going anywhere."

She sashayed down the hallway into her bedroom while I remained seated on the living room couch, listening to Sade's sweet voice. About ten minutes passed, and that's when I heard someone coming up the steps, approaching the door. I heard keys dangling. I assumed that it must be her cousin coming home. The apartment door opened, and in stepped this dark and lovely sister wit' chinky brown eyes, and a wicked figure.

DAMN, I thought.

Whoever she was, shorty was definitely a dime piece. She walked in and peered at me, looking somewhat befuddled.

"Hello," she said.

"Hey," I returned.

"Who are you?"

"Oh, I'm a friend of your cousin, Danielle." Soon after, Danielle strolled into the room wearing a long sleeper white T-shirt that came down to her knees. Shorty looked over at Danielle.

"Um, excuse me. But did I interrupt anything?" her cousin asked.

"No," Danielle said. "Ricky, this is my cousin, Gwen. Gwen, this is Ricky. We're in school together."

"Hello, Ricky." Gwen greeted. "Well, let me get out y'all way. I gotta be at work tonight." Gwen walked off. I tried not to stare because I knew it was disrespectful toward Danielle. But her cousin had a PHAT ASS!!

Danielle looked at me, and then she said, "I saw you staring."

"Me? Nah."

"Yeah, it's cool. My cousin has that effect on everyone."

"What she do?" I asked.

"She's a dancer."

"Dancer?" I uttered. "Oh, she a stripper."

"Yeah, whatever you wanna call her." Danielle moved a little closer to me on the couch, and began to snuggle against me. "We gonna talk about my cousin, or are we going to do us tonight?" she said seductively.

"What you think?" I replied, smiling.

We started to go at it, caressing, fondling, and exploring each other's body. I picked her up into my arms and carried her off into the bedroom. We quickly undressed and I slid in between her inviting thighs.

I'd been out almost two months now, and this was my first piece of pussy since I'd been home. Shit, I missed the feeling of pussy. I damn near melted in between her warm legs. Danielle wrapped her warm smooth thighs around my naked physique and allowed me to thrust my hard-on deep into her, which caused her to moan and scratch my back. I felt Danielle's thighs press tighter against me, and her moans became louder and louder. The pussy was that good. Fo' real. I clutched the sheets, and being the quick nigga that I was, I shouted, "I'm cumming." I was backed up. I quivered and grunted wit' each nut I let off.

After I came, I laid next to Danielle for an hour and we talked. It felt so good to lay next to a beautiful woman. I cherished her company. I knew she would become a positive influence in my life. I didn't want to leave, but it was getting late. I started getting dressed while Danielle lay in bed. I kissed her goodnight and promised to call her when I got home.

When I walked out of Danielle's place, I saw a phat Benz parked outside on the street. A little jealousy stirred up in me. It was a champagne color wit' 18-inch rims and tinted windows. My father's Cutlass was parked behind it. I hated getting into that bucket. But it was my ride home.

Driving home, I wondered if I could keep this image up. Could I go back? Money for me was stressed right now. And school, I was doing fine now, but could I keep it up for four years?

I was probably kidding myself. Mr. Jenkins was asking me to become something that I never was in the first place—an upstanding citizen. I kept saying to myself, "It's gonna be cool, have faith." How much faith can a penniless nigga have in his life?

I didn't want to end up like my father—wife gone, sick wit' masses of medical bills stacked against him, and struggling for cash all the time.

I was scared.

EIGHT.

It was April, and Danielle and I still had a tight relationship. We would see each other almost every day, and I found myself spending most of my time and nights at her place. I also became cool wit' her cousin, Gwen. She was cool peoples.

Danielle was becoming a big help for me wit' school, especially in math. Our relationship was in the open, so niggas knew she was my girl. But did that stop most of them from trying to still holla? Hell no—hating-ass niggas.

I finally got to introduce Danielle to Mr. Jenkins, and he loved her. He even told me that she was the right woman for me. They got along great. Mr. Jenkins treated us to dinner wit' his wife at Red Lobster.

My life seemed to be on track. I had Danielle in my life. I had a 3.5 grade point average, I was on track to making the Dean's list soon, and Mr. Jenkins promised to hook me up wit' a job. It was something decent he said, to hold a nigga down wit' paper.

Everything seemed to be going okay wit' me. But wit'

life, you always gotta expect shit to happen. We gotta go through hell for us to appreciate heaven.

One Wednesday morning I was coming from seeing my parole officer. I gave him the up and up. He gave me a drug test and I passed wit' flying colors. I updated P.O. Grey about my high grades and he was very pleased.

I had just gotten out of the dollar cab and was heading into the buildings when I heard a horn blow. I turned around and I saw this fool Kinko rolling up on me in a yellow Ferrari. This nigga was pushing a fuckin' Ferrari in Queens, of all places. *What the fuck was going through his head?* I thought.

He parked the car and jumped out. "What up, nigga?"

"Yo Kinko. You bugging?" I asked. "Fuck made you buy that?"

"I got it like that, Ricky. I got bored. So what's good, Ricky? You still playing *School Daze*, nigga?" he mocked me.

"You funny, nigga."

"Yeah, I should be on Def Jam."

I glanced down at his watch, fuckin' gold diamond bezel Rolex around his wrist, diamond pinky ring, and a colossal diamond gold Jesus head hung from around his neck. I ain't gonna front, a little envy started to surface, especially when I saw the nigga in a Ferrari.

"Yo, Ricky, you ain't never got back wit' me about that proposition I pulled your coat to. You still down, nigga? My uncle ain't gonna be waiting forever, you hear?"

"Yeah, I've been a little busy."

"Busy? Nigga I'm giving you a chance to make that paper again. You see that?" He pointed to his Ferrari. "That could be you soon, nigga. I know you like it. Shit is tight, right? I'm doing it, Ricky. You hear me? I'm venturing into everything. This is us, Ricky, and don't try to deny it. This is how we're supposed to live, like muthafuckin' kings, nigga. What, Mr. Jenkins got you on the straight and narrow now? That muthafucka is telling you how to live your life, huh, nigga? What the fuck he got to show? He ain't nuthin' but some underpaid school teacher, and that's all he's ever gonna be: a broke-ass teacher, nigga. And he wants you to be a broke-ass nigga, too. He hating on you, son. He can't never be us. He can't never do what we do, and he hating on you now because he know he will never be able to live like us.

"I'm giving you a chance to come back again, Ricky," Kinko continued. "Don't fuck this shit up for yourself. Look at you, who the fuck you supposed to be in your run-down, played-out Boss jeans, unemployed, trying to be the Good Samaritan?" He laughed. "It ain't you, Ricky. I see it in your eyes, that ain't you. You supposed to be out here getting that money. You feel me? Don't let that bitch bring you down."

I nodded my head slightly, looking at Kinko. He seemed to have it all right now, and I helped start this nigga. He was living on top of the world, and I was fuckin' struggling like some bitch-ass nigga.

Kinko's pager went off, and he glanced at the number.

"Yo, I gotta take this," he said, walking back to his flashy ride. Before he got in, he looked at me and said, "Ricky, holla, nigga. I need you, son." He then got in his ride and sped off down the street.

I began thinking as I walked up the steps to my apartment. I had twenty dollars on me right now, and I wanted to cop something really nice for Danielle's twenty-first birthday next week. I didn't even have enough cash to get her something nice, or even take her out somewhere.

I thought, *how can any man live like this?*

I entered my apartment and it was quiet. I knew my pops

was home. He had lost his job a week ago. They fired my father over some dumb shit. The boss called here and told him don't bother to come to work anymore because he had missed too many days because of his illness. That was some bullshit. The man was really sick, and his employers knew it too. But they didn't give a fuck, just another black man gone and lost to them. Some mornings he couldn't even get out of bed. He'd been really down and out. And I felt so bad. I couldn't do anything for him right now. His medical bills exceeded twelve thousand dollars and he didn't have health insurance. And I didn't have the finances to help him out.

"Hey Pop, I'm home," I shouted out. "Hey Pop, where you at?"

I walked through the living room and into the kitchen. I figured Pops was still in bed asleep, and probably upset about losing his job after he done worked for them people for ten years.

I poured myself a glass of orange juice and walked into my father's bedroom. It felt still in his room. I saw him lying in bed. It was almost noon. I opened the blinds to let a little sunlight in.

"Pop, you gonna sleep all day?" I asked. "It's too nice outside for you to be shacked up in your bedroom all damn day." I looked at him again, and he seemed a little too still for me.

"Pop, yo, get up." I nudged him, trying to get him to move. He didn't. "Yo Pops, get up!" I nudged him harder and harder until I damn near pushed him out the bed. "Pops, man, get up! Come on, get up! I know you hear me!"

He didn't move. Tears welled up in my eyes. I didn't wanna accept the fact that he was gone. He couldn't be.

"Pop!" I shouted out again. By now, tears were flowing down my cheeks.

He was dead.

I had to give Pops a cheap funeral because I didn't have the money to bury him the suitable way. He was placed into the ground in a cheap casket, barely any flowers by his grave, and only a little over a dozen people showed up at his funeral.

Mr. Jenkins came to pay his respects, along wit' Danielle. She tried to comfort me the best way she knew how. She was there to hold my hand as I watched them lower my father, Anthony Pablo Johnson, into the ground.

I couldn't stop the tears from falling. I loved that man, and it pained me watching my father suffer the way he did during his last days on this earth. It seemed like no one cared—no one.

He died alone.

When the casket was put into the ground, Mr. Jenkins and his wife came over to me to show comfort. Mr. Jenkins put his hand on my shoulder. I didn't say anything, and neither did he at first. Danielle began to grip my hand tighter as I cried louder.

"Ricky, it's going to be all right," Mr. Jenkins said.

I picked my head up and looked over at him, my expression like 'What the fuck is you talking about?'

"All right? All right how?" I asked.

"You'll get through this," he assured me.

"Fuck that!" I cursed. Danielle looked at me. "Fuck that, Mr. Jenkins. My pops, he in the ground right now. That man been through hell all his life."

"He's in a better place, Ricky," Mr. Jenkins said.

"Better place? My father died a broke man. He died alone, Mr. Jenkins. He died penniless and alone. How the fuck can anyone live like that? I watched that man suffer from the beginning to the end. Nobody cared for him." I shook my head. "I'm not gonna go out like he did."

"Ricky, don't start talking that nonsense. He didn't die alone. You were with him."

"Fuck that!" I released my hand from Danielle's. "I can't go out like that." My tears began to flow even harder. "I can't become like that man who died. I can't die the way he did. It's not me."

"Ricky, you're doing so good. Don't begin to mess it up now," Mr. Jenkins said.

"I gotta get outta here," I told everyone, and suddenly I bolted out of the cemetery. I heard Danielle calling for me, but I ignored her calls and kept running.

I needed to get away from her, Mr. Jenkins, every fuckin' one. Why was this shit so hard? Shit was easier for me four years ago. I thought that if I were rich, my father wouldn't have suffered the way he did. He would've been taken care of, that's for sure. His bills would have been paid, and he wouldn't have had to stress his job or any fuckin' insurance. Money took care of everything.

Money made the world go round, and money gave you that respect—money and power. I said it before, and I'll repeat it again—without money, you ain't shit. Don't no one give a fuck about you. Why should they? You can't pay 'em. And if you can't pay, then they can't do.

Simple as that.

NINE.

For days I isolated myself from everyone: Mr. Jenkins, Danielle, even school. I remained locked up in my apartment and thought about all of the crazy shit I'd been through during my twenty years on this earth. My life was drama. I thought about options. I needed a serious change right now. I needed something to get my mind off the pain. I needed to get my mind off my father.

Kinko stopped by the apartment, gave his condolences, and said that if I needed anything, he was there.

Danielle was constantly calling my crib, but I wasn't in the mood to talk. I just let the answering machine pick it up. Mr. Jenkins refused to leave a brotha alone. Every day he would call or come by, but I wasn't in the mood to be dealing wit' him. He told me he wasn't going to give up on me. He said he was going to do whatever it took to get my mind back on track. He didn't understand that a nigga needed a serious break from everything. Shit was moving too fast for me. I needed to slow down and rethink shit.

It was three o'clock in the afternoon on a Thursday when I heard a loud knock at my front door. I was in my bedroom watching daytime television. I got up off my bed and walked to my door in a pair of brown boxers and a wife-beater. I glanced through the peephole and saw Danielle.

"Shit!" I muttered.

"Ricky, open the door, it's Danielle."

I let out a quick sigh and unlocked the door. She rushed in and gave me a hug.

"Ohmigod, baby, I've been so worried about you. Why haven't you answered any of my calls?"

"I don't know."

"I've been calling and calling. You haven't been to class. I haven't seen or spoken to you in almost a week. What's going on, Ricky?"

"My father just died," I said sarcastically.

"I know, baby, but I'm supposed to be your girl, and you're keeping me at a distance. I'm trying to be here for you."

"Well, I don't need anyone to be here for me right now," I said wit' an attitude. She gave me this unpleasant look, then moved back and placed both her hands on her hips.

"Ricky, I know you're hurting right now, but you don't have to come out your mouth wit' a funky attitude toward me. I love you, and I want to see my man get out of this slump he's going through. But if you don't appreciate a sister caring, then I'll leave!"

"Danielle, I'm sorry. I'm just losing it right now. I got a lot of shit on my mind right now."

"I understand. Just talk to me, Ricky," she said. She came up to me and embraced me in another loving hug.

We went into my bedroom. I sat her down on my bed and took a seat next to her. I explained to her about my past, my drug dealing, the money, the violence, and my incarceration. I told her about everything, even the many women I had been wit' in my past, and how I was a constant showoff. I had to tell her the truth. She deserved to know. After everything was said and done, Danielle stared at me without saying a word.

Danielle took her hand and grabbed my chin gently, staring at me wit' her lovely brown eyes. "Ricky, that was your past," she said. "You're a changed man now, a better man now. What's done is done. I can't change it, you can't change it, so let it be and move on to better things for yourself."

I nodded my head, agreeing to what she was saying. But deep down in me, I felt that I wasn't a changed man. I saw the way Kinko was living, and I wanted to live the same way again. I wanted that fast money along wit' the fast cars. To me easy money was the best way to make money.

I was trying to come correct for Mr. Jenkins, Danielle, my P.O., even for my father, but I wasn't happy. Honestly. I hated my new life. I be putting on fake smiles and pretending everything was good, but I was dying inside. I was used to living like a fuckin' king and now here I was struggling like I got a nickel and dime hustle.

"You okay?" Danielle asked.

"Yeah, I'm good."

"I'm always here for you, Ricky. Remember that."

"Thanks. I love that."

We stared at each other for a quick moment. Our attention didn't divert from one another. She was beautiful. I gave her a smile. She smiled back, and then started to move a little closer to me.

"Happy Birthday," I said, remembering that today she turned twenty-one.

"Thank you, baby."

"I'm sorry I couldn't get you a gift, but I've been busy and you know shit's been happening," I lied. Truth was I couldn't even afford to buy her a nice gift right now. I hated that feeling.

"It's okay, Ricky. I understand," she replied, smiling like everything was all good.

But for me, it wasn't. A man isn't a man if he can't afford to buy the things his woman needs and deserves. How can a beautiful woman like Danielle, or any woman on this earth, love a broke nigga who can't do shit for her, but promise her something he know he can't give out now, and probably not in the future either? I knew that there weren't too many females out there who ain't trying to live off any nigga's pipe dream.

I needed to change my situation for the better. I knew for a nigga like me to keep Danielle around, I had to offer her the world. I had to give her things that I knew the next man couldn't buy.

I've always been about seeing action. I hated all talk. It's always about action, not talk.

On Friday Kinko came to pick a nigga up in his Beamer. We needed to talk.

"What's good, Ricky?" Kinko asked, sounding exuberant. "You ready to get this money wit' a nigga or what?"

I looked over at him and answered, "No doubt."

"That's what I'm talking about," he replied. "You got tired living that average life. 'Bout' time you crossed over again and start living like you should. I saw that shorty of yours. What's her name?"

"Danielle."

"Damn, she finer than a muthafucka. You hitting that, nigga?"

"What you think!"

"My nigga!" he said, giving me dap. "Shorty is fine. You got taste, Ricky, that's for sure. So what's the pussy like?" he bluntly asked.

"Nigga, that's my business."

He laughed. "I hear you. Her shit is that good, huh?"

"You don't need to know."

He laughed again. Kinko continued to drive around Queens, going nowhere in particular. It was midnight, nice and warm out this bitch. I stared out the window, thinking about different shit, wondering about my shorty. I wanted the best for her, so I planned on giving it to her, and soon. I couldn't be waiting around doing four, five years of college, and then searching for a job afterwards wit' a piece of paper that's supposed to open doors for me. They say having a degree can give you the American dream—money, house, cars, etc. Bullshit. My American dream was what I did best—hustling. I made fast money well.

Kinko stopped at a barbershop on Linden Boulevard that was still open at midnight. There were about three people inside, wit' only one barber cutting hair so late.

"Yo, what we doing here?" I asked, staring inside.

"You need ten G's to get down with my uncle's place, right?" he asked.

"Yeah, and your point is?"

"There's your money right there." He pointed at the shop.

"What, that barbershop?"

"Yeah, nigga!"

"What, I'm supposed to cut niggas hair now?"

"No, nigga. We gonna rob them niggas."

"A fuckin' barbershop, Kinko? How much money do you think we gonna get from out there?" I asked, giving him a baffled look.

"That barbershop ain't nuthin' but a front, Ricky. Those muthafuckas are moving serious weight up in there. The owner got a safe downstairs containing serious cash. He's competition right now. He's becoming a serious fuckin' headache. We gotta handle that nigga, kill two birds wit' one stone. I get rid of my problem and you get your money. Simple as that, Ricky. You down?"

I looked at him for a moment. I knew Kinko. He was ready to go up in there and cause some bloodshed. That was always his way. He was never the one to do shit clean and simple. Making a mess was his signature way of telling niggas, "don't fuck wit' me!"

Get this money right, no matter how, I thought. So I looked over at Kinko and said to him, "Yeah, I'm down."

"My nigga. It's good to have you back." He gave me dap and pulled off. "Remember what I always said, in dis game, do onto others before they do onto you."

We ended up on Farmers Boulevard, near Hollis. Kinko pulled up to another spot that was dark and looked kinda remote from all the other establishments on that block.

"What's this place?" I asked.

"This my uncle's spot. He selling it. What you think nigga?"

"It looks ayyite."

"Yo, we gonna make lots of money up in here. You know, bring the hoes up in here, have 'em do they thang and charge niggas at the door. Yo, I'm telling you, Ricky, this a new business for us."

"What, you a pimp now?"

"Money's money, nigga, no matter where it comes from."

"Yeah, I hear you."

He pulled off again, and we got something to eat at this all night diner in Long Island. We chatted for two hours, drinking and taking in the morning. Kinko paid for our meals, pulling out a wad of hundreds. He even tipped the waitress a fifty because he thought she was cute. I knew that made her night.

I didn't get in the crib till eight that morning. After we left the diner, Kinko and I hit up this club in Brooklyn, which was poppin' mad bitches inside. We got in for free, being that I was wit' Kinko, and we got V.I.P. treatment the entire night.

I ain't gonna front, I had a really good time. We drank Moet, chilled wit' dime bitches, and danced all night.

When Kinko dropped me off that morning, I was surprised to see Mr. Jenkins sitting out front in his old blue Chevy. He saw me get out of Kinko's BMW and he quickly jumped out of his car and came toward us.

"Ricky!" he shouted, looking upset.

"Mr. Jenkins," I said, "what you doing out here so early in the morning?"

I glanced at Kinko and he had this huge smirk on his face. Mr. Jenkins came up to the car and I stood there like a young child waiting to get smacked upside his head by his father.

"Ricky, I haven't heard from you in a while. I came by to see if everything was okay," he explained, and then he gave Kinko an appalling look.

"I'm ayyite, Mr. Jenkins. You ain't gotta worry about me all the time."

"Yeah, old man, you ain't got to worry about him. He a man, not a child. So mind your fuckin' business!" Kinko cursed.

"You stay away from him, Pinko, Linko, whatever your damn name is! You're no good for him. He doesn't need men like you in his life. You're poison!" Mr. Jenkins shouted.

Bad move, I thought.

"What you say to me, old man?!" Kinko shouted back, stepping out of his car. He looked offended by Mr. Jenkins' words. "You know who the fuck I am? You know what I'm about?"

"You're a damn menace, that's what you are!" Mr. Jenkins shot back. "You don't care nothing about your peoples. You're out here flooding these streets wit' that crack and heroin. Selling that stuff doesn't make you a man. It makes you a fool."

"Nigga, I'm more man than your pussy ass will ever be. Fuck you got, nigga, huh? Fuck you got to show for yourself? Fuckin' schoolteacher. Get the fuck out my face!"

"I got my soul and dignity," Mr. Jenkins sternly replied. "You're a fool, and you'll continue to be a fool. Look at you, dapper down in that devil jewelry and living that devil lifestyle. I feel sorry for you. You're an idiot, and I don't want you around Ricky anymore."

"Nigga, don't you ever disrespect me like that again!" Kinko angrily shouted. He walked torward Mr. Jenkins and reached for his gun. I stepped up to Kinko, not wanting Mr. Jenkins to get himself hurt.

"Yo, Kinko, chill," I said to him, holding him back.

"Yo, Ricky. You better check that nigga before I put a bullet in his sorry ass!" Kinko yelled.

"And that's how you solve all your problems, huh, by killing?" Mr. Jenkins asked.

"Damn right, nigga. Proves a point, too. Don't fuck wit' me. You better show me some got-damn respect, nigga."

"Yo, Kinko, chill, son. I got this. Go home." I tried to calm the situation.

"Men like you don't deserve respect!" Mr. Jenkins replied.

Kinko gave Mr. Jenkins a grisly stare as he slowly backed away from him and headed back to his car. But before Kinko got in, he warned, "Yo, watch your fuckin' back, nigga!" and he quickly sped off down the street.

I turned to Mr. Jenkins and shouted out, "Yo, what's your problem? You could have gotten yourself killed just now!"

"Men like him are my problem. They're the reason why

my son is dead today. He's bad news, Ricky. I want you to stay away from him. That man got nothing but disaster heading his way."

I shook my head. "Mr. Jenkins, I'm not your son. You're not my father. You can't tell me what to do."

"So you're just going to throw everything you've worked so hard for away so easily, to be like your friend who just left?"

"I ain't sayin' that."

"So what are you sayin', Ricky?"

"I don't know!" I shouted. "I just want everybody to leave me the fuck alone for now."

"Ricky!" I heard Mr. Jenkins shout as I headed for my apartment. "Ricky, things are hard now, but you got strong and positive people by your side. You'll prevail through this. Don't give up."

I got inside my apartment, flopped down on my couch, placed my hands against my forehead, and wondered, *what the fuck is going on wit' me?*

TEN.

Tuesday night was the night Kinko wanted to hit up the place and get that money. It was just us two seated in an old gray Toyota across the street from the barbershop. I glanced at the time. It was ten minutes past midnight. Linden Boulevard was quiet. No cops, no people, no witnesses. I knew what it was going to be about the minute we stepped up in there. Straight bloodshed. That's the way Kinko liked it. The sick fuck called it his calling card. We were both dressed in black hooded sweatshirts and jeans. Kinko passed me the nickel plated nine and asked was I ready for this. I nodded. I remembered the last time I was in this position, back in Far Rockaway, and the robbery didn't go over too smoothly. We made too many fuckin' mistakes that night.

Kinko cocked back his nine and stepped out of the car. I followed. As we crossed the street, we both pulled our hoods over our heads and continued hastily across Linden Boulevard. I had the gat down by my side and glanced around, making sure no one was around.

Inside there were four men and the same barber I saw

from the previous night, a stout dark-skinned man. Everyone was seated, gazing up at the mounted television while the barber began to shave the man's head he had in his chair.

Kinko and I peered into the barbershop for a quick moment. Everything seemed to be on point.

"You ready, Ricky?"

I nodded.

We quickly rushed into the shop wit' our guns raised and ready to pop off.

"Everybody get the fuck down!" Kinko yelled, catching niggas' attention instantly. Suddenly a gunshot went off, startling me. Kinko had fired a shot into a nigga's dome and dropped him to the floor.

I was shocked.

"I ain't playin' wit' y'all niggas!" Kinko continued to yell. Everybody stood around in total awe, including me. *What the fuck?* I stared down at the dead body on the floor that was now covered wit' crimson blood pouring from his head.

"Yo, y'all niggas know who shop this is?" the barber warned, staring at us wit' resentment in his eyes.

"Fuck you think muthafucka," Kinko said. He walked up to the barber and bashed him in the face wit' the gun, causing him to bellow out in pain as he clutched his nose.

"Ricky, lock them doors and turn off them lights," Kinko said, snapping me back into reality. I was fucked up by how Kinko just came up in there and shot one man in the head so easily.

"Everybody down in the basement. Hurry up!" Kinko shouted.

I locked the front doors, turned off the lights, and headed down into the basement behind Kinko. Kinko made everybody lay down on their stomachs against the concrete floor.

Everyone, that is, except the barber. His nose was oozing blood, and his jaw was coated wit' the blood from that hard blow.

"Yo, where the safe at?" Kinko asked, his gun pointed at the barber's head.

"What safe?" the barber countered, giving Kinko a hard stare.

"You trying to be funny!" Kinko said, and then aimed his gun down at one of the men lying face down on his stomach. He fired a fast round into the back of the prone man's head, killing him instantly.

"Oh, shit," the next man on the ground sobbed out, thinking he was next. "Yo, Manny, just tell him where the safe is at. I don't wanna die, man."

"Listen to your boy, Manny. Where the safe at? I know y'all got that shit hidden down here somewhere."

Manny continued to give Kinko a hardened stare. The room was tense. I felt my heart beating rapidly, seeing that Kinko just killed two men, leaving only three alive.

"The safe, nigga!" Kinko repeated, now aiming the gun down at the sobbing man's head. "Tell your boy, yo, or you gonna die tonight. And you know I mean it."

"Manny, tell him, man. Tell him where that shit is at, yo." The man pleaded, helplessly staring up at Kinko and Manny.

"5, 4, 3, 2. . . ."

"Ayyite, ayyite, yo. I'll show you," Manny yelled. "Follow me."

"Yo, Ricky, watch these two niggas, ayyite? If they move, pop two in they head, ayyite? Don't hesitate on these niggas."

I nodded. I pointed my nine down at the two sobbing men on the floor and watched Kinko disappear off into a back room.

"Yo, man, y'all ain't gonna kill us, right? Manny showing y'all the money," the man asked, looking up at me wit' his eyes stained wit' tears.

"No, I ain't gonna kill you," I said to him.

About four minutes passed, and I was starting to feel uneasy about the situation. I felt Kinko was taking too long back there. Suddenly I heard three shots and I jumped. I stared at that back room, hoping Kinko was the one who stepped out alive.

I don't need this shit, I thought. Soon after, Kinko emerged carrying a black garbage bag I assumed was filled wit' the money.

"That's it?" I asked.

Kinko nodded, smiling.

"Good, let's be out," I said and began to head for the stairs.

"Hold on, one more thing," Kinko said. He then shot the last two men in the back of their heads. "There, we out."

"Damn, nigga. You had to shoot them?" I asked.

"Yeah, they heard me say your name."

Before I went up the steps, I looked down at the three dead bodies in front of my eyes. I thought about the barber in the back room and the man upstairs. I wondered if it had to be this way for them. Couldn't this shit have gone down any better?

Sixty-five thousand dollars. That's how much we got niggas for. We counted the cash up at my place because I was alone. There was no one to bother us, so we poured the money out on my bed and it took us three hours to count everything up.

It was three in the morning. I was so tired I couldn't even keep my eyes open. I ended up falling asleep on the floor, leaving the cash on the bed.

I woke up five hours later to the sound of the phone ringing. Then there was a loud knock at my door. I got up and looked to see who it was. Danielle.

"Shit!" I mumbled, wishing she wasn't here right now. Kinko was still in the bedroom asleep wit' the money. I put on a pair of jeans and answered the door.

"What you doing here, Danielle?" I asked.

"I came to see you. I've been calling you all last night, and this morning, and you wasn't picking up."

"I was knocked out."

"You okay?"

"Yeah. I'm good," I said, taking a seat on the couch.

"Mr. Jenkins gave me a call last night."

"What the fuck he call you for?" I asked, sounding a little angry.

"He was worried about you."

"I know he's got a good heart, but the man needs to stop sweating me so fuckin' much. I got a life. I mean, I had more fuckin' freedom in prison," I stated.

"He cares about you, Ricky. The same way I care. Lately you've become so distant from us. I don't even know what's up with you anymore. You just lay around here wasting your life everyday. You haven't been to school in weeks and you don't come by anymore."

"I've been busy," I said, getting up off the couch.

"Busy doing what?" she asked.

"Danielle, listen, things are about to change for us. I mean, I wanna look out for you. You're my lady and I can't even buy you nice things."

"I don't need nice things right now, Ricky. I need you."

"Yeah, whatever. Last week was your twenty-first birthday and I couldn't even afford to buy you a nice gift. You think I wanna continue to live like this, not being able to treat my lady to nice things and take her out to nice places? I'm not a man. A man doesn't live broke. A true man is supposed to live like a king," I proclaimed.

"A king?" Danielle asked. "You are a king, baby. Money and nice things don't make you what you are. I love you for you." Danielle started peering out the window.

"What's wrong, baby?" I asked, walking up to her.

I saw a few tears trickle down her face, and I started to become a little more worried. She turned her head to face me, staring me in my eyes. Then she said, "Ricky, I'm pregnant."

"What?" I said, shocked. "You're pregnant?"

"Yes. I'm six weeks."

"What you gonna do about it?" I asked.

"I'm gonna keep it. It's yours."

"I know that, but . . . but . . ." I didn't know what to say or do.

"I need you, baby," she said. "The baby needs you."

"Damn." I rose up, clasped my hands behind the back of my head, and paced around the room.

I'm about to be a father, I thought.

"We gotta get on the ball, Ricky. I'm scared," Danielle said. I turned and looked over at her. She seemed so innocent, so beautiful.

I went over to her, crouched down in front of her, grabbed her hands softly and said, "Everything is gonna be all right, baby. I promise you that. I'm gonna take care of us."

She smiled and gave me a hug. "You promise?"

"I promise. I love you, girl. You're the best thing that ever happened to me."

After Danielle left, I went back into the bedroom where Kinko was up and counting money.

"That was your bitch?" he asked.

"My girl," I corrected him.

"Yeah, whatever," he sarcastically countered. He had a stack of money in his hand, mostly hundreds, and he handed it over to me. "Here. That's twenty thousand for you."

"Damn, twenty," I said, looking flabbergasted.

"That's your cut, nigga. You did good last night, Ricky. So, you're definitely in wit' my uncle's club, right?"

"No doubt," I said, giving him dap.

Kinko placed the rest of the cash into the garbage bag, hurled it across his shoulder and started for the door. Before he left my place, he turned to me and said, "It's good to have you back in the game, Rick. We gonna do us again. Oh, and take your girl out tonight, somewhere nice. You can afford it now." He smiled and left.

Damn, I was holding twenty thousand dollars in cash in my hand. It'd been so long since I had this kind of money on me. It felt good. I had a huge smile plastered across my face as my fingers ran through the stacks of bills. I thought about what to do, what to spend it on. I felt like a kid. It felt like a brand new day.

I gave Danielle a call and told her we were going out tonight, somewhere special. We were gonna do us.

I got dressed and drove my black ass to Jamaica Avenue to do some shopping. I needed a fresh wardrobe. My shit was looking raggedy. It was nice out, the sun shining fiercely down on us, and the warm wind blowing against my skin. It was the perfect day to go shopping.

I parked my father's Cutlass and went into the first sneaker/clothing store I came across. I copped me a pair of Timberlands and a pair of blue and white Nikes. After that, I went into a clothing store and copped a denim jean suit, a few football and basketball jerseys, some jeans from every brand imaginable, a few baseball caps, and these twelve hundred dollar diamond earrings.

I was on a high that afternoon. I was walking around wit' serious cash in my pockets, and spending money like it was water. It felt good shopping like a bitch wit' money to burn.

I went into the Coliseum Mall on 165th Street, went downstairs to the jewelry department, and copped me the phattest Cuban link gold chain, a diamond ring, and a gold bracelet. I was on a high that entire day.

Later that evening, after I parked the car and was about to head up to the apartment, I noticed four men quickly get out of a black Benz and hastily start to come my way. *What the fuck is this about?* I thought, looking somewhat baffled. I stood there holding many shopping bags in my hand when this big, 6 feet, 6 inches, Shaq-looking mutha-fucka grabbed me up and slammed me against the brick wall.

"Yo, what da fuck! Get da fuck off me!" I yelled out, struggling to get loose from the powerful grip he had on me.

"Shut da fuck up, nigga!" the large man shouted, glaring at me.

"Yo, what y'all niggas want?" I asked, trying not to look paranoid. After I asked that, this slender nigga in a gray sweat suit and wearing dark shades came strolling up to us.

"Your name, Ricky?" he asked, sounding a bit more casual than his man who had me hemmed up and shit.

"Yo, who da fuck is you?"

He took off his shades and revealed his eyes. He had one glass eye, but the rest of him looked to be normal. "I'm looking for your friend, Kinko. I believe that him and an acquaintance ran into one of my establishments, killed everyone inside and stole a hundred grand from me," he explained calmly.

"A hundred grand?" I said, sounding surprised. "I don't know what da fuck you talking about."

"Is that true?" he asked. He glanced down at my shopping bags, and then took notice of the jewelry I had on. "Nice things. You definitely got good taste. And you've been out of jail for how long now?"

"Man, listen, I don't know nuthin' about no hundred

grand being taken from you. I don't rock wit' Kinko like that anymore," I told him.

"This nigga lying," one of his men shouted out. "I say we cap him right now, and find that bitch-ass nigga Kinko ourselves."

"Calm down, Ray."

"Yo, look, I just got home," I said. "I ain't trying to get into no shit. Whatever happened last night, I ain't got shit to do wit' it. I swear!"

"You sure about that?" he said, coming closer to me and staring me in my face. "I hate liars. There are two things that I despise the most, thieves and liars. And you better not be both," he threatened.

"I don't know what da fuck you're talking about. I told you. I don't rock wit' Kinko like that anymore." I stared him in the face, giving him direct eye contact to let him know that I was serious.

"Let him go," he ordered his man who had me hemmed up.

"What, Charlie?"

"I said let him go."

I caught a breather as King Kong lost his grip on me and backed off. Glass Eye, or Charlie, or whatever his name was, peered at me wit' his one good eye and then said, "We find out you're involved and we will be back around, and when we do, I promise you our next visit won't be so pleasant."

I didn't respond to his threat. I just stood there, massaging my neck. I watched him and his goons retreat back into their Benz and pull away.

What the fuck did I get myself into, fuckin' wit' Kinko?

I dashed up to my apartment, locked my door, and gave Kinko a call to let him know what the fuck just happened to me. I didn't know no Charlie wit' a glass eye, and why the fuck was he coming at me?

Then he said Kinko took a hundred grand from him. I could have sworn we counted sixty-five thousand dollars last night. But that muthafucka probably said a hundred just to see if I would be stupid enough to correct him and blow my spot up.

That night I was gonna continue wit' my plan to pick up Danielle and take her out somewhere nice. I tried not to stress glass-eyed Charlie and his fuckin' goons. The nigga didn't have shit on me. Everyone in the barbershop was dead, and Kinko was the only soul who knew I was involved. The murders in the barbershop hit the evening news, but so far, nothing connected back to us. I felt we were in the clear.

I stepped out into the parking lot and observed everything around me, watching my back cautiously. I didn't want any more surprises coming up on me tonight, so I had a small friend tag along wit' me: the 9mm Kinko gave me the previous night.

I was looking sharp, dressed down in some black slacks, a gray silk Italian shirt, and some nice polished shoes, kinda looking like my old self. I walked up to my father's old Cutlass and shook my head in shame. Here I was, looking like I should be stepping into a fuckin' limousine; but instead, I was stepping into a damn hooptie. The first thing I did was conceal my gun under the driver's seat.

I got to Danielle's around nine that night. Gwen answered the door, and my fuckin' mouth dropped and started to water. Shorty was standing in front of me in a pair of red panties and a flimsy white t-shirt that barely covered anything. My eyes were fixated on her meaty thighs and that phat ass.

"You're here for Danielle, right?" she asked.

"Yeah, luv," I said, trying to play it cool.

"She's almost ready. Come in and have a seat."

I did, and the way her ass bounced when she walked—
ohmigod. I had to tell my dick to lay low. Shorty was definitely raw, the way she walked around the apartment
almost naked in front of me like it was nothing to her. But
then again, she was a stripper, so it probably wasn't nothing for her.

"Bitch, won't you go put some fuckin' clothes on!" I
heard Danielle bark. "Why you gotta be walking around
like that in front of my company?"

Gwen sucked her teeth at her cousin, rolled her eyes, and
returned wit', "He a man. It ain't like what I got is something new to him. Ricky, you seen it all before."

"Go put some clothes on, Gwen," Danielle repeated,
sounding a little more agitated.

Gwen leisurely walked past me, almost like she was trying to flirt wit' a nigga, and my eyes stayed glued to the
booty.

"Sorry about that, Ricky. My cousin can be so stupid
sometimes," Danielle said.

"Nah, it ain't nuthin. You ready?" I asked. I stared at
Danielle and smiled. She looked so exquisite in her black
sheath dress that hugged her curves right.

"Almost, can you give me a few more minutes?"

"Yeah, no problem."

Danielle went back into her bedroom to continue to get
ready. I swear, you tell a female a certain time to be ready,
and your words be falling on deaf ears the majority of the
time. I didn't care, though, especially after her cousin came
walking back into the living room. This time she had on
some tight blue jeans that accentuated her thick hips and a
bigger sized t-shirt.

She looked over at me and then asked, "You got a cigarette on you?"

"Nah, I don't smoke," I said.

"Damn, I gotta go to the corner store now." She walked into the kitchen. "So, where you from cutie? I heard you were on lockdown for a minute."

"Who told you, your cousin?" I asked. I was kinda curious about shorty being up in my business.

"Nah, I heard from around the way. You get around. You from Queens, right?"

"Yeah, why? You be out there a lot?" I asked, staring at her.

"Yeah. I dance out there."

"Word, what club?"

"The Sugar Shack. I know you heard about it. It's a famous club down Rockaway Boulevard, near the airport."

"Yeah, I heard of it. Never been there, though."

"Why not? You should come check it out sometime, come see a sista dance. Believe me when I say that I'm worth the trip."

"Oh, you are?" I said, staring into her lovely hypnotic brown eyes. "What you go by?"

"I go by the name Darkly Luscious," she said, placing her elbows on the kitchen counter and peering directly at me, smiling.

"I'll stop by to come check you one night," I said.

"You promise?"

"I promise."

"Don't lie to a sista. Believe me, if you don't come down, you'll be missing out on a lot. I'm famous down there. I'm the baddest bitch they got dancing down there," she said.

"I hear that."

"I'm ready, Ricky," Danielle said, coming from out the bedroom. Gwen removed herself from the counter top, left the kitchen, and walked past her cousin into her own bedroom.

"What was she in here talking to you about?" Danielle asked.

"Nothing. She was just telling me about her job," I said.

"Um hmm, whatever!"

We walked downstairs together and I opened the passenger door for her.

"So, where are you taking me?" Danielle asked.

"Somewhere special to make up for not having a gift for your birthday," I said, starting up the car.

"Ricky, I told you I don't care about you getting me anything for my birthday. I'm spending time with you, and that's all that matters to me, okay?"

"Yeah, but I still feel bad about it. So tonight, it's about you. I'm taking you somewhere special. I don't want to hear about you complaining about the expense. I got everything covered tonight."

She smiled and said, "All right, you're my big man tonight. I'm with you all the way." She then leaned forward and gave me a tender kiss on my lips.

"That's my girl."

I took Danielle to this exquisite seafood restaurant at City Island. It was very nice and serene, and the food was great. I spared no expenses when it came to my baby because she was about to have my baby.

After dinner at City Island, I took her into the city and we stopped at a bar and grill located in downtown Manhattan. Then I drove over to Roosevelt Island and parked the car in an isolated spot that gave us a great view of the Eastside of Manhattan, along wit' the FDR. We talked, joked, and then ended up fucking in the car. When she asked where the money came from, I lied and told her that my pops had a little cash saved up under his bed. I told her it was about two grand. She believed me.

My shorty ended up staying the night wit' me at my place, and we nestled and caressed against each other till dawn.

I met up wit' Kinko two days later and told him again about my rendezvous wit' glass-eyed Charlie, who turned out to be a local thug who ran the pimping business in Queens, along wit' trafficking a few narcotics on the side. Charlie had a string of underground strip clubs that promoted prostitution, drug use, and sometimes violence if you crossed him. I found out that Gwen worked for Charlie in one of his clubs. In fact, Gwen was his main bitch. That bitch pulled in at least two thousand dollars a night. I asked about her around the way, and she definitely had a rep—a notorious reputation for being a bitch you didn't want to get involved wit'. She was Charlie's bitch, and he had a very deadly jealous side to him.

And yet, here I was, fuckin' wit' her cousin.

Kinko and I sat up in his Beamer, parked around the corner from my place, talking.

"Yeah, we gonna get this nigga, Ricky. He short-lived right now, believe me. He comes at you like that. Don't worry about dat nigga, son. He gonna get dealt wit'."

"He was serious, Kinko."

"And what am I, a fuckin' joke, Ricky? That nigga's trying to fuck up my money, and you know how I am about my money. Now when I tell you don't worry about it, don't fuckin' worry about. It's gonna get handled right. Now this shit wit' my uncle, we trying to get this shit poppin off by the summer. I need bitches up in my club. And I ain't talking about these hood dirty bitches wit' gunshot and stab wounds. I need the finest hoes up in our shit. You feel me?"

"Yeah, I feel you. In fact, I know just the right girl who can get this shit started for us. We get her, and we get the rest of 'em. Because from what I'm hearing she got clout in the game. She can bring bitches."

"Ayyite, that's what I'm talking about. You on the money, Ricky, definitely. I want you to handle this shit for us. Be on it, Rick," Kinko said, giving me dap and letting me know that he had confidence in me to set this thing up.

I got out his car and walked into the building. It was afternoon out and hot. May was around the corner, which meant summer was not too far away. I made a vow to myself that when the summer came around, I wasn't trying to be a broke-ass nigga. I wasn't trying to live like that. It felt too good to have a bankroll of hundreds in my pocket. That was a feeling I was trying to keep for a long time, and I was willing to do whatever it took to maintain the wealth. I also saw how happy Danielle was the night we went out to eat at City Island, and when we toured the city sparing no expenses. It was great to see my baby having a good time, without, for once, money being an issue for us.

"Ricky," I heard someone shout. I knew the voice. I wasn't surprised to turn around and see Mr. Jenkins coming my way.

"Hey, what up, Mr. Jenkins?" I greeted, flashing him a smile, but really not happy to see him right now.

"Is this what you're about now!" he said, taking my seventeen-hundred-dollar gold chain into his hand, quickly glancing at it, and then letting it fall out of his fingers. "I thought you were better than this."

"Ah man, Mr. Jenkins, what do you want from me?" I dragged out, staring at him.

"I want better for you," he said.

"Better? And what is better for me, huh? An education, school, becoming a working man for the rest of my life? Huh, you want me to become like you? I can't bust my ass every day for some nine to five and making shit pay. That's not my style, Mr. Jenkins, and you know it."

"Then what is your style? Killing yourself? Going back to prison, huh, Ricky? That's your style because that's where you are headed. I thought you were better than this. I looked out for you while you were in jail. I still believe in you, Ricky."

I just stared at him. I didn't have a response. Looking at Mr. Jenkins brought up some guilt in me. If it wasn't for

him, I'd still be on lock down today. He hooked me up wit'
the GED program in prison and I was eligible for parole
through that program. If Mr. Jenkins didn't come through, I
woulda done the entire five.

"I gotta go, Mr. Jenkins," I managed to say.

"Before you walk inside, answer me this: do you truly
care and love yourself?"

"What?"

"Because, if you do, if you love life, the choices you are
making today, right now, are going to affect you in the long
run. Every man has a choice. Every man has a road to take.
You choose your own way, and you accept your own fate.
I'm here for you, Ricky. I'm gonna always be here for you,
but if you're not willing to accept my help and help yourself, then there isn't much I can do for you."

The only thing I could say to him in return was, "I gotta
go, Mr. Jenkins," and I walked into my apartment, closing
the door behind me.

ELEVEN.

Friday night I went up to the Sugar Shack where Gwen worked. I went solo, which was crazy of me, already knowing it was one of Charlie's spots. But I had to go check out Gwen and see if she was that good on stage and banking dough like that from niggas. Shit, this bitch had been on my mind all fuckin' week.

Outside the Sugar Shack was lookin' crazy. There was a line of niggas ready to get in, standing around and waiting to see some pussy, and there were cars of all makes and models parked outside. I even noticed a silver Bentley parked out front—lucky bastard, whoever owned that car. I wondered about that, though, since this place was supposed to be so low-key.

I stood at the back of the line and noticed these two ladies stroll by dressed in tight fitted jeans and wearing nothing but a bra or a swimsuit top. Both of 'em had phat asses. They looked like strippers, but they were fine. Every man's head turned quickly as soon as they passed by.

"How much?" I asked the beefy bouncer at the door.

"Twenty," he answered, and started to search me for any weapons.

After the search, I gave him a twenty and headed on in. I passed through the foyer and entered through another set of doors that led me into where the action was. It was enormous inside. This place could hold up to at least five hundred heads. I started to gaze at the scantily clad ladies who walked back and forth collecting their tips, giving niggas lap dances, and politicking wit' other niggas who bought them drinks from the bar. I felt my dick getting excited. But my main purpose for coming was to check out Gwen and see what she was about.

I walked over to the bar and ordered myself a quick drink, then turned around and started to gaze at the seminude females again. Yo, they were fuckin' fine. Never in my life have I seen this many exquisite looking females crammed together in one room. Bitches were in thongs, wit' the string getting lost up in their asses 'cause some of they asses were so phat. Now these were the type of bitches Kinko and I needed to have in our place when we opened—fo' real.

I started to walk into the crowd, you know, get my feel and fondle on wit' some of these shorties up in there. A nigga like me couldn't resist the temptation any longer. Girl or no girl, I was about to play, just a little. The place was loud, the DJ was bumping some new joint from Biggie, and the lights were dimmed down low, allowing one's actions to be more discreet.

The first ho who came my way, I quickly pulled in my direction and demanded a dance from her. I wanted her to tease my dick somewhat. She was a Spanish ho, and she smiled and led me to a nearby wall so she would be able to grind up on a brotha. She only had on a pair of panties and this white T-shirt that barely covered her petite breasts.

Shorty backed her ass up against my dick and started to

gyrate her thick hips against a brotha something lovely. I took it there and stuffed my hand down her panties and started to fondle her pussy, grabbing a handful of pubic hairs and letting my fingers dance around in her pussy. She smiled and allowed me to do whatever I wanted to her body.

Ten minutes later and minus fifty dollars from my pockets, a nigga was horny. The bitch was doing me right and had a nigga all worked up. That was her job in the first place, and she was doing it to perfection.

"You want a private dance?" she asked.

"How much?"

"The room is twenty and for me, it's a hundred and fifty. I'm worth it, baby, believe me," she assured me, wit' her fingers dancing on my chest.

"I'll think about it," I told her.

"It's on you, cutie," she said, and strolled off into the crowd.

I had to admit, it was tempting, but I had to stay focused and remember that I was here on business. I glanced around the room looking for Gwen, but there was no sign of her. I went back to the bar and ordered myself another drink.

Forty minutes later, the music changed from loud rap to some smooth R&B. The DJ decided to throw on some Sade, which surprised me. The crowd didn't mind. Them niggas were probably too tipsy and high off pussy to notice anything unique.

"Ayyite, for y'all niggas out there, I got a special treat for y'all," the DJ announced through the mic. He had my full attention. "Yo, shorty coming to the stage right now is what's up. She's one of the hottest bitches I've seen come through here in a long time. She's been in *Black Tail* magazine *Pictorial*, even *Hustler*, so y'all know she's a bad bitch.

128 *Erick S. Gray*

Yo, check it out. I know y'all horny muthafuckas been waiting, so here she is: Darkly Luscious, coming to the stage."

That what's up, I thought. I casually made my way to the stage to get a full view of this. Sade's lyrics played throughout the crowd. I had my drink in one hand and a bunch of Washington's in the other.

Gwen came through the crowd in her sliver stilettos and a long green and white Jets jersey that came down to mid thigh. She got up on that stage and immediately began to do her thing. She started seducing niggas in the crowd by flirting wit' them, grinding, touching, rubbing on herself. Shit, in the first five minutes she already had a hundred dollars on stage.

Soon that football jersey came off, and she was ass naked wit' her petite breasts in full view. But it was her ass, hips, and thighs that niggas were making noise over. When it all finally came into view, more money came out. I mean niggas started tipping big—tens, twenties. Even the ballers in the club threw out fifties and hundreds. She was definitely the best dancer in the club, and everyone knew it. That's why she was constantly getting the big money.

Our eyes met, and she saw that I had showed up. She flashed me a quick smile and focused back on her job. Once Gwen got onstage, it seemed like all the money stopped for the other dancers. She was that ill.

After about forty minutes, and wit' her pockets about five hundred dollars richer, she gathered her things and walked off the stage. She came straight for me in all her naked glory.

"Hey, you made it," she said, throwing her arms around me and giving me a hug in front of everyone.

"I told you I would come."

"So, what you think?" she asked.

"You were good, really fuckin' good. Damn, your body is

tight," I complimented, staring down at her nude and wonderful hourglass figure.

"Thank you. So, what's up? You gonna come through more often?"

"Maybe."

"I can't get a tip?" she asked, flirting a little.

I couldn't refuse. I pulled out my bankroll in front of her, hundreds mostly, and peeled off three hundred, and passed them to her.

"Damn, nigga," she said, "you ballin' like dat?"

"I'm doing me, luv."

"I see dat."

"So what you doing after you leave here?" I asked her.

"Why you wanna know?"

"Because, I wanna pull your coat to sumthin'."

"And what might dat be?"

"I don't wanna talk here. Somewhere quiet and more private," I told her. "So you down?"

"I don't know. I'll think about it."

"Don't let me down, Gwen." I smiled.

"I won't."

"So, meet wit' me, tomorrow night, maybe."

She glanced around for a quick minute, like she was looking out for someone. "Listen, I gotta go. But I'll definitely talk to you."

"Well, take down my number."

"I can't right now, it's too risky. But we'll hook up. I promise."

She walked off quickly, back to the dressing room. I watched her until she disappeared into the crowd, and then I started to focus my attention somewhere else, mostly wit' these naked hoes around. I pulled one to the side and got another lap dance.

It was about two in the morning when I was ready to leave. I had my fun for the night, a little too much fun, and

I was down twelve hundred dollars. But I knew I'd make the money back, so I wasn't sweating it. I was exhausted, and I had seen enough pussy for one night.

Before I even got to the door, these two niggas quickly grabbed me by the arms and said in my ear, "Charlie wants to see you." They didn't even wait for my response. They just dragged me off like I was one of these bitches up in here.

I was tipsy and shit, and all I wanted to do was go the fuck home, but muthafuckas didn't care. They took me to a private back room, and knocked twice on the door. I got dragged inside.

I saw Charlie sitting behind a desk, reclined back in a La-Z-Boy, looking like he supposed to be the Godfather or sumthin'.

"Here he go, Charlie. The piece of shit you asked for," one of the men said.

I glanced around and noticed that I was outnumbered five to one. I didn't even have my gat on me—big mistake.

"Nigga, is you stupid?!" Charlie barked, frowning at me.

"What?" I responded.

"You come to my club when your boy Kinko takes a hundred large from me, kills my cousin, and then I see you hugged up on my bitch, too. You must be either stupid, dumb, or crazy, which one?"

"Yo, Charlie, I told you, I don't know anything about dat," I said to him.

"You don't, huh? Then why I see Kinko come out your crib a week ago?"

"What?"

"Nigga, don't be fuckin' naïve wit' me," he shouted, "because you're this close from getting your head blown off right now. I want my money, Ricky. And if dat nigga, Kinko, don't come forward wit' my shit soon, then I'm holding you responsible. And if I ain't paid by next week, I'm killing you and Kinko. And just to let you know that I ain't playing wit' you, yo, y'all niggas fuck his ass up right now."

"What?" I replied in shock, and soon afterward, felt a hard blow to the back of my head, which dropped me down on my knees and stomach. I looked up, which was a mistake, and caught a size thirteen Timberland across my face. Blood shot from my mouth. I got into the fetal position and felt critical blows hitting me all over. I tried my best to cover my face, but one nigga caught a lucky hit across my eye, which felt like it had blinded me. The beating felt like it went on forever. I wanted it to stop. I bellowed and bellowed until the hitting suddenly stopped. I opened my one good eye and saw Charlie standing over me wit' a black 9mm gripped in his right hand.

"Hurt, don' it?" he said, smirking down at me.

I started coughing, spitting up blood and holding my side. Shit was blurry all around me. I was in serious pain. Charlie squatted down in front of me and shouted, "Open your fuckin' mouth!"

I didn't—fuck him!

"Nigga, you keep thinking dat I'm a joke. Open your fuckin' mouth, or you won't have a week left to live," he demanded.

The gun was aimed inches from my eyes. I slowly opened my mouth, and my entire jaw felt like fire. I couldn't even whistle.

"Suck my dick, nigga!" he yelled.

I stared at his gun and then him, feeling like shit.

"Nigga, open your mouth and suck my dick." I looked down the barrel of that 9mm, and all I could think of was revenge. I wanted to kill this bastard. I had never killed a man in my life, never found a reason to. Tonight I had a reason to.

Noticing my reluctance, Charlie quickly cocked the gun back, allowing a round to enter the chamber as he glared at me.

"I ain't gonna say it again," he warned.

I leaned forward and slowly placed the tip of the gun into my mouth. My jaw was aching. "Some more, deep throat dat shit." I placed half the barrel into my mouth, gagging. I heard his goons laughing. Charlie laughed too.

"Dat's what you are, Ricky, a bitch. You always been a cock-sucking bitch. Fat Tony ain't here to have your back anymore. You on your own now, right bitch? You a faggot. You lucky I don't have my boy Gutter fuck your asshole out right now. He fresh out the joint a month now. But I'm gonna let you be for now."

I still had the gun jammed in my mouth, gagging. I was embarrassed, angry, and wanted retribution for what Charlie had done to me. He humiliated me.

"Get the fuck out my building," he yelled.

I was thrown out the back door. I struggled to get to my car, staggering and falling against parked cars. My ribs felt like they were broken, and my vision was blurry. My eyes were swollen like I don't know what. I was a fuckin' mess. I got ten feet to my car and collapsed in the middle of the street.

I woke up in a hospital room. When my eyes opened, the first person I saw standing over me was my girl, Danielle.

"You're awake," she said, smiling down at me.

I let out a cough and felt this unbearable pain on both sides of my ribs. I tried to get up, but Danielle stopped me, telling me that I needed to rest. She also told me to try not to move around so much. My sides were bandaged. My face was mostly covered, and I felt like shit.

"What happened?" I asked.

"I should be asking you that," she said. "I get a call, and they tell me my man is lying in a hospital."

"I got robbed and jumped," I lied.

"They found you outside the Sugar Shack. That's where my cousin dances. Why were you over there?" Danielle asked, as she held my hand softly.

"I went wit' a friend, next thing you know, I'm coming out the club and I'm getting pounded on."

"The doctor says you got four broken ribs. Besides that, a few bruises. You'll be okay. The doctor said you can leave tomorrow."

"Cool."

"I want you staying with me, Ricky."

"At your place?"

"Yes. I'm pregnant, and I'll be damned if my child grows up not knowing who his father is because he's out here doing dumb shit."

"I told you, I got robbed and niggas jumped on me. Why da fuck I gotta lie for?"

"Um huh, whatever! I also found this on you," Danielle said, holding up a stack of money, hundreds mostly. "Where did it come from?"

"You going through my pockets now!"

"Ricky, I found twelve hundred dollars in your pockets. You ain't working, so where did the money come from?"

"C'mon Danielle, why you beefing? You see me lying up here in a fuckin' hospital, and you bitching at a nigga instead of trying to comfort a nigga. I don't need this shit right now. I told you about the money my pops had."

"I'll stop bitching when you come straight with me. You got robbed, yet you still got your jewelry, this money, and your wallet."

I sucked my teeth, knowing that she had caught me in a lie. But I wasn't about to tell her the truth. She didn't need to know the truth. She was pregnant, and all she needed to know was that I was going to take care of her by doing whatever it took.

I started to cough again, and grabbed my sides—shit, it hurt. I peered over at Danielle, and she just stood there, scowling at me.

"I called Mr. Jenkins," Danielle said. "He's on his way here."

"What da fuck you called him for? I ain't in the mood to see him right now."

"Maybe he can put some sense into that thick head of yours. You hustling, Ricky. I know it. I'm not stupid."

The room got quiet for a minute. I stared up at the mounted TV over my bed and thought about the previous night. The coughing continued. Not only was my pride hurt, but my body was numb.

"You hungry, Ricky?" Danielle asked, rising from her seated position next to my bed.

"Nah, I'm good."

"I'm going down to the cafeteria. You sure you don't want anything to eat or drink?"

"I'm good, Danielle."

She walked out the room, and I felt myself about to doze off again as I stared up at the television.

"Wake up, nigga!" I heard someone yell out five minutes after Danielle done walked out. I turned my head and saw Kinko standing over me, along wit' some dude I ain't never seen before.

"Kinko, what's up?" I said, sounding tired.

"Who did this to you?" he asked.

"Fuckin' Charlie and his goons, dat's who," I answered.

"Damn man, you all fucked up. They worked on you good. I heard you were down at the Sugar Shack. Why da fuck you went down there for in the first place? You know we got beef wit' the nigga."

"Nigga probably went down there to check some bitch," the stranger standing next to Kinko said.

"Yo, who this nigga?"

"Yo, Ricky, dis my boy, D'Angelo."

He was tall, slim, and had long braids. He had on a gray sweat suit. I didn't know him, and didn't want to know him. He looked sneaky, and I didn't trust him from the start.

"What's up?" he greeted, extending out his hand, waiting for me to give him dap like we were cool like that. I just nodded my head and ignored his salutation.

"When they letting you out?" Kinko asked.

"Tomorrow."

"Ayyite. You think you ready to put some work in when you get out this bitch? We gonna hit up Charlie, let that muthafucka know his reign is over. We taking control now. You feel me, Ricky?"

"I feel you. But you know dat nigga stay around protection," I added. "He got security around him all the time."

"I got dat covered, nigga," D'Angelo chimed in, smiling.

"We got da guns, Ricky. I know you want that revenge. I see it in your eyes. I want you there when Charlie goes down. We gonna shoot out the one good eye he got left," Kinko said.

I chuckled. "Yeah, I want in."

"Dat's my nigga talking," Kinko said. "I let you know when and where. But in the meantime, get your rest, baby. We need you." After that Kinko and his boy left, but not before they were met on their way out by Danielle and Mr. Jenkins.

"Hey there, schoolteacher. Haven't seen you in a while," Kinko said, as he glared him down.

"Get out this room," Mr. Jenkins replied. "I don't want you here or anywhere near this boy again. I'll call the cops on you."

"What?" Kinko asked before stepping into Mr. Jenkins face. "You gonna call da cops on who? Word of advice, schoolteacher, stay out my business, or I'm gonna have my business come visit you." Kinko rolled out wit' D'Angelo.

I lay in bed, knowing that I was about to hear the bullshit from both Danielle and Mr. Jenkins.

"Ricky, what you got going on with him?" Danielle asked, staring at me nervously.

"Nothing, Danielle."

"Then who was that, that just left here?" she asked.

"Bad news," Mr. Jenkins chimed in. "What's going on, Ricky? You looking for revenge now, huh? Eye for an eye."

"It's in the Bible," I countered.

"Why can't you just open your eyes and see, Ricky? Stop being so blinded all the time. The only ones who truly care about you and your safety are the people standing in this room right now."

"And?"

"Boy, why are you so hard-headed? I thought being locked up was going to put some damn sense in your head. It seems like you're getting worse. Why don't you move in with Danielle? I feel it will do you some good. Stay out of Queens for a moment. This woman loves you dearly."

"I know, but . . ."

"But what?" Mr. Jenkins cut me off. "You're about to have a baby. And the last thing we need is for this child to be brought into this world without having a father. It's got to end. Too many fatherless children, especially among the black community. Your child doesn't need to visit you in jail, or at your grave. You can change that, Ricky. Don't let your baby grow up to be another statistic."

This talk was going in one ear and out the other. My child was going to have a father—a great father. I was going to give him or her the things I never had growing up. I was going to do for Danielle and the baby, and if doing dirt and putting in work was the only way possible to get that stuff, then so be it. I was going to be rich. Nothing was stopping me.

I had business to take care of. My family was going to live wealthy. I was going to make sure they didn't have to put up wit' the bullshit I went through when I was young. I was 20 years old, and I had a lot of making up to do.

I decided to move in wit' Danielle. And besides, I couldn't stay at my place any longer. It was too hot over there, plus the rent was due. And another good thing about staying wit' Danielle—her cousin. It gave me a chance to connect wit' her and talk to her about quitting Charlie's club and coming to work for us at our new club when it opened.

The first week Danielle took care of me while I rested. She cooked for me, massaged my sore limbs, and nurtured me the whole time. I couldn't complain. Plus, I was getting mines when I could.

I kept in contact wit' Kinko through my cell phone. He knew where I was at, but didn't want to risk coming by.

About two weeks had passed, and my wounds were better. I was able to walk around the house without aching and clutching injured limbs when I moved. Gwen and I also became cool. She opted to go wit' us, but she had one problem—Charlie. He wasn't about to let his number one bitch go so easily, especially in our hands. It was going to be problems. That's why I knew Charlie had to go, and soon too—especially after my deadline to pay him back his one hundred thousand dollars expired. I knew he had soldiers at my place waiting to put a bullet in me once I showed up. I told Gwen not to worry because Charlie was living on borrowed time—death was coming for him for sure. It was inevitable.

The one bad thing about Charlie was that he was a hard to get at muthafucka. The nigga was never alone. He was constantly surrounded by niggas, or his soldiers. Kinko had someone follow Charlie around to check out his routine. The nigga didn't have a routine. He was unpredictable, and that was a problem for us. So Kinko decided the only way to get at Charlie was when he exited the club—shoot it up. It was going to be messy, but it was our only option. Word got back to Kinko that Charlie was in his club one Thursday night/early morning. Kinko called me up and told me that it was going down that night. I had one problem—Danielle. Ever since I left the hospital, Danielle had been on me like a fuckin' hawk on its prey. She wouldn't let a nigga breathe. She be thinking I was constantly getting into trouble or some shit. Frustrated and needing to get out the fuckin' house and handle my business and get this money, I just flipped out on Danielle while she was on the couch watching television. I started cursing at her about some dumb shit, and we started to argue. It got to the point where she started to throw things at me. I got fed up and bounced, jumping into my father's Oldsmobile and leaving.

I had my .45 under the seat as I raced to Queens. I met up wit' Kinko and D'Angelo on Supthin and Foch. They were parked outside a corner bodega. The minute I pulled up to them, it started to drizzle. I thought maybe this was a sign from above that tonight was going to be bad news for me. But my hard-headed ass didn't pay it any mind. I just didn't give a fuck. I hopped into Kinko's car, and we all headed for the Sugar Shack. I knew Gwen was dancing tonight. I wished she wasn't because I didn't want her to get caught up in what was about to go down.

It was about one something in the morning when we arrived. D'Angelo parked across the street from the place, a good and safe distance where we weren't so easily spotted. We all sat, waited, and contemplated. It started to rain a little harder. Raindrops started cascading off the front windshield, and then heard some thunder.

"You ready for this, Ricky?" Kinko asked, turning back to face me.

"You know what's up," I said, nodding my head and showing him my .45.

"Scrap that," Kinko said. "We got something better for tonight. Show him, D'Angelo."

D'Angelo leaned forward and picked something up off the floor. Then he showed me what he had in his hands, and I was in total awe. The nigga was holding a black Uzi.

"Everybody lies down tonight!" Kinko proclaimed, looking possessed.

"Damn!" was the only thing I was able to say at the time.

"We ain't playin' wit' this muthafucka, Ricky. He's dead, and every other muthafucka that's around him is dead."

I felt my heart racing faster as I sat in the backseat. I peered out into the hard rain that began to fall, and I took in a quick deep breath. Mr. Jenkins edged into my thoughts—don't know why. Maybe it was my conscience talking to me. But it was too late to turn back now, no matter what my mind was saying. I looked at tonight as an opportunity. This was my chance to finally get mines. And if a nigga gotta die so me and my family could live, then so be it. In this game, it was you or him—whoever is quicker wit' the sword, rules. That's life, that's the streets. That's how it is now, and how it will be forever. Kinko's motto was: do unto them, before they do unto you.

"What time he gets out?" D'Angelo asked, looking antsy and shit.

"The club closes around four, five, but the nigga don't stay all night," Kinko said. "That's what I heard. He's out around this time, wit' a bunch of muthafuckas around him."

The club's front door opened and out stepped Charlie and his entourage of hit men.

"It seems that this nigga ain't all dat unpredictable after all," Kinko said.

D'Angelo passed me an Uzi, and Kinko had one too. We were definitely well equipped wit' fire power, and wit' these guns we couldn't miss.

"Y'all niggas, let's finally toe-tag these muthafuckas," Kinko said and quickly stepped out into the rain. D'Angelo and I soon followed. We were getting drenched from the heavy rain, but we held our Uzis and approached Charlie and his men.

We looked like madmen as we loomed closer to our targets, using the rain and thunder as a distraction. Kinko raised his weapon and D'Angelo and I did the same.

About fifteen feet from our targets, Kinko cried out, "What now, Charlie, huh!"

Charlie and his boys turned around. Our guns were quickly extracted, and the manslaughter began.

Loud and intense gunfire erupted from our guns as we quickly mowed down Charlie's men. They didn't have a chance against us. We were too heavily armed. It was loud and abrupt. Niggas tried to run for cover, including Charlie, but we cut those niggas down to the floor, having machine guns tear their backs up. Blood and pandemonium were everywhere. Bystanders near the entrance rushed back into the club and closed the door. You could hear the partygoers screaming, probably fearing that they were next, but we didn't come for them.

We continued to approach our targets. I saw Charlie was still alive, bleeding excessively, and crawling on his hands and knees—to where, I had no idea.

"Fuck you, nigga!" I shouted out at him, seeing him weak and helpless. "Who's the bitch now, huh!" I then let a few more shells eat up his back, making him look like Swiss cheese, stopping him still.

"Ricky, c'mon, we out," Kinko shouted.

I didn't hesitate. I began to run back to the car, and D'Angelo was right behind me. Suddenly I heard a burst of gunfire. I turned around and saw D'Angelo on the ground. Someone we had hit was still alive, and he had the strength to fire off his weapon and strike D'Angelo in his back.

Fuck him, he ain't my man, I thought, and I continued running. I saw Kinko didn't care either because he was already in the car 'bout ready to drive off wit' or without us. I jumped in on the passenger side, Kinko made a quick U-turn, and we sped off.

I was soaking wet, and the rain was still coming down heavy. What we did tonight was going to go down in history. We gunned down a major playa in the game. You couldn't get any more gangsta than that.

I didn't even go straight home. I crashed the remainder of the night over at Kinko's crib in St. Albans. We stashed the Uzis, changed clothes, and pretended like tonight never happened.

Two days later, it was all over the news and in the papers. "GRUESOME MULTIPLE MURDERS OUTSIDE A NOTORIOUS QUEENS NIGHTCLUB," the headline read. We made front page and our work was aired all over. I wasn't a proud man for what I had done, but it was surprising to see that killing an infamous drug dealer and pimp made serious headlines throughout the city.

I lay low for weeks.

I couldn't help but think it was a new day, and I was about to begin a new life. Money, money, money—that's what makes the fuckin' world operate. C.R.E.A.M.—cash rules everything around me. After Charlie's death, I knew a new chapter was about to start for me.

TWELVE.

June 1997

It was Greek Fest, the last Saturday in June on a sweltering afternoon. Kinko and I attended the event in style. We pulled up to Jones Beach in my new burgundy '97 Jaguar XK8. I had on a pair of Hilfiger shorts, a wife-beater, a pair of Nike sandals and some tube socks—the simple look. But the sun wasn't the only thing shining that day. My jewelry was ridiculous—five-thousand-dollar platinum chain around my neck, the twenty-two-hundred-dollar diamond pinky ring, wit' the diamond bracelet to match, and diamond studded earrings in both my ears. And Kinko was just as bad as me. We both looked like rap stars.

We were top notch out there on the beach and in the parking lot. All eyes were on us. Bitches craved our attention. If you were cute, sexy, and had a nice figure wit' a dynamite booty, we gave you love. But some of the beasty looking bitches tried to holla, too, thinking they had a chance. I laughed. I ain't had to say a word. Kinko quickly put them ugly bitches in their place, letting them know

what time it was. If they got their feelings hurt, too bad—
acting like they don't see their reflection in mirrors—ugly
bitches.

But on the real, Kinko and I were out recruiting bitches to
come work down at our club. Our minds stayed on money.
We passed bitches our cell phone numbers and told them to
call us up anytime. There was this one bad bitch—damn,
she was bad. She definitely caught eyes and hate. She came
sashaying past my ride wit' her friends, acting like they
weren't interested, looking stuck up and shit. I knew she'd
noticed Kinko and me, but she wanted us to sweat her.

I called the bitch over, you know, the gentle way, saying,
"Hey, beautiful, can my man and I holla at you and your
friends for a minute? Can you spare us a minute of your
time?"

She turned, glared at me and replied, "For what?"

I smiled. "You look good, dat's why."

And yes she did. Shorty was brown skinned, and had tall
legs that stretched out to heaven. She had on stilettos—at
the beach. I don't know why, but she looked good in them.
And her bathing suit, it was a scanty one piece wit' a thin-
ass string covering her nipples, which came around and got
lost in between the crack of her bodacious, round, phat ass.
The bitch was practically walking around butt naked. She
had long, sensuous, auburn hair that stopped down the
middle of her back, and you could see the tattoo of a rose
on her right ass cheek. This bitch was thick and curvaceous.
Every nigga, and I do mean every, snapped their necks
back when she passed. They all tried to holla, but she wasn't
showing niggas any love like that.

"I'm saying, beautiful. I just wanna talk," I said.

Her friends looked willing, but they didn't move until
she moved. I guess she was the leader of the pack. Kinko
stood next to me. I was waiting for him to open his mouth
and say something smart. He had a way to either piss a

bitch off, or make bitches wanna have his baby. And he didn't care how pretty or cute you were, if you were a stank bitch wit' an attitude, he was gonna diss you for sure.

"Why it gotta be like that, shorty? You see my man wanna holla," Kinko shouted. "We don't bite. What you acting like a stank bitch for?"

"What? Niggas be playin' themselves. Fuck I look like to y'all?"

"A slut," Kinko insulted.

"What nigga, fuck you!" she countered back at him. I saw Kinko's eyes flare up, and I knew I had to step in before Kinko ended up slapping and hurting this bitch in the parking lot.

"Yo, chill, Kinko. I got this," I said. I walked up to shorty and said to her, "Excuse my man for being so rude. You know it's hot and shit, and you looking good. I just wanted to get to know you better."

"Yeah, whatever! You see all this," she boasted about herself, "and you just looking for some quick pussy."

"Nah, luv, it ain't even like that. I'm sayin', you the baddest shorty out here, coming out here dressed in a string and shit. I know you got these bitches hating because your shit is tight."

She peered at me wit' her three home girls standing behind her. I heard one of her friends say, "Oh, he's cute."

"Um-hum, whatever. What's all this?" she asked, gently clutching my exquisite diamond pendant in her fingers and staring at it.

"You like it? I can buy you one just like it."

"It's too much for me. I like simpler things," she stated.

"How simple?"

"I don't know. Why? You think you can afford me?"

"Maybe, if you tell me your name," I said, staring into her lovely brown eyes.

"What's yours?" she asked.

"Ricky."

"Cute name. Where you from?"

"I'm from Jamaica, Queens, but I stay out in Brooklyn."

"Oh."

"Iris, we'll be back. We going over to the beach," one of her friends said, revealing her name. And then the three of 'em walked off. They were all cute.

"Iris, huh? That's a cute name."

"You happy?" Iris snapped.

"Damn, luv, why da attitude? It's Saturday, nice out, you looking good, so enjoy da day. Shit, luv, you too pretty to be acting dat nasty."

"Nah, I'm just sick of niggas always grabbing on me like I'm some slut. I wear what I got on because I feel comfortable in this. I don't give a fuck what y'all niggas think! My body is tight, and I like showing it off."

"I feel you, luv. You do your thang," I responded. I glanced over at Kinko and saw him hollering at these two light-skinned bitches by the car. He was doing his thang, too.

"So, how long y'all gonna be here?" I asked.

"I don't even know. But I'm bout ready to leave. We been here since eight."

"Damn." I glanced at my watch, and saw that it was three in the afternoon. I also observed the area around me and saw a lot of niggas were screw-faced when they saw that shorty was actually giving me her time and her attention. They could hate all they wanted. I had the .45 in the car in case niggas wanted to act da fuck up.

"So, Iris, what's da deal? I definitely wanna link up wit' you soon. You ain't got a man, right?"

"No, niggas out here too cheap for me. You probably got a girl anyway."

"Nah. I'm single right now," I lied.

She stared at me. I wanted to fuck the shit outta this

bitch. Just standing here talking to her and looking at her was making my dick hard.

"Give me your number," she said.

"I get yours too, right."

"I don't give out my number like dat," she stated.

"Why not?"

"Because, I don't know you."

"So, I don't know you either."

She sucked her teeth real hard, staring at me. Nah, if she got my number, I was taking hers, too. This wasn't gonna be one-sided.

"Why you so stubborn?" Iris asked.

"Because I know what I like, and I definitely wanna holla at you, take you out somewhere nice. But it ain't gonna be you call me and I can't contact you. If it ain't an even exchange, then we both might as well call it a day and go our separate ways," I said to her, being serious.

"Ayyite, take down my number then. You got a pen?"

"I'll just store it in my phone," I said, pulling out my cell. She told me her number and I quickly stored it in my phone. I then walked over to my Jag, retrieved a pen from the car, and wrote down my cell phone number on a small piece of paper.

"Don't lose it," I told her, because looking at her, she had no pockets, and nowhere to put my number in a secure location.

When we exchanged numbers out in the open parking lot, I felt that hate on my back. Fuck 'em, just shake it off.

We continued to chat for about an hour and a half more. I had her seated on the passenger side of my Jag while I was reclined in the driver's seat. She admired my ride, and we listened to CDs—mostly rap. Come to find out that Iris was from South Carolina, but been living up here for a minute now. She didn't even have an accent though.

At about five PM, and I was ready to bounce, and so was she. We had a good time just talking and chilling. Before she got out my ride, she gave me a quick kiss on my cheek, then she strutted away to meet back up wit' her friends. I watched dat ass wiggle and sway away from me, hearing her heels click against the pavement, and thinking about dat pussy. Damn, it felt so good to be me.

Around six that evening we drove out to Nassau Road and profiled out there for a minute. My Jaguar was gleaming, and we brought some serious attention on ourselves as we parleyed near a McDonalds. Kinko and myself had the serious dice game going down in the parking lot wit' five thousand dollars cash up for grabs. We had a group of bitches around us as we were shooting dice, drinking, and getting high. We had a great time, especially when everybody came through like a hundred deep, showing off their tricked out bikes, roaring their engines, and popping wheelies in the streets.

I never rode a bike, never had the interest to, not until I saw how all them bitches in the parking lot got so hyped when niggas on bikes came through and started wheeling they shits. Bitches began getting on the back of bikes and niggas took them for a ride down the strip at top speeds. I got hyped myself, and thought about getting a motorcycle. I wanted to show off like these same niggas who were in these biker clubs, sporting their motorcycle jackets.

Later in the evening, around ten, shit started to die down. I was ready to go. The hoes were getting boring and I had lost three thousand five hundred dollars shooting dice. And besides, we had business to take care of at the club. We'd been open for a few weeks now, and it was poppin'. We had the baddest bitches working for us, and niggas were spending an ample amount of cash on hoes every night, making our pockets richer.

"Yo, Kinko, you ready to go?" I shouted, leaning against my Jag, drinking a Corona. I was a little tipsy, but I was still able to hold my own and drive back to Queens.

"Give me a minute, Rick," he shouted back. He was hugged up on some light-skinned shorty.

"Hurry up, nigga. I'm ready to go."

"Ayyite, Rick."

I threw away my beer, got into my car, and started the ignition. I reclined the driver's seat and threw in a Biggie CD. I had the top down, and the night was still warm. It felt good just to sit there in my expensive ride and enjoy life a little, knowing dat I was able to afford to live the finer life now.

As I was in my chillin' mood, eyes closed, enjoying that warm summer night and listening to Biggie's lyrics, Kinko hopped into my car and slammed the door. "Let's be out."

"Damn, nigga, don't be slamming my got-damn door like dat. You know how much this car cost!"

"Nigga, just fuckin' drive. Don't nobody give a fuck about your Jag," he said.

"Yeah, whatever! You gonna be paying for my shit."

"Nigga, be out already."

I pulled out the parking lot and took the Southern State Parkway coming from Long Island back into Queens. We were five miles from home when I noticed Po-Po pulling a nigga over on the Belt Parkway. They had their overhead blue and red light flashing and stayed close behind my ride, indicating that I should pull over to the side of the highway.

Ain't this a bitch, I thought.

I wasn't nervous. I had no drugs, and I had my .45 concealed safely in a stash box I had installed in my ride when I first got da shit. And ain't no way police was gonna find my shit, no matter how hard they tried.

"What da fuck these bitch-ass niggas want?" Kinko cursed. He was laid back in his seat wit' a cigarette dangling from his lips.

"Chill, Kinko," I told him.

"Fuck a cop!"

I just looked at him. Yeah, I might have been tipsy, but a nigga was still in his right frame of mind to know I didn't wanna get locked up over some bullshit tonight.

The cop dragged himself outta his squad car and came walking his way toward us. He was alone. I stared at him from my rearview mirror. I saw that he had his hand near his weapon as he approached us.

"License and registration, please," he said, peering into the car wit' his flashlight beaming in on us.

I know how it works, so I didn't say anything. I passed him my legit license and the registration. Everything was clean, so I wasn't worried about shit. After I passed him everything, and he stared at it, I asked, "Why did you pull me over?"

His excuse was, "You were doing 75 in a 55 zone."

"You sure, officer?"

He didn't say anything. He stared over at Kinko, who was seated quietly in the passenger seat, smoking his cigarette and keeping his cool like I asked him to.

"Where y'all coming from?" he asked.

"Jones Beach," I replied.

"Is this your car?"

"Yes, officer."

"You've been drinking?"

I didn't wanna answer that, but I did. "Yeah. I had about two beers."

"Step out the car, please," he said, stepping back from the door wit' his hand still placed near his weapon.

"C'mon officer. I ain't do nothing wrong."

"I said, step out of the car, please," he sternly repeated. I looked over at Kinko, and he had a frown on his face, I didn't want any trouble, so I slowly did what the officer ordered and exited my car carefully. Soon as my feet hit the pavement, another squad car pulled up in front of us, and another officer stepped out.

"Everything okay here?" the second cop asked.

"Driver, come around to the trunk," he ordered.

I sighed, not believing this shit. I didn't argue. I just tried to do what I was told. I saw the second cop standing by Kinko's door, and he was ordering him to step out the car.

"Why y'all fuckin' wit' us for? We ain't done shit wrong!" I heard Kinko bark.

"Sir, can you please step out of the vehicle?"

"C'mon man, we got rights too. Y'all fuckin' wit' us cause we some rich niggas pushing a car dat y'all will never be able to fuckin' afford no matter how many niggas y'all arrest! Fuck wrong wit' y'all racist bastards?"

"Kinko, chill, and do what they say, so we can be out," I said to him, almost pleading because I didn't want any sudden beef tonight.

"Man, fuckin' dumb-ass cops about to ruin my day," Kinko said, stepping out from the passenger seat. He came and stood next to me behind the trunk of my car. I knew they were 'bout ready to search through my ride, seeing if they could find something, anything illegal, so that they could make their collar for the night and probably charge me wit' a felony for something. One cop stood, watching us wit' his light shining on us as the next went searching through my Jaguar. I heard him going through my shit while Kinko and I faced the opposite way, staring at the front of the first police car.

I wasn't worried though. I had da .45 in da car, but I knew they weren't gonna be able to find it. Stash boxes, them shits came in handy for situations like these—random stops for DWB—driving while black and in a luxurious Jaguar, too. Yeah, they pointed us out, especially since I had the top down. We definitely stood da fuck out.

The cop continued to ransack my car, hoping to find something. I knew he was becoming frustrated. I heard him mumble something, and then he cursed out loud. I let out a huge smirk, which seemed to get the second cop's attention. He put the light in my face and angrily asked, "What the fuck you find so funny?"

"Nothing, officer," I replied.

It was frustrating, especially in a situation like this, but what could we do? Lose our temper, wild out, and we would get our asses locked up. They had the upper hand, and I'd let them have the upper hand tonight, knowing that they didn't have shit on me or Kinko. They had the badge, the right to carry a weapon, and the right to also be a dickhead and fuck wit' a brotha because I was driving around in a nice car. Let 'em hate. I wasn't one of these brothas to go off on a cop and act a fool by carrying on and giving them a reason to assault and arrest my black ass. Nah, I played the nonchalant role, being easy and also a little sarcastic, too. I knew by being that way, it pissed them off even more by letting them know they weren't getting to me. I was the better man.

After going through my ride for at least fifteen minutes, the cop gave up and came over to us.

"Find anything?" I asked a little sarcasticly.

He didn't say anything. He had the light in my face and in Kinko's.

"Empty y'all pockets," he demanded.

"What?" Kinko shouted.

"Chill, Kinko," I said, emptying my pockets. I pulled out a wad of hundreds, some coins, and a pack of chewing gum and placed the items on the trunk of my car. Kinko pulled out another wad of cash, some keys, and his I.D.

Seeing that our pockets were clean, the officer shouted, "Ya'll two can leave now."

"Fuck you stop us for in the first place?" Kinko asked, glaring at the officer.

"We had a report of a stolen car that fit your vehicle's description," he stated.

I looked at him and said, "I thought dat it was for speeding."

The cop turned, glared at me, and still let us be on our way without the ticket. Fine wit' me. I was about to get into my car and noticed all these passersby in their cars slowing down on the highway to see a young black man getting harassed by these two white officers. It made me feel like I was part of some exhibit.

I drove off slowly, easing my way back onto the highway.

"Fuck dat, Ricky. I swear, I don't give a fuck, badge or not, if a cop ever tries to put me in a fuckin' cage, I'm gunning them da fuck down. For real, nigga! They gonna feel my wrath. And you need to stop acting like a bitch. Po-Po can get theirs, too, nigga. Dat badge and gun don't mean shit to a nigga like me!"

I paid Kinko no mind as I continued to drive to Queens.

I drove to our club on Farmers. We had named it "The Down Low." It was catchy and business was booming. Investing into Kinko's uncle's club was the best thing I had ever done. I mean, pussy was bringing in some heavy cash for us, at least three to five thousand a night off admission, liquor sales, and V.I.P.s.

We became large quick. Ever since we took out Charlie, our main competitor, no one could even compare to our numbers, or come at us on some takeover shit. Kinko was the main reason for that. He became feared throughout the neighborhood—terrorizing, killing, and even bribing a few local officers who wanted to shut our place down. Kinko would grease their palms here and there, and it kept the heat off our backs.

Our spot was official. Bitches came because they knew that they stood to make a decent amount of cash when they danced nude in our joint. We had the major ballers, players, and occasionally a few celebrities/rap stars come through and they would tip the ladies lovely—shoving fifty- and hundred-dollar bills down their G-strings.

For niggas, admission was ten or fifteen dollars, and for strippers, they tipped the club thirty dollars up front. Some strippers complained, saying it was not fair to them. But these same hoes that was complaining about the tip in or tip out, were making at least three to five hundred dollars a night. So you knew we had to get our cut from these hoes. They kept what was theirs, and we got our percentage. It was fair to us. Plus, it allowed them to keep dancing at our club and make their money.

We were killing it in the V.I.P. Those hoes, they charge whatever they want to charge to suck and fuck a nigga in the V.I.P. rooms, but the house had to get paid first. For a muthafucka to come use our rooms to get his dick wet, it was twenty-five dollars per room. And that was our main bread and butter, pimping out those hoes.

There were four V.I.P. rooms located in the basement. We had each room tricked out wit' leather couches, red carpeting, and a small mattress. We had a nice décor, you know, to make these tricks and johns feel a little more comfortable.

And the strippers, we obtained the finest hoes from all five boroughs. They came in all different sizes and races. We had black, Latino, Caucasian, Puerto Rican, and Russian. Shit, the list went on and on. We established a rep and a serious name for ourselves. The Down Low was well-known throughout the tri-state area.

Kinko and I walked into the club around eleven that

night, and it was packed as usual. We had this kid from Hollis managing our place and making sure our money was right and shit was ran tight. He was cool, this nigga named Linden. Linden wasn't no joke. He had street cred- itability and knew how to hold it down when shit got rough. Linden was six feet, two inches, slim, and had defi- nite hand skills because he used to box. And the kid had heart. He was only nineteen and had many grown-ass nig- gas fearing his name out there like he ol' skool. He took a liking to us, and we took a liking to him. We were like older brothers he looked up to, so we gave his ass a job. The nigga was making money. Linden was an ex stick-up kid, who constantly lived his life by the gun. I met the nigga up- state during his brief time in Woodbourne Correctional Fa- cility in Sullivan County. He was doing a two-year bid for a gun charge because he had priors.

"Linden, what's good?" I asked, observing my club and the activity that was going on around me.

"Same ole, same ole, Rick. These bitches trying to get their paper on, niggas trying to get their dicks hard and feel on some titties. Oh, yo, some dude came by the club earlier looking for you, Rick."

"Who?"

"Don't know, da nigga didn't give his name, just asked for you. Some bum lookin' nigga. I ain't see him as no threat, or I woulda bodied the nigga. You know what I'm sayin', Rick?"

"Yeah, I hear you."

"Yo, Rick, I'll be in the office," Kinko said.

"Ayyite."

"So what's good, Rick? How was Greek Fest? Mad hoes out there, right?" Linden asked, smiling broadly.

"It was cool," I nonchalantly replied.

"Nigga, I know you got numbers wit' your fly ass."

I chuckled, and then said, "Yo, get back to work."

"Yeah, whatever. You know you a fly nigga, Rick."

I shook my head and laughed.

"Hi, Ricky," one of the strippers greeted me as I walked by the active bar.

"Hey, Star." Star was a new girl. She'd been on the job two weeks, and the bitch been trying to fuck me ever since.

"Hi, Ricky."

"Hey, baby."

"Ricky, umm, why you don't call a bitch?"

"Ricky, I need to talk to you."

"Ricky."

Damn, I had a million and one hoes constantly chatting in my ear, begging for my attention. I hardly ever paid these strippers any mind except one, and that was Gwen. At that moment I noticed her flirting wit' some ugly nigga at the end of the bar. She saw me coming and started to smile.

"Hey, Gwen," I greeted, touching her thigh gently.

"Hey, Ricky," Gwen said, giving me a kiss on my cheek.

"Come see me in my office soon," I said, giving her a smile in front of her male company.

I retreated to my office that was located in the back of the club. Kinko was on the phone wit' someone. I took a seat at my desk and started browsing through some paperwork.

"Whatever, nigga," I heard Kinko shout, and then he slammed the phone down into the cradle.

"What's dat about?" I asked.

"Nothing, yo. Just some bullshit. Yo, you gonna maintain things tonight? I gotta go take care of something."

"Yeah, I got it."

"Ayyite, my nigga," he said, giving me dap.

After Kinko left, Gwen stepped into my office, smiling broadly and looking so fuckin' sexy in her thigh-high red leather boots and coochie-cutting shorts.

"You wanted to see me, Ricky?" she said, closing the door gently.

"Yeah." I got out my leather swivel chair and approached her. She stood by the door and gazed at me wit' her beautiful brown eyes.

I stepped closer to her until I was up in her face, feeling her sugary breath blow against my skin and lips.

"You look good tonight," I complimented, taking a quick step back and gazing at her figure from head to toe.

"I always look good. So how was Jones Beach?" she asked, but I knew she didn't really care.

"It was cool. You know, half-naked bitches roaming around and niggas trying to bag every bitch's number."

"What about you? You get numbers?"

"Why should I?" I said, stepping closer to her and gently placing my arms around her waist, pulling her closer to me. "I'm fuckin' you, right? Pussy is tight."

"And you better remember that! I can be stingy with my shit."

"But you won't, not wit' me anyway," I joked as I backed her against the door, and started to pull off her shorts, exposing her shaved pussy. Our tongues met and we began to kiss eagerly. I felt Gwen unbuttoning my jeans, putting her hand in my pants, and fondling my dick. I started to grope on her tits, kissing, sucking, and licking on her dark, erect nipples, and grasping her firm ass. I had my pants down around my ankles, and I picked Gwen up wit' her back against the door. Her legs straddled around me and I started to push my dick deep into her wet and inviting vagina. She moaned and clutched my back as I thrust my hard-on deep into her.

"Ooh . . . .da pussy so good . . . .damn, da pussy so good, baby," I whispered, feeling her strong womanly bliss.

"Take it, baby," Gwen panted. "Aah. Um, take it, Ricky. Da pussy is yours."

I continued to fuck her dat way for ten minutes, then I turned her around, stretched her arms flat against the wall, and penetrated her from behind. I gripped the booty tightly as I vigorously began to fuck da shit out of her. I was not worried about anyone hearing us because the loud and thunderous bass from the club drowned out our moans of ecstasy.

We ain't use no condoms. It was just straight raw rough sex wit' Gwen. I was buggin', especially wit' it being Danielle's cousin.

"I'm cumming," I shouted as I squeezed Gwen's phat ass tightly. Gwen continued to work dat ass, backing it up intensely and working a nigga.

"I'm cumming!" I repeated. Perspiration trickled from my forehead down the side of my face. Her pussy was getting tighter and wetter wit' every stroke.

"Shit, aah, damn, yes, baby. Ah fuck, yes!" I screamed, letting out a powerful nut up in her. Afterwards I didn't pull my dick out. I just let it marinate in the juices as we both panted loudly. I then collapsed to the floor and tried to catch my breath. The pussy was good. Nah, her shit was off da fuckin' hook.

Gwen lay down beside me and asked, "You okay?"

I took another breath and answered, "Yeah. Whew! Damn, Gwen, you gonna give a nigga a heart attack wit' pussy dat fuckin' good."

She laughed. "As long as you can handle it, then we're okay."

"I guess so."

I continued to lay around my office, nearly butt naked for another fifteen minutes, and then I got up, buttoned my pants, and went back to work.

Ever since the club opened, I'd been fuckin' Gwen. Shit, I knew it was gonna happen. The pussy was too fuckin' tempting. And the way she was flirting and throwing it at a nigga, how could I resist? Now I saw why Charlie tried to have her under lock and key. Gwen was a bad bitch, yo.

Gwen went on to do her segment on stage, and I was about to go home to Danielle, my wifey and soon to be mother of my child.

I told Linden that I was going home. I knew he had everything under control, so I wasn't worried. I jumped into my Jag and rushed home.

I shared an apartment wit' Danielle, subleased of course. I got her a two bedroom apartment out there in the exclusive co-op buildings. We had a tenth floor terrace overlooking Jamaica, Queens, a furnished living room wit' an Italian décor, a big screen TV wit' the cream of the crop entertainment center, marble kitchen floors, and a king-size bed. Because of me, Danielle was now living the good life. She was living like a queen. All my baby had to do was go to school, cook, clean, and take good care of my unborn child.

I paid her tuition and any other school fees that came up. I took Danielle out of Bushwick and moved her up first class, and I felt good doing it.

Danielle didn't have any idea about my life in the streets. And if she did, she acted like she didn't care. She ignored it. You know why, because when dat money started flowing in, her eyes became blinded. She finally accepted the fact that she didn't have to live the poor way—financially unstable, constantly beefing about bills and other dumb shit dat concerns money. Instead she could live like Lil' Kim— diamonds, minks, pearls, money, cars, and jewels.

I didn't give a fuck. Any bitch is gonna complain about your life on the streets if there ain't no money coming in, and ain't shit stable. But the minute you place around her neck a twenty-five-hundred-dollar princess cut Sapphire, diamond, eighteen karat gold necklace and diamond earrings to match, she gonna love you real good, and forget all about your life on the street. That money changed her way of thinking real quick.

I walked into the apartment around three AM, being careful not to wake Danielle. I got undressed and eased into bed wit' wifey. I noticed she had on my N.Y. Jets football jersey. Damn, she looked good in it. I gazed at her while she slept and blocked out the fact that I had just fucked her cousin. When it first happened, I felt guilty. My conscience was tearing me apart. But now, I was used to it. I came home every night to her and acted like everything was all good. I would stare wifey in her eye and be denying the whole thing and reminding myself, *I ain't a married man, and it ain't like Danielle can just walk away from all this.*

I threw my head back against the pillow, stared up at the ceiling, took a deep breath, and dozed off. Tomorrow was a new day.

THIRTEEN.

"I love you, Pop," I proclaimed while standing over my father's grave on a calm and warm Tuesday afternoon. I stood there talking to my father for at least fifteen minutes, reminding him how much I was missing him. He was a great man, but he let life push him around too much. I think that's why he died broke, sick, and alone.

I stood there staring at his grave until my cell phone rang. I glanced at the number and it was Gwen giving a nigga a call. I ignored it. I wanted to be at peace, so I switched my phone to voicemail.

"Pop, you should see me now," I said. "I know you probably would have been proud of me. I'm coming up, and if you were still alive today, you wouldn't be suffering. I woulda took care of everything. I got my own crib now, and you about to be a grandfather. I think Danielle is having a boy. She's great, Pop. I know if you would have gotten to known her better, you would have loved her. But I know dat you're in a better place now, a much better place than the hell we were living in. You in heaven now, P. Have fun there." I laid a handful of flowers on his grave and walked off.

Dat same evening, I went down to the club and everything was cool. It was kinda slow since it was only a little after eight. I chilled at the bar wit' Linden and watched the strippers arrive for work that night. We both drank Hennessy and *parleyed* in the club.

"Yo Rick, dat same nigga that was looking for you the other night, he came by again," Linden said.

"What he look like?" I asked, being a little curious about this strange man who was constantly asking for me.

"He about your height, a little chubby too. Some ugly black lookin' muthafucka," he informed me.

I thought about anyone I knew who fit that description, but no one came to mind.

Fuck it, I thought. I brushed it off and focused on business.

"Hey, y'all," one of the strippers greeted. Her name was Cindy, but her stage name was Sparkle. She was light-skinned and a big booty cutie.

"Cindy, what's good?" Linden greeted, smiling from ear to ear.

"Hey, Linden. You got me tonight?" she asked.

"Of course, luv," Linden flirted. "You know you my lady."

Cindy smiled, and then looked over at me and asked, "So what's going on, Ricky? You sitting there ignoring a sista. Buy me a drink."

"I got you on the rebound, luv," I responded, then got up off my stool and headed for my back office. It was definitely a slow night. A little too slow for me. I sat back in my leather swivel chair and stared at the walls of my office.

Two hours later things got a little livelier, and more girls showed up, including Gwen. She came into my office dressed in her stage outfit—a tight skirt, blue thong, and a flimsy, short, sexy, red and white T-shirt.

"Hey baby," she greeted, coming up to me and taking a seat on my lap. She gave me a passionate kiss on my lips and threw her arms around me.

"What you up to?" I asked, while sliding my hand up her skirt and feeling in between her warm thighs.

"'Bout to get on stage in another hour. But I got time to spare," she said. She got off my lap and rested down on her knees while I was still seated in my chair. She unzipped my pants and slowly pulled out my slight erection while caressing my dick in her hand. She then leaned forward, put her lips to it, and started to suck me off nice, slow, and easy.

"Mmm, damn," I moaned.

I sat back and enjoyed the blowjob from Gwen. Five minutes later, my cell phone rang. I looked at the caller I.D. and saw it was Danielle.

"It's your cousin," I said.

"What da bitch want?" Gwen asked as she stopped sucking me off for a quick minute.

"Hold on," I said, and answered Danielle's call. "Yeah, baby, what's up?"

"You gonna be out all night, Ricky?" she asked.

"I don't know yet. I gotta lot of work to take care of tonight."

"I miss you, baby. I don't get to see you anymore," she said, sounding glum.

"I miss you, too, baby, but you know I gotta handle business."

She sighed. "Ricky, you still love me?"

"What kinda question is that? Of course I love you, baby."

"Well, you're not acting like it. I'm pregnant with your

child, and I don't get to see you anymore. I'm bored, Ricky."

"Call up a friend of yours and go hang out," I suggested.

As I was on the phone wit' Danielle, Gwen took the initiative to continue her sexual act and started licking and kissing on and around my navel. She caused me to let out a slight giggle.

"Stop," I mouthed down to her.

"What's so funny, baby?" Danielle asked.

"Nothing. Listen, I'll try to be home earlier to keep you company," I said.

"Ricky, I'm bored sitting in this apartment without you. I'm pregnant, and I'm getting fat . . ."

"Danielle," I interrupted, before she even got into one of her mood swings, "You still look lovely. I told you to stop being so insecure all the time. You're having a baby. I want you to stop being so damn stressed out. I'll be home tonight."

"Promise?"

"I promise, baby," I said, and then we hung up.

"'Bout' time. Fuck her!" Gwen said after I hung up.

I focused my attention back on Gwen and asked, "Why you keep disrespecting your cousin, my woman, like that? What you got against her?"

"We cousins and all, but I ain't gotta like her. We get along okay, but my cousin be acting too fuckin' prissy sometimes, like she ain't from the hood. I swear, that shit be getting me sick."

"That's your cousin," I said.

"And?" she asked wit' much attitude. "We lucky my mother and her mother are sisters."

"So why you fuckin' me, huh? To get back at your cousin or something?" I asked.

"No, I just like the dick. Why? You want me to tell?"

"Hell fuckin' no. No matter what you think of your cousin, that is still my woman, and she's having my child, and I love her."

She sucked her teeth and replied wit', "Whatever! You wouldn't dump Danielle for me? I mean, I'm a better bitch, right?"

Her hand reached for the dick again, and she started stroking me gently causing a slight moan to escape my lips.

"See, you like that. I do the dick justice," she added, then stood up, pulled off her thong, lifted her skirt, and climbed on my dick nice and slowly. She straddled her legs around me as we pressed against the cold leather, and I felt my hard-on disappear into her vagina.

"Fuck me, Ricky," Gwen muttered. "Fuck me good, Ricky baby."

She gripped my shoulders and moved slowly up and down on my lap. I gripped her ass and became lost in her bliss. I popped out both titties and started sucking on her dark and erect nipples.

"Does Danielle give it to you this good?" she asked as she kissed and nibbled my ear.

"Don't worry about Danielle," I said. "Worry about us."

I reclined my chair back and let her ride me until my eyes started to roll into the back of my head. We got so lost in the sex that everything around us didn't matter. Suddenly I heard my office door open and in stepped Linden.

He saw us fuckin' in my leather chair and said, "Oops, my bad, Rick. I see now is not a good time. I'll come back."

Gwen and I stopped as we watched Linden quickly exit, and we both began to laugh. I didn't give a fuck. Linden knew what was up between Gwen and I. We didn't keep any secrets. Well, except for Danielle.

Ten minutes later, after I came and got mines, I was back on the floor checking out the club and seeing that everything was on the up and up. It was going on eleven. When I noticed that everything seemed cool for the night, I decided to make good on my promise to Danielle, leave early, and spend the night wit' her.

"Linden, I'm out for the night."

He smiled and said, "Yeah, you good now. Don't worry Rick, I got things around here. You go do you, son."

"Ayyite, yo."

We walked to the door together and Linden was chatting in my ear about this and that. He was telling me about this new ho that was supposed to start next week, telling me she was a bad bitch. He wanted me to check her out for my approval. I told him no problem.

We both stepped outside—Linden for some fresh air, and me to head home.

Out of the corner of my eye, I peeped a strange figure in the dark. Before I could even speak or act, I heard the all too familiar sound of gunshots. Sounded like hundreds of 'em. I fell to the ground in a pool of my own blood before everything went black on me.

FOURTEEN.

My eyes slowly opened. At first everything was blurry. I strained to see and to focus on my surroundings. I knew I was in a hospital, but I didn't know what the fuck had happened. I looked over and saw my sweetheart, Danielle, seated next to my hospital bed. She was holding my hand gently, wit' her head lowered. It looked like she was praying.

She looked up, saw me awake, and smiled.

"Oh, thank God," she whispered. She picked herself up out of the chair, leaned over me and placed a kiss on my forehead.

I didn't speak. I just gazed at Danielle and admired her lovely beauty. It was good to wake up and have her next to my bed.

"Ricky, you scared the living shit out of me," Danielle barked.

I still didn't mutter a word. I just looked at her. I was a little dazed. Danielle was the only person in the room. I looked around for Mr. Jenkins and was a bit surprised he hadn't shown up.

"You were shot, baby. Four times. You're lucky to be alive," Danielle said.

The only thing I remembered that night was getting ready to leave the club, talking to Linden, and now waking up in the hospital.

"Linden," I said. "What happened to Linden?"

"Baby, he didn't make it," Danielle stated, staring at me sadly.

I felt fucked up. He was only nineteen, a year younger than me. And even if I didn't know him long, his death was bad. I felt I was somewhat responsible for his death. He lived by the gun, and he died by the gun.

Danielle stayed to keep me company throughout the entire afternoon, but it felt awkward because she didn't say much to me. She would just sit there staring up at the television and trying to feed me.

Two bullets went straight through me, one exiting out my left side, and the second through my shoulder. The third bullet was embedded in my left thigh, and the fourth missed my heart by one inch. The doctors informed me that I was lucky. That one had barely missed arteries and shit.

As if my situation wasn't already fucked up, I had two suit-and-tie homicide detectives come visit me in the hospital. These two white male cops entered my hospital room, flashed their badges, announced who they were, and wanted to know what happened that night

"Ricky Johnson?" they inquired.

"Yeah, what y'all want?" I asked, screwing my face up at them while I lay helpless in my bed.

"We're here to ask you a few questions about the night you were shot," one asked. He was the tallest, wit' slick black hair, a goatee, and was casually dressed in black slacks and a button-down shirt. His partner looked the same, but he had silver hair and wore a gray suit wit' a black derby.

I knew the deal. They wanted information. It wasn't like

they cared who shot me. They didn't give a fuck about me. They didn't care if I lived or died. It was just a job to them. They wanted information and an arrest. They wanted to lock a nigga up. And if these two detectives had anything on me, which I knew they didn't, they would have probably locked my black ass up right then, injured or not.

"How you holding up?" the silver haired detective asked.

"I'm ayyite," I said, being short and simple with them.

"I'm detective Freeman, and this is my partner Nordic," the silver-haired man informed me. "We wanna find out what happened to you that night. Do you have any idea who could have done this to you?"

"Nah, don't know, yo," I said.

"Look, we gonna keep it real with you," the taller slick hair detective chimed in. "It's rumored out in the streets that you were responsible for killing a gangsta named Charlie a while back."

I sighed. "I don't know what y'all talking about."

"Yeah, whatever! We know you're dirty, Ricky. And we know your partner, Kinko, too. If you don't get your own self in trouble, he will definitely get you in trouble. Now look, we're here to help you. You think the people responsible for getting you shot are going to give up when they find out you survived? They're going to come back." Detective Nordic said this as if he was trying to scare me. "Now, you have two choices, either help us out, or you're a dead man."

I let out a heavy sigh and shook my head like I couldn't believe this shit. I glanced over at Danielle, and the look on her face let me know she wasn't pleased with me.

"Excuse me, gentlemen," Danielle said before rising from her seat and quickly exiting the room.

I folded my arms across my chest and continued to listen to their bullshit. Like I said before, if they had anything on me, I woulda been handcuffed to the bed railing and charged. These two continued to pound me with bullshit after bullshit. The one thing I'd learned was to keep your mouth shut, and never volunteer information. You slip up and say the wrong things, and the cops will use that against you.

They kept pressuring me to talk, but I wouldn't. I didn't even know who was responsible for shooting me that night. I had my suspicions, but I wasn't one hundred percent sure. And where I'm from, we don't go to cops and snitch. We handle our problems out in the streets.

The last thing I needed in my life was for niggas to suspect that I was snitching. Kinko was a paranoid fool already, so for my safety and everybody else's, my best option was to stay far away from cops and shut da fuck up!

They passed me their cards, told me to call 'em when I decided to talk, and left the room. I knew that they both were frustrated wit' me. But cops will get you in more trouble than they're worth.

After they left, Danielle came back into the room wit' her face still looking upset. She glared at me while she stood over my bed, folded her arms across her chest, and said, "Ricky, I can't take this anymore."

"Say what? What da fuck you talking about?" I spat back, staring up at her.

"You could have been killed. Every night I'm in that apartment carrying your baby, worrying about if you're gonna make it home. This is the second incident with me having to come visit you in the hospital. What's going on, Ricky?"

I sighed. I wasn't in the mood to be hearing this shit. Somebody tried to body me the other night, and hearing Danielle's grief wasn't my main concern right now.

"What you want me to do, Danielle? This is who I am."

"What happened to that man in college? The one I met, who was humble, nice, and was still in school? These past five months, you've changed so much, Ricky. I don't know what to do. I don't know who you are. Are you out here killing people, Ricky?"

"This is me, Danielle. This is the man I am. You either deal wit' it, or be gone. I've been this way before I met you, and I'll continue to stay this way after you're gone. I'm out here trying to get this money so that we can live. Look at you, trying to criticize what I do. But I don't see you taking off that diamond necklace around your neck, or that platinum ring off your fuckin' finger. You're still out here spending my money, and living like a queen, but the minute something fucks up, you're on my ass about stupid shit. I just did four years in prison, and now I'm trying to play catch up. I'm supposed to own these streets by now, but instead, I've been playing Little House on the Prairie wit' your ass!"

Danielle's eyes widened. "I can't believe you, Ricky," she said before snatching off the necklace and ring. She threw them at me.

"Fuck you, you fuckin' asshole!" she cursed. "I don't care anymore."

She stormed out of the room.

"Danielle, I'm sorry. Danielle!"

I tried calling out to her, but she was out of sight. I knew I had fucked up. I was just upset. I caught four shots, and I was kinda scared that I'd almost lost my life. I leaned back in my bed, and knew that I'd probably fucked up the one thing that was truly good to me. Damn!

As the hours passed, I oddly waited for Mr. Jenkins to show up and have him ask me how I was doing. I knew I wanted him to chill for a minute, but when he didn't come, I felt fucked up. I thought maybe he had truly given up on me. Double damn!

Two weeks passed, and my wounds were healing. Too bad I couldn't say the same for my heart and my relationship wit' Danielle. I had hurt her bad. Since I'd been home, she'd been walking around the apartment ignoring me. I tried to apologize, but she wasn't hearing it. She threatened to leave, maybe go move in wit' her moms who lived out in New Jersey. But for her, that was too far from school, and she was almost finished wit' school. So she stayed in the apartment and made me pay—no sex, no loving, no hospitality at all. She was completely cold toward me. I mean, not that I could blame her, but damn, how many times can a man admit his mistakes and apologize?

Word on the streets was that Charlie's younger cousin Nino set up the contract and the hit. He wanted Kinko and me dead, and he wasn't playing. He almost came close wit' me. We had killed his older cousin in the most heinous way. We gunned that man down in front of his place of business on a dark and rainy night. Kinko sent out a message to everyone that we were taking over the streets, and if you came fuckin' wit' us, then it would be a bloody massacre.

But I knew that day was coming, that retribution was gonna come for us sooner or later. It was the law of the streets—an eye for an eye. See, you don't gun down a man like Charlie and his men and not expect for his peoples to come gunning for you. It's street physics, a recycling killing spree—if you kill me, my boys are gonna kill you, and so on and so on.

I got word from Kinko that he was already on it. He had his soldiers out on the streets looking for Nino or whoever was associated wit' him. He also apologized for not coming to see me in the hospital. There were too many cops around, and he couldn't fuck wit' it like that.

Now Nino, I heard the name in my ear once or twice, but his name didn't ring bells like that. Nino was some young eighteen-year-old fool who wanted nothing but a name and reputation for himself out there on these streets. And he figured that the best way to attain that was coming after the men responsible for killing his cousin. Well, Nino was a fool, and a soon to be dead fool at that. When Kinko caught him, I wanted to pull the trigger on him my damn self.

"I'm going out," Danielle said.

"Where you going?" I asked.

She had on a spring jacket, loose-fitted jeans, and a baseball cap.

"Out, that's all you need to know," she replied.

"Damn," I muttered as she left the apartment, slamming the door. A black woman, boy, I'll tell you, they are something else. Why we gotta deal wit' them?

A few hours later the door bell sounded. I got out of bed, limping to the door wit' a cane in one hand, and my gat in the other. I didn't trust anyone. Danielle went out for the day, so I was alone. I was in the bedroom watching TV when I heard someone at the door. I slowly crept my way to the front door, yelling out, "Hold on, I'm coming!" I got to the door and shouted, "Who is it?" I was even scared to looked through the peephole, fearing that someone was gonna put a bullet in my eye.

"Ricky, it's Mr. Jenkins."

I let out a sigh of relief and slowly opened the door. Thank God. When I finally saw his face, he didn't seem too pleased wit' me. His face was in a scowl as he stood erect at my doorway, and he didn't blink once.

"Hey, Mr. Jenkins," I greeted feebly.

"What's wrong with you, boy? You ain't gonna be happy till you end up dead, huh?"

"Mr. Jenkins . . ." I started to say.

"Why do I gotta keep hearing about you ending up in hospitals, or hear about your name constantly in the streets from my students? Ricky, do you want to go back to jail? Do you want to ruin your life? Because if you do, then you're on the right track."

I didn't answer him. There was an awkward silence between us as he still stood out in the hallway. I then asked, "Do you want to come in?"

He let out a quick sigh and stepped into my apartment. Mr. Jenkins gave me this unpleasant look. I caught him staring down at my left hand wit' the .380 gripping it.

"And this is how you wanna continue to live? Answering your front door with a gun in your hand?" he asked. "This is the life you so longed for, huh? Watching your back constantly, not knowing who's going to put a bullet in the back of your head one day, ducking the cops, selling that poison!"

"Mr. Jenkins, it ain't even like that," I stated weakly.

"Then what is it like? Because from what I'm seeing, you're on your way to hell, Ricky. Look at you. Paranoid. You can't even come and answer your apartment door in peace without holding a gun in your hand."

I had to admit that I felt a little ashamed. Why did he have to see the gun? I tried to hide it behind my back, but I knew it was a little too late for that. My business was out in the open.

"You want coffee or something, Mr. Jenkins?" I asked, attempting to relieve some of the tension in the room, mostly with me.

"We don't have time for coffee, Ricky. Have a seat. I want to have a talk with you."

I did what he said despite the fact that he suggested, or *demanded*, a talk wit' me in my own home. I took a seat on the couch after concealing the .380 somewhere safe. Mr. Jenkins took a seat across from me. I don't know why, but I was truly nervous. He didn't attempt to say anything for a few minutes. He just glanced around my apartment, observing certain items, especially the big screen TV I had in the living room.

"Nice," he said.

I didn't respond. I just sat there like a disciplined child.

"I want to ask you something, Ricky, and I want the truth from you." He started focusing his attention back to me. "Are you out here killing people?"

I was stunned wit' that question. I just looked at him, not sayin' a word. My heart began to race. *Why da fuck did he ask me that?* I wondered.

"Why you ask that, Mr. Jenkins? You know I ain't a killer. You know what I'm about."

"Don't lie to me, Ricky. I hear things on the street. I'm hearing terrible things about you, and if you've become a killer, Ricky, if you have crossed that line . . ." He suddenly paused, shaking his head. "I pray to God you have better sense than that. A life; you can never bring that life back. I've lectured this to you kids over and over, Ricky. Money is not worth taking a life. It's not worth it!" he shouted, startling me a little.

"C'mon Mr. Jenkins, I ain't never killed anybody," I lied. "That's not my style."

"Somehow, I don't believe you. I want to believe you, but my mind is telling me different."

"What? You came to my crib to judge me now? You asked me a question, and I gave you an answer," I said through clenched teeth. "Now if you don't believe me, then that's your business, but I told you I ain't never killed anyone."

I knew I couldn't tell Mr. Jenkins the truth. That was one part of me I didn't want him to see. I wanted that secret to be buried wit' me. If Mr. Jenkins found out about the bodies I had on my soul, somehow I felt that he'd never forgive me. He would probably blame his son's death on me too. He would judge and say that I might as well have pulled the trigger on his son because I was out here doing the wrong, too.

So I stood my ground and maintained my innocence in

front of Mr. Jenkins. I didn't want him to see that side of me.

Mr. Jenkins went rambling on about the Bible, and other shit like that—about how thou shalt not kill, and so on and so on. He talked about why the black youth couldn't stop killing each other. We hard-headed, that's why.

But you know, I felt what he was sayin', but I wasn't listening. I don't know why. Maybe I was confused, lost even. But deep down inside, I knew that I was still gonna continue to do me, and live the way I wanted to live. That being righteous shit, I knew it wasn't swinging my way anytime soon. But I sat there and listened to Mr. Jenkins preach to me about loving thy brother, and blah, blah, blah. I gave him respect and sat there for the next hour or two, because he had always helped bail me out of difficult situations.

Around four that afternoon, Danielle came strolling in. She saw Mr. Jenkins and a huge smile emerged across her face. She went up to him and greeted him wit' a strong loving hug and quick kiss on his cheek. And as for me, I got nothing when she turned to notice me. I got greeted wit' a huge grimace and attitude.

"Everything okay with y'all two?" Mr. Jenkins asked.

"No, Mr. Jenkins," Danielle quickly said and started informing him about our business. I was tired, and here this bitch was, starting him up again. And of course, he started preaching to me, again. He started saying I was lucky to have a beautiful and supportive woman like Danielle. And how it was important for me to keep her around, and to change my sinful ways because of the baby, and he kept on pounding into my head that I needed to be a good and supportive father.

Oh, God.

So, of course, I went through another lecture wit' Danielle sitting next to my side, agreeing wit' Mr. Jenkins.

"I love him, Mr. Jenkins. God knows I do. But lately, he's become a real asshole," she proclaimed.

"I've become a real asshole?" I rhetorically asked back. "What is this, Marriage Counseling 101?" I added. I abruptly got up and walked off into the bedroom, slamming the fuckin' door. I was sick of this shit.

I heard them talking in the living room, but I had a lot of shit on my mind and none of it dealt wit' giving a fuck about them.

FIFTEEN.

I got the call the following night right after Mr. Jenkins' visit. It was Kinko on the other line, informing me that he got wind of Nino's whereabouts, and he wanted to hit 'em up real hard tonight. Kinko wanted me to tag along wit' the crew and pull the trigger on Nino my damn self. Of course, when he called, Danielle was lying in the bed next to me. When she heard me talking over the phone, she looked at me wit' a suspicious gleam in her eyes. I told him to call me back later, or I'd hit him up later.

Now of course, I was excited. They got that nigga. He tried to end my life real swiftly and ain't give a fuck how he did it. I probably deserved it after what we did to his cousin. But yo, these were the streets, things fuckin' happened, and if you ain't careful, things might happen to you.

"Who was that?" Danielle asked, staring at me wit' attitude and shit.

"Nobody, just some bullshit," I tried to explain.

"Ricky, stop lying to me. That was Kinko, right? What he want from you now?" She rose out of her laying position, propped herself against the headboard, and stared uncertainly at me.

"Danielle, don't stress yourself. You got the baby to worry about."

"I got two babies to worry about," she replied.

I just looked at her. "Whatever!" I jumped out the bed and began dressing.

"Ricky," Danielle called out wit' pleading eyes. "Don't go. Stay home with me tonight, baby."

I stood there by the bed, in my jeans, about ready to throw on my shirt, and here she was showing me some love and a little bit of hospitality. It had been about two weeks since I'd received that.

She came up to me, clad in her cotton pajamas, looking so cute wit' her long black hair falling down to her shoulders. She started kissing me on my neck and touching me. I let out a slight groan, enjoying the way her warm lips slowly saturated my neck and worked their way up to my chin and onto my lips. I seized her pregnant figure into my arms and returned the favor little by little. I slowly undressed her, pulling off her lengthy pajama bottoms and exposing that she didn't have on any panties. I then pulled off her top and had Danielle ass naked in our bedroom. Her belly had started to protrude a little, but she wasn't showing much. Her figure was still looking sexy. I kissed and felt around her belly. I knew it was too soon for me to hear any movement or a heartbeat, but I became exuberant just knowing that a life was forming inside her stomach. My life, my child, my seed.

I laid Danielle across the bed. I parted her smooth brown thighs and kissed and licked my way down them until my face and tongue were pressed against her moist and soft womanhood. She let out a blissful moan as she gripped the back of my head and whispered, "Aah, I love you, Ricky. Don't ever leave me."

I didn't respond to her. My face was too busy in between her legs, eating her out. That's how I wanted to show her my love, which was rare for me. I continued tasting her for the next ten to fifteen minutes, and then I came out my clothes, climbed on top of her, and slowly pushed my dick into her. She caused me to groan because her pussy never felt so good. It's true what they say—pregnant pussy is the best pussy.

An hour later, we were both sprawled out on the bed, sweaty and still naked like the day we came into the world. It was some great sex. I wasn't complaining and neither was she. We didn't say a word to each other. We both just lay there side by side and looked up at the ceiling, panting and breathing hard.

The phone rang. Danielle looked over at me, and said, "Don't answer it. Please, baby, don't answer it. I want to continue to enjoy this night together." And after that was said, she started to cuddle against me, getting all cozy against my naked frame. She began to touch and kiss me in all the right places. I completely forgot about the phone and Kinko, and began round two wit' my girl. It had been too long since I had that. I guess she had finally forgiven a brother.

Thank God.

Now that I had things right wit' Danielle again, here came Gwen, bitching at a nigga. I finally left the house and went down to the club after I done been shackled up in my apartment for numerous weeks, and was in the hospital before that. So a nigga needed some fresh air and I needed to see how things were going. I still had a business to run regardless of being shot four times.

Kinko hit me up beforehand and asked what happened to me that night they got at Nino. I told him I couldn't get out. Danielle held a nigga up, but that didn't stop the nigga from breaking me off the details about what had happened that night.

He went on to explain about how Nino didn't even see it coming, just like his cousin Charlie.

"I blew the side of his face the fuck off," Kinko ecstatically told me. "You should have been there, son. The nigga was sitting alone in his ride. We just rode up on the nigga, opened fire, and ate his face up. It was definitely a closed casket for that nigga." He paused and then said, "For my nigga, Linden, word. He was a good brotha."

I had no words. When I heard the events, I just shook my head. Kinko took murder to a completely new level. But it's funny, I thought hearing about Nino's death would make me feel better, but it didn't. I thought about what Mr. Jenkins said to me the other day when he came over to my apartment—about brothers killing brothers. Would it ever stop? I wondered if that nigga Nino truly deserved getting his head blown off. I was just feeling guilty.

I stepped into the club around eleven that night and it was poppin'. Nothing had changed since I left. The minute I walked through the doors, I was greeted wit' love, respect, and awe.

"Ricky, baby, it's good to have you back," the first bouncer greeted.

"What up, Rick?" the second bouncer said, giving me dap and embracing me in a manly hug.

I strolled into the club, and the look on these bitches' faces, you could have sworn they seen a ghost enter the place.

"Ohmygod, Ricky!" Cindy merrily greeted, coming up to me wit' her titties free and bouncing. She embraced me into a hug. More of the ladies started to come over. They trotted off the stage and came up to me, pressing their scantily dressed selves against me, and showing a nigga much love.

"I thought you were going to die," one of the strippers said, looking at me like I was a fuckin' miracle.

"I'm glad you're back."

"You okay, right? No problems anywhere else?"

I had to pry myself away from the ladies. They wanted to know all of my business, and they couldn't keep their hands off me. They all treated me like I was a ten dollar tip. I barely made it to my office in one piece.

I asked around for Gwen. They told me she was downstairs in the dressing room changing outfits for the night. She didn't know I was in the building. Well I was sure she knew now because one of them hoes had to open up their mouths and tell her that I was back.

And sure 'nuff, about ten minutes later Gwen came strutting into my office in a pair of clear stilettos, a pink thong, and her breasts mashed together in a skimpy bikini top.

I stood by my desk. She looked at me and I looked over at her. Neither one of us said a word. She came over to me, and I was taken aback when she slapped me hard across my face.

"What the fuck," I said.

"Fuck you for scaring the living shit out of me," she cursed, and then forced herself against me, throwing her arms around me and surprising me wit' a passionate kiss. "I thought you were going to die."

"Never that," I assured her. "I'm here till the end."

"You better be. I see my cousin took good care of you at the apartment. I woulda came by to see you, but you know, me and her don't rock like that anymore. And I didn't want the bitch to get suspicious and shit."

"Understandable. I'm good, though."

"Good enough for a quick fuck?" she asked, wit' her fingers touching my body seductively.

I let out a slight chuckle. "Damn girl, you don't play around."

"I've been worried sick about you for the past few weeks. I've been missing mines."

"Yeah, I see."

"Yeah, whatever, ummm," she moaned as she gripped my penis through my jeans. "Yeah, I see he's been missing me too." She felt my man about to rise.

I didn't want to get anything started tonight. I just got back and I wanted to chill out and take care of things here down at the club. I needed to make sure the money was still correct.

"Next time, Gwen. I promise," I said, backing away from her.

"Next time?" she asked, sounding irritated by my choice of words. She sighed, folded her arms across her breasts, and returned wit', "What, you get shot four times, and now all of a sudden you don't want the pussy no more? Huh, that's it, Ricky? Or does my fuckin' cousin got you strung out on her weak shit?"

"Gwen, what da fuck, yo? I just came back. I don't need the drama coming from your fuckin' lips. Chill out, ayyite!"

"Whatever, Ricky," she replied, and then quickly strutted out my office.

I just shook my head and let out a colossal sigh. Damn!

I was alone in my office for twenty minutes when one of my workers came in interrupting me. Manny was his name.

"Yo, Rick, we got a new girl today. I thought you might want to check her out," he said, smiling from ear to ear.

"Oh, word. She bad?" I asked.

"Shorty is off da fuckin' hook. Her body is tight, Rick. She got my dick hard just by staring at her."

I smiled. "Ayyite, Manny. I'm a check shorty out. Where she at?"

"She downstairs changing clothes. We can make some serious money pimpin' her Rick. Whew, niggas is lovin' shorty."

"Ayyite."

"For real, Rick . . ."

"Manny, ayyite. I'll be out there," I said, cutting the nigga off because he be talking too fuckin' much sometimes.

I took care of what I had to take care of in the office, then headed out to where the music, pussy, and action were. The D.J. had some Biggie rockin' hard in the club, and I glanced around lookin' for a new face. I spotted shorty on stage wit' her back turned to me. Ohmygod, shorty had the phattest fuckin' ass, fo' real yo—thick like a muthafucka. Her body was glistening wit' baby oil under the dimmed lights as she clutched one of the two poles set on the stage. She extended her arms out and had her ass out to the public. She had on a pink thong that got lost in the crack of her ass, stilettos, and this skimpy lookin' top, wit' her long, curly, auburn hair falling off her shoulders.

She had the niggas going crazy. I mean I saw fives, tens, even fifty dollar bills being thrown on stage. I thought, Gwen got herself competition because this ho was a bad bitch, fo' real. I was in awe over her body.

She still had her back to me. Suddenly she dropped her booty down to the floor and quickly went into a complete split.

It was on and poppin'.

Manny came up to me, tapped me on my shoulder, and nodded his head, saying, "I told you so."

I couldn't stop staring at her. She made my dick hard, and I hadn't even seen her face yet. The stage was crowded wit' niggas holding money in their hands and hollering and cheering shorty on. And of course, shorty got hate from the other bitches because she was the new girl and making all the money.

When she finally did turn around and I got to see her face completely, I was in total awe again.

"Oh shit," I muttered. "Word. Not Des."

Yes her, my ex-girl from four years ago.

She spotted me looking and smiled. Seeing me didn't stop her from continuing her routine on stage. She went on performing, acting like we didn't see each other.

I was like, DAMN! I mean Des always had a nice, bangin' body when she was young, but now her shit was like whoa! She'd definitely become thick in all the right places, that's fo' sure.

She spent about another fifteen minutes on stage, getting that money and driving nigga's crazy wit' her fine sexy ass. Afterward, she collected her money and clothing and strutted off in her heels. She immediately came up to me, smiling like she had won the money and embraced me wit' a strong loving hug.

"Ohmygod, Ricky. How you been, baby?" she asked as we rocked back and forth in each other arms.

"What's good wit' you?" I replied.

"I've missed you," she said.

"Damn girl, when did all that happen?" I asked her. I stepped back a few and peeped her lovely and well-rounded figure.

She laughed and returned wit', "You always knew that I had a tight body, don't be actin' brand-new and shit."

"Yeah, but you're thicker now in all the right damn places. Shit," I said, lustfully staring at her.

"Well, things changed."

"Let's go somewhere and talk private, where it's quieter. Follow me to my office," I said.

She sashayed right behind me into my office. I closed the door, drowning out the thunderous bass from the club, and took a seat on my desk.

"So, what's good, Des?" I asked.

"You tell me? You makin' dat money right now. I see you doing fine for yourself," she said, staring me up and down.

"I'm doing ayyite."

She sucked her teeth and uttered out, "Whatever!"

"What's up wit' the slight attitude?" I asked.

"No reason."

"Shit, I should be the one wit' the fuckin' attitude, Des."

"Why is dat?"

"Because while I was locked away for four damn years, I ain't get not one letter, none of my collect calls were accepted, and if so, your moms picked up to curse a nigga out, and not a got-damn visit from your ass once. What's up wit' that, huh? You left me in there to rot. Dat's fucked up, Des. You were my girl. You were supposed to hold a nigga down."

"Please, Ricky, don't even start trippin' about dat shit. You knew how ill and strict my moms was. Dat wasn't even my fault."

"If you really loved me, you woulda found a way to come see a nigga, or hit a nigga up."

"I wanted to. Believe me, Ricky, I wanted to. But both our situations were fucked up. When I heard you were locked up, I cried, baby, fo' real. I wanted to come see you so damn bad that I almost ran away from home."

I looked at her.

"Come home wit' me tonight, Ricky. I need to show you something."

"Tonight?" I instantly thought she wanted me to hit her off wit' a little something, sexually speaking. It had been four years.

"It's really important for you and me, Ricky," she added.

"Important?"

She gave me this serious look, cutting her eyes at me. "I gotta get back to work."

"Work? I'm the boss. Chill for a minute."

"I'm getting off at three. Can you drop me off tonight?"

"Yeah, I can do that for you."

"Thank you," she said, and then strutted out the door in her sexy stilettos.

After Des left my office, I took a seat in my chair and thought about her for a quick moment. Damn, she was fine. Her body and her beauty were embedded in my mind.

Did I miss her? I asked myself.

I stared at the walls of my office. It looked like Des had matured quite a bit these past four years. I started thinking crazy shit, like fuckin' and maybe dealin' wit' her again.

My little trance ruptured when Gwen came storming into my office and shouted, "Who da fuck is dat bitch?"

"Excuse me?" I asked, looking at her like she done lost her fuckin' mind.

"Dat bitch I saw you hugging and kissing on, and then you took her into your office. You fucked her, too, Ricky? That's why I can't get no dick because you fuckin' that stank skeezer now. You sorry, Ricky!"

"Gwen, you need to calm da fuck down and chill."

"Fuck you, Ricky! I should tell my cousin about us since you wanna be on some grimy shit like dat."

I jumped outta my chair and went straight for her. I forcefully grabbed her by her neck and threw her against the wall. "You gonna say what! Fuck is wrong wit' you, bitch! This is my business. You ain't my girl. We just fuck. Don't forget dat. And don't you dare bring Danielle into our business. And who I bring into this office, that ain't none of your fuckin' business either."

"Can you please let go of me," Gwen whimpered, clutching my wrist and staring into my eyes wit' tears trickling down her face.

I stared at her for a moment wit' my face twisted wit' anger. I knew I had the look of a madman. I slowly began to loosen my grip around her neck, letting her breathe. She huffed, rubbed her neck and didn't say a single word to me. I saw the look of fear plastered across her face. I had never reacted like that toward her. I don't know what da fuck came over me. I just fuckin' snapped like that, and I didn't even know why. All I heard was her telling Danielle about us, and I lost it.

"Get da fuck out," I said to Gwen, and she quickly left my office. I took a seat back in my chair and laid my head on my desk.

"Yo, what's up wit' shorty?" Kinko asked, coming into the office.

"Nothing, the bitch is just stupid," I replied, picking my head back up and staring at Kinko.

"Word, Ricky, you got these hoes trippin' over you?" He took a seat on the couch, pulled out a wad of cash from a small bag, and started counting big bills. "See this, nigga. Money, nigga."

"How much?"

"About twenty thousand."

I nodded.

Kinko was hustling the streets hard and fast. He didn't spend that much time in the club like me. He was mostly on the streets, making sure his workers, product, territory, and his street reputation were in order.

I knew he used this club as a front. And he had other businesses that he laundered money through, like his barbershop on Rockaway Boulevard and his small restaurant/lounge on Jamaica Avenue.

I didn't operate or care about any of his other businesses. My main focus was this club and makin' sure it operated properly. We both were like the dapper Dons of Queens. Our reputation was fierce and steady. No one fucked wit' us, not even cops. Kinko had connects and his money had reach, sometimes to the most unreachable places.

It was a little after three in the morning. I called Danielle and told her I was staying out late. She got pissed, but hey, I had to do me.

Des was already dressed and waiting for me outside the club. She had on tight blue jeans that accentuated her figure, Nikes, and a white t-shirt. She was still looking cute, even in regular gear.

"You ready?" I asked.

"Yeah."

I walked her to my car.

"Damn, you rolling like dat?" she asked as she admired the Jag.

"Gotta be on top of things. My shit is tight, right?" I boasted.

She smiled.

Being a gentleman, I opened the passenger door for her and allowed her to enter my ride like a lady. I got in and asked, "Where to?"

"I stay in Flatbush now."

"Ayyite." I started up my car and bounced.

We got to Flatbush in no time, being that it was three in the morning and traffic was sparse. I pulled up to this six-story building and left my Jag double-parked out front while I walked wit' her to her apartment.

I didn't plan to stay long. I thought Des was gonna bless a nigga wit' some quick ass, maybe head too, and then I'd be on my way. That's how she got down. Lookin' at her, I was so fuckin' horny.

"You're not gonna park?" she asked.

"Nah. I ain't staying long."

She shrugged her shoulders and I followed her into the building. I walked three steps behind her the whole time because I wanted to see that ass switch left to right, right to left while she walked. And it was looking so fuckin' juicy and phat. Damn, she had my dick jumping.

We got to her fifth floor apartment and stepped inside. It was dark in the hallway. Des reached for the light switch on the wall and turned on the hallway lights. I quickly studied the layout of her crib while she went into the bedroom to change clothes. She stayed in a two bedroom apartment wit' a small-ass kitchen and a small-ass living room. And the bathroom, it felt like you were in a hallway closet. Her shit was tiny. I was scared to stretch, fearing that I might knock down something.

I began to hear two voices coming from the bedroom. It sounded like a woman. My ears perked up because I was trying to be nosy and shit. Moments later this elderly lookin' lady came out of Des' bedroom.

"Hello," she greeted politely, wit a West Indian accent.

"Hey," I greeted back.

"You must be Des's friend. I'm Nikkei," she introduced, shaking my hand. "Such a handsome fellow."

I smiled.

Des stepped outta the bedroom dressed in this long pink t-shirt that stopped at her knees. The lady left when Des came out of the bedroom.

"Who was dat?" I asked.

"The babysitter," she informed me.

"Babysitter? You got a kid?"

She nodded. "He's three. You wanna see him?"

"Hey, I don't mind."

She led me to the second bedroom, clicked on the lights, and I saw the most handsome young man sound asleep in his bed.

"What's his name?" I asked, peering down at him.

"Raheem."

"Raheem, huh? Cute name."

"So what's up wit' you and the baby father?"

"He ain't been around."

"Why not?"

She shrugged. "I don't feel like talking about him right now."

"That's cool."

We left the child's tiny bedroom and walked back into the living room. I took a seat on the couch and thought about Des having a baby. Damn, some lucky nigga knocked dat up and gave her a son. He musta been enjoying that pussy. Shit, I woulda probably knocked her up too if I didn't get locked up. The way we were fuckin', it was definitely gonna happen sooner or later.

"You want something to drink?" Des asked from the kitchen.

"Nah, I'm cool."

I was still horny, and seeing Des walk around in the apartment wit' that long pink t-shirt on and her breasts protruding through the shirt, I knew she didn't have a bra on. I thought about her not having on any panties either.

Yo, I'm fuckin' tonight.

Des came back into the living room wit' a glass of juice in her hand. She sat down next to me. *That's what I'm talking about.* She looked over at me and said, "We need to talk."

I smiled. "About what?"

She paused and diverted her eyes from me. I knew she had something on her mind. I didn't stress it. I waited for her to continue. She stared back at me and said, "We need to talk about your son."

"What?" I replied, staring at her like she was fuckin' crazy. "My son?!" I repeated.

"Yes, Ricky. Your son."

"You trying to tell me that's my son in dat room?"

She nodded.

"Get da fuck outta here! Why you trying to play me, Des? What's dis about, huh? Money? You need fuckin' money? If you do, then just say the shit. Don't come at me wit' games and shit, telling me I got a son."

"But he's yours," Des tried to explain, taking my hand into hers.

I jumped up and stood over her wit' my face scowling. "Yo, fuck you. I'm out."

"Ricky, please don't go. Wait!" Des shouted.

I stood in the hallway.

"Please, don't leave me. He's your son, believe me."

"How da fuck do I have a three-year-old when I was locked up for four years? Huh, Des? Explain dat."

"I got pregnant before you were incarcerated. You got locked up in May. I found out that I was two months pregnant in June. He's yours, Ricky. I wasn't with anyone else when I was fuckin' you."

I just stood there, glaring at her, thinking, *I don't believe this bitch.*

Des continued, "I had Raheem in January. He was born on January 12, 1994. I had him alone, Ricky. I got no one."

"What happened to your moms?" I asked.

"The bitch kicked me out her fuckin' house when she found out I was pregnant. I was fifteen, scared, alone. And my moms just deserted me. You were locked up, so where was I gonna go? What was I gonna do? I was so scared Ricky. That's why I didn't write or come see you. I couldn't."

"I had no money, no job, nothing," she said. "You know what happened to me, Ricky? I had to fuck this thirty-year-old man so I could stay at his crib. He took it from me every night, but what could I do? I had to fuck him or I was gonna end up homeless. But two months later, I guess he got tired of the pussy, so he kicked me back out onto the streets.

"I stayed from one friend's house to another's house. And where were you, Ricky? You thought I abandoned you, huh?" she said and continued, "I needed you so much, Ricky. I missed you. I was out there alone, struggling, pregnant wit' your baby, fuckin' niggas for cash, sucking dick so I could be able to live and feed myself. I even sold crack and dope."

She started to tear up as she sat there on the couch telling me her sad story. I ain't a ruthless and heartless person like Kinko, I thought. I do have a heart and if her story was true, then damn, if that was my son, then I gotta hold it down for him.

I didn't move. Des just sat there, crying. "If you wanna leave, Ricky, then leave. Raheem and I managed without you these past years, and I'm sure we can manage without you a few more years. I just thought you needed to know the truth. You have a son in this world. A beautiful baby boy, and I want him to have a father in his life. But that's your decision."

I sighed.

"And don't get it twisted, Ricky. I'm not that same materialistic, young bitch who stayed on your dick just for a few dollars. Having Raheem changed my life so much. I strip and dance because the money is good. I'm trying to get my GED and go to college soon, so if you think any less of me, fuck you. I'm not after you 'cause of your money, your cars, and your jewelry. I'm just trying to do me, so I can live and get mines."

I was quiet during her whole speech. Des had changed a lot. She was nineteen now, looking like she had a head on her shoulders. I went up to her, sat down near her, and pulled out a wad of bills. I peeled off five hundred, pushed the money in her hand, and said, "I'll call you."

She gave me this nasty smirk, but I took down her number and left her in the apartment.

I got to my car and thought about Raheem. Damn, I went up there expecting to have some wild and crazy sex, and I came back out her crib having a son—fuckin' ironic. But I knew one thing—my pops didn't raise me to abandon my kids. He didn't abandon me when shit got rough wit' him, and I knew I was gonna do the same wit' my child. I was gonna be in that child's life, fo' real.

That same morning around eight, I stopped by Mr. Jenkins' crib and told him about my situation wit' Raheem and Des. He was a bit amazed by the news, and he remembered Des from when I was in high school.

"Ricky, I hope you don't have any more kids springing up on you. You need to keep it in your pants," he said.

"Nah, Mr. Jenkins, it only happened one time. And I was locked up when she was pregnant. I think it's mine. I'm not sure though. I told you, Des used to be a wild girl back then."

"So you're sayin you're having doubts. It might not be yours. Do you want it to be yours?"

"I'm sayin, he's cute. I see a little of my qualities in him."

"Talk to her, Ricky. You're a young man, and I'm trying to lead you right, but you got to make your own decisions and trust the choices you make. I can't guide and hold your hand forever. Stay off these streets, and stay away from certain individuals, Ricky. You possibly got one son and another child on the way. I want you to be around to see your children grow up, and it's up to you to mold them into the men and women you want them to become."

"I understand, Mr. Jenkins."

It was early, but Mr. Jenkins always said that his door was always open. I damn sure just took advantage of his open door policy. I'm probably one of a few students who had kept in contact wit' him since high school.

Damn, now I had to tell Danielle about Des and Raheem. I figured she couldn't get mad because it happened way before we even met. But knowing Danielle, she wouldn't care. She'd probably still flip the script on a nigga. I had to think on that.

SIXTEEN.

The next few weeks were crazy. I kept seeing Des at the club every night, and it was awkward for me. My baby mama—maybe. I had my uncertainties about having her continue to dance there. I still had some lust for her. But I also understood that she needed to make that money, for herself and Raheem.

I tried staying away from her. The less contact between us, the better. I didn't know what to say or do. I would just come into the club and chill out in the back office.

Now Gwen, I guess she got the point because she wasn't any trouble to a nigga at all, which was a shock to me. After our little incident in the office several weeks ago, shorty began to act like I didn't even exist. I would come in, and she wouldn't even look at me.

Now I can't front, Gwen was still looking good and shit. Her body was so fuckin' tight, and there would be moments when I would wanna call her into my office, spread apart her thighs and have my way wit' her like before. I probably still could, I thought.

It was August, and the heat outside was unbearable. It

felt like the sun was coming toward the earth, and wit' Danielle fuckin' stressing a nigga all fuckin' afternoon about her pregnancy and me being out all the time, I had to get da fuck outta the crib.

I went down to the club around seven that evening dressed in a drenched wife-beater, some jean shorts, and a pair of Nikes. I thought about Des and Raheem, and promised myself to make a trip to her apartment to see 'em. It had been weeks, and I knew Des was definitely cursing a nigga out, and probably putting curses on me. Her family was Haitian, and you know how they got down. I had to chill for a minute and think about my situation. I had a three-year-old son, and I still hadn't mentioned it to Danielle.

I pulled up in front of the club and noticed Kinko's BMW parked out front. Usually the nigga was never here that early. Sometimes he was never there at all. But I paid it no mind and headed for the club.

I walked into the club and it was empty, not a soul around. I headed to the back office and when I walked in, I caught the bombshell of my life. Gwen was bent over my desk, butt naked, wit' Kinko standing behind her and fuckin' her brains out in the doggy style position.

"Damn nigga, you don't fuckin' knock," Kinko barked, glaring at me, and pulling up his pants.

"Yo, what's up wit' this?" I asked. "Damn, Gwen, you get down like dat!"

"Whatever, fuck you!" she cursed while reaching for her clothes.

"I don't know why you're reaching so fast for your shit. It ain't like I never saw it before. You a stripper, bitch!"

"Yo, Ricky, why da fuck you here so early?" Kinko asked, fully dressed now.

"Nigga, I'm about business. I don't know what you're about. I see you was getting your ho on," I said, peering at Gwen.

"Fuck you!" she cursed again.

Gwen stormed by me, leaving the office. At that moment I decided to move on. I didn't know about her, but it was for the better for me.

Kinko lit a cigarette and stared at me.

"Um, damn dat pussy good, Rick," he said. "What's up wit' you and her? Y'all ain't fuckin' no more?" he asked.

"Nah, been there, done dat," I said.

"Ayyite, don't come crawling back to shorty when I'm beating it up, you hear?"

"Nigga, I ain't even stressing the bitch."

"Whatever, nigga."

I took a seat in my chair while Kinko went into the bathroom. I picked up the phone and started to call Des, but I thought against it, and hung the phone back up. Lil' Raheem had been on my mind for the longest, and I thought that it felt good to find out I had a son out there, by Des too—pussy was that good four years ago.

Kinko came out the bathroom and he went straight for the hidden safe under the floor mat in the office. He pulled back the mat and dialed the combination to the safe. Inside the safe we both had one hundred fifty thousand dollars stashed away. Most of it came from crack/cocaine, and the rest from the club and bitches.

"What's good?" I asked, curious as to why he was going into the safe.

"I gotta take care of business tonight, hit up my new connect."

I just sat there and watched him. I invested into the drug game wit' Kinko, but he ran the streets and took care of the product. I just sat back and handled the money runs wit' the sales and other investments. Being out on the streets and handling the product, that wasn't me anymore, and Kinko knew it. I didn't want to touch or go near that stuff most of the time. It had gotten me four years in jail.

"I got a line on this new dope connect," Kinko informed me as he pulled out a stack of bills bonded together. "He up in Connecticut. I'm supposed to meet duke out there by midnight. You wanna roll, Rick?"

I was surprised. Kinko never asked me to roll wit' him when it came time to meet up wit' his connect. That was his business and his business only.

"Dope, nigga? When did you start fuckin' wit' heroin?" I asked. We never fucked wit' dope. To me, it was too risky, too much work, and got you more years in prison. Shit you get caught wit' one kilo and that's ten years mandatory up-state.

"I got things starting up, Rick. I got a good plug in, and plus, I got more territory I'm about to jump off wit'," he explained. "I'm moving in on Hollis Avenue and 201st Street. That dope game is definitely moving over there."

"Nigga is you crazy? That's Ra-Ra's shit. If he finds out you're moving weight up in his hood, he gonna flip and try to murder us both. He an ol' skool gangsta, Kinko. This ain't Charlie we dealing wit'. Ra-Ra will go out and try to have you and your whole family killed if you fuck wit' him."

"Nigga, do I look scared?" Kinko asked and the crazy thing is he didn't look scared for nothing. "How many bodies do I got on my hands? Dat nigga bleeds just like anyone else. I got soldiers too, Ricky, don't forget dat. Money is definitely out there, and I'm getting mines. Besides, dat nigga getting too fuckin' old to be running shit like he a young nigga. Now you down, nigga? I know you feeling all cozy and comfortable chilling and running things up in this club, but I need you back out there in the streets wit' me in case shit gets ugly. You my number one, Rick. What's up?"

I sighed. This nigga was wilding right now. We both were eating and living lovely right now, and he wanna go out and cause a war. I mean, c'mon what's the point in getting involved wit' the dope game? We had everything else on lock: weed, crack/cocaine, shit even pimping these bitches and selling methamphetamine and LSD to these Long Island white boys on a regular. Dope, that shit was pure evil, and too much fuckin' trouble for me.

See, business for me was good. I pushed my weight too. We had this connect out in South Jersey, you know get them birds for a decent price from these Dominicans for $17.5 thousand. But Kinko mostly dealt wit' the serious weight. I pushed eight balls and ounces, or half ounces on niggas. From me, you could get an ounce of coke for $950, maybe $900, and for an eight ball, I pushed that for $175. But my main focus was the club and dealin' wit' these bitches. I made lots of money from these hoes—pussy sells, and it will always sell. I even had bitches who made house calls.

I looked over at Kinko and responded, "Shit, I don't know, Kinko. I ain't down wit' dat shit."

"Fuck you talking about, Rick? You a drug dealer, nigga. You need to start dealing some drugs and making more money out this bitch. Why da fuck you limiting yourself, huh, nigga? I'm in this game to win, take over, and eat as much as possible. You, I don't know what da fuck is up wit' you!"

"Nigga, I ain't trying to go back to jail, or get killed out this bitch, you hear! I got a baby on the way."

"Nigga, I got three kids. You don't see me bitching and complaining and scared to make that money."

"Dat's you, nigga!"

"What da fuck you talking about, nigga?! Your heart starting to pump out Kool Aid now, huh? Let me know, Ricky, fo' real!"

"Nigga, I'm still dat down-ass nigga. I'll still get down for mines, don't get it twisted, Kinko. To me, it seems like you're getting just a little too fuckin' greedy. We don't need to fuck wit' that dope right now. We're eating lovely."

"And I'm gonna continue to eat lovely," he said, while placing the small bundle of bills into a small black bag. "Now I got business to take care of tonight, either you're in or out. Let me know now, muthafucka," he said, wit' his face twisted up at me.

"Nah, I'm out wit' that." I let it be known.

"Fuck you then, nigga! I do you a favor, and bring you back into this game to make money, and I even blow off Nino's face after he put four shots into you, and you wanna front on a nigga now. Fuck you, Ricky!" He then walked outta the office.

I just leaned back in my leather swivel chair, blew air out of my mouth, and became frustrated. This nigga Kinko, I see now, he was gonna become out of control. He was hot-headed, greedy, a cold-blooded killer. And worst of all, he was fuckin' arrogant and stupid.

How long would this last? I wondered. I'd been in the game for only seven months, and in these past seven months, life had been good. I felt I'd accomplished more within these months than I did the whole time before I was incarcerated. I was doing me when I was young. But now, I was ballin' like a muthafucka.

I had the phat apartment in Rochdale, pushed a '97 Jaguar, and was about to cop this Range Rover soon. I had money to burn, and my girl Danielle, she was a dime piece to sport and have under your arm. I was proud to get a bitch pregnant. No regrets wit' her.

But I remember, shit don't last forever. And the way Kinko was acting, I saw our shit crumbling soon. Kinko didn't know how to chill and relax, and make and invest money the easy way. He wanted to get this and that real quick and get it by any means necessary. Sometimes he killed without thinking, and he was becoming too wild. Everybody knew his name and his reputation on the streets. Everybody feared him, and now he wanted to get involved wit' the dope game and start stepping on the wrong toes. That was a bad idea. Especially if he wanted to step into Ra-Ra's territory.

Ra-Ra was in his mid forties and had been around from the days of Nicky Barnes, Guy Fisher, Fat Cat, Pappy Mason, and other infamous niggas. He was known for many crimes and many bodies. He was infamous for putting the murder game down. I heard once he walked into a diner in broad daylight and in front of a dozen witnesses, and shot two of his enemies in the head while they ate. And he got away wit' the crime. I never met the man in person, but his name definitely did ring bells in niggas' heads.

It was a beautiful Saturday afternoon and I had decided to spend my day taking Des and Raheem shopping. It was time for me to spend some time wit' them and do right by my son. I finally gave Des a call and told her about my plans. She was really cool wit' it.

By three that afternoon I was at Des' apartment door. I knocked twice and Des answered wit' Raheem in her arms.

"Hey," she greeted, smiling.

"What's up?" I greeted back, planting a quick kiss on her cheek. "Raheem, what's up lil' man?"

"Hi," he replied. His voice was so gentle and innocent. He stared at me wit' his big pure black eyes, probably wondering who this man was who was standing in front of him.

"Y'all ready?" I asked.

"Almost, come on in," Des said.

I stepped into her apartment and took a seat on her couch. One thing I give Des, even though her place was small, she kept it looking immaculate. There were no dirty dishes, no dirty or clean clothes lying around the place, the floor was spotless, and there was a sweet smell that lingered throughout her place. I definitely admired that.

Lil Raheem wasn't a shy or hyped child. He was cool, and he became really comfortable around me. While Des was in the bedroom still getting ready, Lil' Raheem sat next to me on the couch and showed me his toys, some children's books, and talked about his friends and teachers in daycare. By the conversation we were having I could tell Raheem was a very intelligent child. I knew he was my son.

"I'm ready now," Des said, coming out of the bedroom. She definitely looked good. She had on this purple short slip dress that highlighted her bodacious butt and tits. She wore fresh white Adidas, and I swear Des musta put some baby oil on her legs because they were glistening and turning me the fuck on. Des' legs had definition and perfect structure—my point, she had a gorgeous set of legs on her. DAMN!

"You look nice, Mommy," Raheem complimented, staring at his mother.

"Thank you, baby," Des said, smiling.

"Yeah, you do. Dat's for sure."

"Thank you. Y'all ready?"

"Been," I said, getting up off the couch. Raheem did the same.

We all exited the apartment and went downstairs to where my Jag was parked. I strapped Raheem in the back, buckled his seatbelt, and opened the door for Des.

"Thank you," she said.

"Of course."

We drove to King's Plaza Mall on Flatbush Avenue. The first store we went into was a clothing store where I purchased a few outfits for Des. Then we went into the Gap and I bought Raheem some gear. After that I got both of 'em some sneakers. I also bought Des these expensive pair of shoes that cost $350.

We ate lunch at Burger King. After that Raheem wanted

to see a movie, so we took him to see _Men in Black_. He had a
ball watching the different aliens and Will Smith up on the
screen battling.

When we came out of the theater, it was going on eight. I
didn't realize it was so late in the day. I had gotten a call
from Danielle. She left a message on my voicemail inquir-
ing as to my whereabouts, but I didn't return the phone call
till nine-thirty that night.

"What's up?" I asked while I was in the mall bathroom.

"Where are you?" she asked, having a little attitude in
her voice.

"I'm taking care of business, why? What's up?"

"I don't see you all day, and it's almost going on ten. I
want you home, baby."

"I'll be home soon," I said.

She sucked her teeth and replied wit', "Everything is always business with you. You forget you have a pregnant
woman at home? Huh? Everybody gets your time except
for your pregnant woman who you keep alone at home.
Fuck you, Ricky!"

She hung up.

"What da fuck!" I muttered, looking at my cell phone
like it was possessed. It had to be her hormones or something talking, fo' real.

I met back up wit' Des and Raheem and we left for her
place.

Raheem was asleep in my arms as I carried him into the
apartment. He had a busy day, and he fell asleep during the
car ride home. I put him to bed and looked down at him
while he slept. Des went into the bathroom, so I was alone
in the room wit' my son.

It felt good today. It felt like Des, Raheem, and I were a
family. Damn, if being a father felt like this, then I couldn't
wait till Danielle had my next seed.

I leaned over, kissed Raheem on the forehead, and quietly told him goodnight. I walked into the living room and sat on the couch. I wasn't ready to leave yet. I had a good time, and I wanted to chill and talk wit' Des. I thought about her a lot. She changed so much that it was unbelievable she was the same woman who four years ago asked me for money every passing minute.

The apartment was dimly lit and quiet. I put my phone straight to voicemail. I didn't want the loud ring to wake up Raheem. I slouched against the couch and felt a little exhausted.

A few minutes later, Des came out the bedroom clad in this purple silk sheer burnout sleep-shirt wit' the sexy side slits. The minute I saw that, I knew what time it was. I rose and stared at her. She smiled as she came toward me. Her legs shimmered in the dim room. She came up to me, climbed onto my lap, and straddled me. Slowly she started to kiss on me. I returned the kisses, and we passionately embraced.

"I missed you Ricky, so damn much," she soothingly whispered in my ear, and then put her tongue in it.

"I missed you too, Des," I replied, feeling the moment.

We continued to kiss and fondle each other. I saw that she had no panties on underneath her sheer sleep shirt. That just got me more excited. Next thing I knew, she started unbuckling my jeans, pulling them off, and my dick was in her mouth. After the blowjob, she straddled me again and placed my dick slowly into her, causing me to grunt. It was feeling so good.

We fucked and fucked and fucked till my dick couldn't get up anymore. We both ended up sprawled out on the floor, ass naked, and huffing and puffing—SHIT!

"You okay?" she asked.

"Yeah, I'm good."

She smiled. "You had a good time today?"

"Of course. What about you?"

She nodded. She stared at me. "I had a great time. Thank you."

"You're welcome. It was cool. I'm glad the both of y'all had fun today. He a fun child to be around. Damn!" I stared at Des. Damn, she was beautiful. I had to admit, I was feeling her groove and her style.

I looked at the time and saw that it was past midnight.

"Shit!" I got my naked ass off the floor and searched for my clothing.

"You leaving?"

"Yeah, I gotta go."

She got up off the floor. When I saw her naked figure, I stopped getting dressed and gazed at her. That body, it was a blessing—got-damn.

"So when are we gonna hang out again?" Des asked.

"Soon, I promise."

"Just you and me next time."

"No doubt, luv," I said, throwing on my Timberlands.

Des came up to me and threw her arms around me. Her touch felt so alluring, so warm, so enticing, I felt myself getting a hard-on again. I freed myself from her sweet embrace and headed for the door.

SEVENTEEN.

Damn, this had to me one of the hottest months of the summer. It was late August and the sun wasn't giving us a break wit' the humidity. The temperature had to be in the upper nineties, and I was sweating like I just ran a fuckin' marathon.

I decided to head down to the club around noon that Wednesday and touch up on some things. I saw Kinko's BMW parked out front. The first thing that came to my mind was him and Gwen stinking up my office again having dirty raw sex. But to my surprise, when I walked into my office I saw about ten kilos of raw uncut heroin and a large stack of money on my desk.

Kinko was sitting in my chair talking on his cell phone, and he had some new bitch sitting on his lap. And there were also these two dudes there. I was familiar wit' their faces, but I didn't see them around often. Banks and Lil' Ra. They both were two notorious hitmen who worked for Kinko. They killed at his will, and didn't think twice about it. Whenever I was around them, I got nervous. We weren't cool like that. I didn't say a word to them, and they didn't say a word to me. I tried to keep my distance from the two. They were bad news and too fuckin' deadly for a nigga like me to be hanging wit'.

"Kinko, nigga, what da fuck yo!" I barked. "You can't be having your drugs stashed up in here. What if po-po run up in here?"

I didn't get an answer from Kinko, but I did get an answer from Lil' Ra. "Nigga, calm down. Ain't nobody running up in here. We got this shit on lock, nigga!"

I just looked at Lil' Ra, knowing not to say a word to him because he had a deadly temper. I knew he wouldn't think twice about pulling out his gun if I commented something smart back to him, causing a scene and trying to put a cap into a nigga. I'm not sayin' that I'm pussy, but I did my best to avoid frivolous drama and confrontation. I was about making money, not about getting locked up over dumb shit.

When he saw that I didn't reply, Lil' Ra looked at me and let out a nasty smirk like he had my heart in the palm of his hand. Yeah, let that nigga keep thinking so, he didn't know me—da real me.

Kinko sat in my chair, talking on his celly, wit' this fine-ass light-skinned bitch kissing him on his neck. I just stood there and waited for this nigga to get the fuck off the phone. I was getting irritated. He had drugs up in the club. When we first opened, Kinko and I established that there would be no large quantities of drugs up in this club. We didn't want to make this place too hot. The nigga had stash houses set up, so why da fuck was he here?

Kinko finally got off his phone and paid attention to me.

"What up, Ricky?" he greeted, staring at me wit' no smiles, no hug, nothing.

"Yo, what da fuck, Kinko? Why you trying to play me? Huh? We said no drugs up in this club. So what da fuck is dat shit doing up in here?"

"Nigga, calm da fuck down. I own dis shit too, nigga, don't forget dat. Just because a nigga don't be up in here like dat, don't think I ain't still running shit. I bring what da fuck I wanna bring up in here. I brought you in, don't forget dat, Ricky. I made your ass. So don't be coming up in here getting loud wit' a nigga thinking you da boss, especially in front of my niggas."

I just stood there staring at Kinko while he tried to play a nigga. I didn't know what da fuck was going on in his head, but I saw now, we had our differences.

Kinko continued to talk. "We hit up one of Ra-Ra's spots last night. This his shit."

"What da fuck, Kinko? I told you to chill from dat shit. That ain't gonna do nothing but bring us heat. You stepping on the wrong toes now."

"Nigga, just because you scared to go at the nigga, dat don't mean I am. He too old to be getting dat money. This our time, Ricky. Dat dope game around his way is what's up right now. And I definitely want in on dat shit."

"You know he gonna come back on us. He ain't gonna let this shit slide," I said.

"So," Banks cut in. "We can handle da nigga. What da fuck!" Banks lifted his shirt and revealed to me the .357 he had stashed down his jeans.

Kinko smiled. "See, dat's what time it is! My niggas gonna have this shit on lock completely. You see dat, Ricky. You see how my niggas Banks and Lil' Ra gonna hold it down. We don't back down from no one. You hear me? We running things around here. Ra-Ra, he retiring soon, mark my words."

"That's right baby. You my nigga," said the shorty on Kinko's lap. "You definitely gonna do you, baby." She was cute, but she definitely looked like a hoochie mama, wit' the big earrings, tons of make-up on her face, dressed in tight designer clothes, and looking stupid.

I shook my head and left my office. I didn't want any

part of the drama that was about to unfold. I thought about Raheem and what it felt like to be a father to him. Des was in my life again, and Danielle was about to have my baby.

Now there was this mess that Kinko was unfolding on himself. I knew it was about to become deadly, and when the shit hit the fan, a lot of muthafuckas were either gonna be dead, or in jail. And I didn't want to be either.

Later that night, the club was poppin', and Kinko and his cronies were still lingering around the place. I felt uncomfortable having them around. No telling what might pop off wit' them three around. But I tried to relax and handle business, the women, and a few rowdy customers. In this life, shit, there was always something jumping off—more bad than good.

Gwen came into work around midnight, but she was looking pissed off about something. We hadn't spoken to each other in weeks. So I was surprised when she came up to me. But of course, it was for all the wrong reasons.

"Where da fuck is Kinko?" she asked, looking like a fuckin' madwoman.

"Why? What's going on?" I asked, but I really wasn't concerned. Whatever was going on between them was their business.

"I need to see him. I know he here. I see his fuckin' car parked outside. He in da office, Ricky?"

"Nah, he downstairs handling business," I told her.

"Excuse me then!" she exclaimed, brushing by me and storming down to the basement. I saw a few heads looking. I didn't want any trouble, and something was up, so I quickly followed Gwen into the basement.

I was two steps behind Gwen, coming into the basement where most of the ladies changed clothes when I saw Banks getting head from one of the strippers. He was laid up on the couch wit' his head arched back, and there was Sandy, this busty, fine-ass Dominican stripper, wit' his dick in her mouth.

When she saw me come down, she quickly got up off her knees. I guess the bitch was embarrassed, but for what? I already knew she sucked dick for a living.

"I'm so sorry, Ricky!" she said.

I paid her no attention, like I gave a fuck. "Yeah, whatever!"

The basement was empty. Everyone was upstairs getting paid or getting drunk. Gwen stormed by Banks and Sandy and went toward the private room in the back. She swung open the door and found Kinko wit' his dick in some bitch. In fact, it was that same ho I had seen him wit' earlier. The light-skinned chickenhead.

I wasn't surprised.

"Oh, so this how you do a bitch, Kinko, huh?" Gwen asked. "You out here fuckin' this big-head bitch. I thought we were together."

Kinko glared at her and shouted, "Bitch, take your ass somewhere and shut da fuckin' door!"

Gwen looked at him, shocked. I guess she wasn't expecting those sudden words to discharge from his mouth. But I guess she didn't know Kinko. I knew the nigga for years, and I still didn't know Kinko.

"Oh, it's like dat?" she asked. I knew she was hurt. I saw it in her face. "Fuck you, nigga! Fuck you and Ricky. Y'all think y'all can just play a bitch. You gonna fuck me, and think I'm just gonna let it be like that!"

"Excuse me, I gotta go," Sandy said, rushing up the steps and leaving behind a difficult situation.

"Yo, Gwen, you ain't my bitch. You never were. You were just a piece of pussy. Your shit wasn't even all dat in the first place."

"Bitch, can you please leave so I can finish fuckin' my man," the light-skinned shorty said.

"What bitch?"

Banks stood up, guessing that drama was about to unfold. I stood there wishing for Gwen to stop and let it be. She didn't know Kinko, and by the look I saw on his face, I knew the nigga was getting upset. And Kinko would hit a bitch and wild out on her something terrible.

"Gwen, c'mon, just forget about it," I said, grabbing her by her arm. I looked in her face and saw that she was crying.

"Nah, Ricky," she said. "Why y'all keep trying to play me? You don't wanna be wit' me, and this nigga here, he a fuckin' joke. You little dick nigga. I coulda had better, and then you had your boy rob my shit!"

"Fuck you talking about?" I asked.

"I bring him to my crib, show him around, fuck him in my bedroom, and I come back the next night, and most of my shit is gone," she explained.

"Bitch, get da fuck outta here. Ain't nobody take your shit. You better go somewhere wit' dat!" Kinko shouted.

"Nigga, why you lying? I knew who you had take my stuff. One of them young niggas from around da way. He even told me it was you."

"Gwen, chill for now and we can work this out later," I said, trying to calm the drama between them.

"Nah, fuck dat. I'm gonna work it out all right. I'm gonna work it out wit' the fuckin' cops," she proclaimed.

The room got quiet for a quick minute. I saw the look on Kinko's face and the look on Banks' face and knew Gwen had fucked up.

She continued, "I'm gonna tell 'em what a grimy, bitch-ass nigga you are, Kinko. About the drugs you had in my crib and dat nigga you shot in the face. You keep fuckin' wit' me, Kinko! I ain't the bitch to play wit'!"

Shit, now why did she had to go and say that? Gwen didn't realize she was dealing wit' dangerous people. But she knew she fucked up because the look on Kinko's face said it all.

It happened too quickly. One second Kinko was standing there glaring at her, and the next he was lunging at her, grabbing her throat and plunging his fist against the side of her face. Gwen screamed.

"You gonna do what, bitch? Huh? You wanna snitch on a nigga? You wanna go to da fuckin' cops on a nigga?" Kinko belligerently shouted as he attacked Gwen wit' fierce strength.

Gwen just screamed and screamed while she lay on the floor. She was in the fetal position trying to protect herself while Kinko continued to assault and pounce on her. He kicked and beat the shit outta Gwen. I rushed up to Kinko to restrain him from doing any further damage to her, but Banks pulled out a gun on me and told me to chill and let his man do his thang.

I never felt more disgusted in my life. I wanted to turn that gun against Banks and blow his fuckin' brains out. But I felt powerless. I just stood there and watched Gwen getting her ass beat to death.

Kinko took it to the extreme when he reached for a metal pipe and started striking her against the head wit' it. Gwen's screams became weaker and weaker till there were no more screams at all. The loud deafening music upstairs drowned out Gwen's pleas for help.

After it was done, Kinko was panting heavily. His hands were covered in Gwen's blood. He clutched the bloody pipe and stood over the body. He was gone. His eyes were filled wit' rage and evil. I looked in his eyes, and I swear, I thought the devil himself was staring at me.

I didn't say a word. I couldn't. I felt helpless. And for the first time, I felt I was in danger. I never feared Kinko, but after what I had just witnessed, I didn't know what to think. He beat Gwen to death in a matter of minutes.

I looked over at the light-skinned shorty Kinko was fuckin'. The look on her face was one I couldn't even describe. Her eyes were wide wit' fear and terror. Panic was written across her face.

"Dumb fuckin' bitch!" Kinko yelled, dropping the pipe. "You okay, Rick?"

"I'm cool," I managed to say.

"Damn Kinko, you really fucked dat bitch up," Banks said wit' some sort of pleasure.

"Fuck her! Yo, make sure no one comes down here!" he ordered Banks. "And where's Lil' Ra at?"

"He wit' some ho upstairs," Banks said.

"Yo, Banks, go get dat nigga. Rick you help me wit this bitch here," Kinko said.

"What?" I asked, my voice high.

"Nigga, you heard what da fuck I said. Help me clean this shit up." He glared at me. It was like he was waiting for me to say no to him.

"Ayyite, nigga, whatever!" I said, removing my shirt.

We started to strip Gwen from her clothing. I got a black trash bag and threw all of her bloody clothing inside. Banks and Lil' Ra came back down after locking the basement door and they started to help.

Lil' Ra looked at the body and disdainfully replied, "Damn Kinko, da bitch musta had some really bad pussy for you to kill her! You shoulda passed the ho my way. I woulda took her off your hands."

I looked at Lil' Ra and shook my head. He saw me, stared back, and shouted, "What nigga? Dis too much for you to handle?"

I didn't respond. I was just too disgusted by everyone. These niggas, they didn't have a conscience, no heart, no sensitivity—nothing. They were just ruthless killers.

"Yo, Kinko, what you gonna do wit' dat bitch?" Banks pointed out. We all stared at light-skinned shorty. I didn't know her name, but she looked so scared and frozen. She never even moved from the spot where she was standing.

"I mean, she saw the whole thing happen," Banks added.

Kinko stared at shorty, and the next words that came from his lips were, "Cut dat bitch's throat."

Shorty started to yell and scream. She made a bold move and tried to bolt for the exit, but it was hopeless. Lil' Ra and Banks quickly grabbed and subdued her. She fought, but Banks pulled out a blade while Lil' Ra held her down.

"No . . . please . . . no . . . I won't say anything. I swear on my two children! I won't say anything!" she pleaded and begged.

But her cries fell on deaf ears. Banks put the 3 inch blade to her throat and easily slit her shit open. Blood gushed out from the wound and some spilled onto Banks.

"Damn, this bitch is a bleeder, yo," he said, jumping back from the body.

I'd seen enough. I hated this. It was senseless. Now, instead of one body, there were two.

Reluctantly I helped them strip down both girls, place their bloody garments into the trash bag, and tie it up. I peered down at Gwen and the other dead woman next to her and shook my head in disbelief.

Damn, I thought. It was a waste. Gwen, she never did anything to anyone. She just loved the wrong men, and that cost her life. And the worst part, I had to go home to her cousin, look Danielle in the face, and keep this a secret from her. I couldn't tell Danielle that her cousin was brutally murdered. I didn't want to get her involved, especially wit' Kinko being psychotic. I knew Kinko would be crazy enough to try to kill me and Danielle if word ever got out about tonight.

Around two in the morning we loaded both bodies into the trunk of a burgundy sedan that was parked in the alley behind the club. I scrubbed down the basement wit' some acid and bleach and made sure the smell of death didn't linger.

"Yo, Banks, you and Lil' Ra go dump those bitches somewhere, and be subtle about it. Y'all hear?" Kinko told them.

"Yeah, we got you, Kinko," Banks replied.

They got into the sedan and drove out of the alley. Kinko and me walked back into the club and headed straight for the office. Kinko was nonchalant like nothing happened— this cold-blooded muthafucka. He smoked on a cigarette, got on his phone, and started to conduct business. Then he had the nerve to call one of the ladies into the office and demand a blowjob from shorty. She got down on her knees behind the desk and started sucking him off.

Kinko gave me this uncomfortable smirk, like he was daring me about something. I was so appalled I told him I had to leave. He didn't say anything else.

I jumped into my Jag and took my black ass home.

I was surprised to see Danielle still up. It was almost three in the morning, and there she was sitting on the couch, clutching onto a pillow, and staring at the television.

"Why you still up?" I asked.

"I couldn't sleep," she replied, staring at me. She didn't look angry. She just gave me this casual look. I assumed everything was ayyite wit' her. But as for me, shit was fucked up. I knew she probably saw the anguished expression on my face. I had witnessed her cousin being murdered, and then I helped cover the shit up. Now here I was, face to face wit' the cousin and feeling like I was about to break down and cry. But before that could happen, I darted into the bathroom, turned on the shower, and stripped off my clothing.

"Baby, is everything all right?" Danielle asked from the other side of the door.

I didn't answer her. I just stood quietly in the shower wit' my hands flat against the wall, and let the water cascade against my skin. So much was going on. Too much death, too much drama. I stood in the shower and thought about my life, the victims and the grief I had caused others. I thought about Gwen, and the other woman who was murdered after her. They didn't deserve that. They shouldn't have died that way. And then there was Charlie and his cousin, Nino. It was too much for me. This game was becoming too much for me. For the first time in my life, I wanted out. For the first time, I didn't care about the money, jewelry, fine women and fine cars. I wanted out. I didn't want to be associated wit' none of that shit anymore. I was thinking about my son, Raheem.

I wanted to tell Danielle about my son and Des. Every day it was eating away at me to admit to her that I had another seed out there, and to also admit that I was falling in love wit' Des. I mean, don't get me wrong, I still loved Danielle wit' all my heart and strength, but there was something about Des that I loved more. Maybe it was because of Raheem. That was something, that's for sure.

As I stood in the shower alone, contemplating my thoughts, I heard the bathroom door open. I became wary.

"Danielle," I called out.

I heard someone coming closer. I had this sick thought that it was Kinko or one of his hitmen entering my home wit' a pistol wanting to put a bullet in my head. I got a little scared.

"Danielle!" I called out again, but there was no answer. I prepared myself, naked and in the tub standing my ground. As soon as the shower door opened, I was gonna lunge at whoever was out there. I was determined not to be shot down like a fuckin' dog.

The shower door came back, and right before I leaped forward, I saw that it was Danielle standing before me naked.

"Danielle, what da fuck?" I cursed. "You ain't hear me calling you?"

"Yeah, but I wanted to surprise you," she said.

My heart and nerves calmed down. I was so relieved that it was her and not a killer. Danielle stepped into the shower wit' me. I paid her no attention. My nerves were fucked up. I stood under the running water. Danielle came up to me and wrapped her arms around my waist. She slowly started to kiss me on my back and then said, "You'll be okay, baby. I love you."

That's when I broke down and started to cry. I said in the shower, "I'm sorry, baby. I'm so fuckin' sorry!"

"For what, baby?" she asked.

"I'm sorry."

Danielle continued to hold me in the shower, making sure her man was okay. She didn't even press me about the reasons for my apology.

EIGHTEEN.

Two days later, I was laid up in the crib wit' Danielle all morning. It was just me and her watching TV, talking and spending quality time together. I tried blacking out Gwen's gruesome death, but it was still lingering in the back of my mind.

Around one there was this loud knock at my front door. I got out of bed and proceeded to the door wit' my .380 in hand. The knocking continued. But the chilling shouts of "Police, open up!" caught my definite attention. I froze in place and stared at the door.

"It's the police, baby. What do they want?" Danielle asked, coming out of the bedroom and throwing on her robe.

"Danielle, here take this," I said, passing her the gun to hide.

She took it without any hesitation and hid the gun in the bathroom. I went up to the door shouting, "I'm coming."

I opened my front door and saw the same two detectives who questioned me in the hospital when I got shot. Detective Freeman and Nordic, these two dickheads again.

I sighed and asked scornfully, "What da hell y'all want?"

"We're here to ask you a few questions about the death of a Gwen Meeks."

"What?" Danielle asked, standing behind me wit' a look of shock on her face. "My cousin? Did you say, Meeks?"

"Yes," Freeman replied.

"Ricky, what the hell is going on?" Danielle asked, staring at me, waiting for an answer.

"Baby, I don't know," I responded.

"We need you to come down to the station with us," Detective Nordic said.

"Am I under arrest?" I asked.

"Just come down to the station. We need to ask you a few questions," Freeman said.

I knew that it would be stupid enough for me to resist, so I got dressed, told Danielle it was a mistake, and walked out my crib wit' 5-0. Danielle looked heartbroken when she heard about the death of her cousin. She started crying and asking me if it was true about her cousin. I told her I'd be back. I was going to handle things.

Now these two asshole cops did that shit on purpose. I mean, c'mon, there are better ways of breaking the news to a loved one, rather than in the blunt and disrespectful way they did. My heart went out to her. While I was riding in the backseat of the unmarked car, I thought this had to be a mistake. I knew Lil' Ra and Banks disposed of the bodies correctly, or did they? They were two idiots anyway, so no telling what had happened wit' the bodies.

I was smart. See, in this game you never know what might go down, or who may start snitching on a nigga. So before I opened up my fuckin' mouth, the first thing I asked for was my lawyer.

I had started saving money and hired me a two hundred dollar an hour attorney. He was an old Jewish criminal attorney who represented the best of the worst and saved a lot of niggas from lock up.

I learned my lesson from my first experience wit' the court system. I did four years because I was stupid. I wasn't doing any more time for no one. I was older, more mature, and wiser. But before my lawyer could arrive, Detective Freeman and Nordic bombarded me wit' tons of questions about two nude bodies that were found near Jamaica Bay. They were the bodies of Gwen Meeks and Denise Conway.

"What you know about Gwen Meeks?" Freeman asked.

"I don't know nothing," I said. I stared at him straight in the face.

"Well, that's not what we hear," Nordic spoke up. "We heard she was last seen wit' you down at your club. Witnesses say she was angry about something and left with you to go down to the basement. So that makes you the last person to see her alive. Whoever murdered this girl beat her up pretty bad. Her face was almost unrecognizable."

"Listen, I don't know nothing," I repeated, standing my ground.

"Look, Ricky, you sit here thinking you a tough guy," Freeman said, looking tight faced at me. "When shit hits the fan, it's gonna be your ass. You think you know these streets, huh? You don't know jack shit, my man. I've been in this game longer than you, twenty-five years. I've seen muthafuckas tougher than you sit in that same position and chew on nails. Give up your boy, Kinko. It's him we want. You just did four years upstate for possession. I'm sure you don't wanna see prison again."

I continued to sit there.

Nordic shook his head, took a seat on the table, and stared at me, like these niggas were trying to intimidate me.

"Muthafucka, you can't be that stupid," he said. "You think if Kinko was in the same position, he would be tight-lipped for you! Let me ask you something, Ricky, since you wanna go hard for your boy. I went over your arrest record, found that you got caught with crack-cocaine and possession of weed in your high school. Smart move, my man. Who do you think set you up that day? Ain't it funny, that the day you went to remove the product from your locker, cops and security guards were there waiting? Who do you think snitched on you?"

"Fuck you," I said.

"Ricky, don't be naïve. We know about the hit in Far Rockaway. The streets talk, and we listen attentively. We didn't have enough evidence to charge you to the murders in the apartment, but we knew who set that up," Freeman informed. "I do recall when I used to work in the 113th that there was an anonymous call made about a young man hustling drugs in August Martin. The caller never gave his name, but he did give us your name and a very good description of you. The caller informed us about a pick-up that was being made early Monday morning in a school locker. It's funny, you go to jail, and Kinko remains out on the streets getting richer and richer off the money the both of y'all stole."

"Whatever," I said, shaking my head, blocking out every damn thing they said.

"Your boy is selfish, Ricky," Nordic stated. "He don't give a fuck about you or anyone else. You know who his best friend is? Money, the almighty dollar. He's a killer, and if you don't fuckin' wise up, you're going back to jail for that fool. Give him up, Ricky. He's grimy, selfish, and dirty. Don't take the fall for him."

"I don't know nothing," I said.

"Are all y'all niggas just as stupid," Nordic shouted.

I just sat there, holding my ground. Shit, I didn't know if they were playing me or speaking the truth. Cops, they'd use anything against you, especially if you had a record.

They'd tell you that this one is snitching on you, that they got evidence against you for this crime and that crime, but yet, I was never placed under arrest. I'll tell you this, the fact that Kinko may have snitched on me did linger on my mind.

My lawyer finally came. The first thing he asked both detectives was, "Is my client under arrest for a crime?"

"No."

"Then let him go. Get up, Ricky, and leave."

And I did that. I quickly got up and bounced. Muthafuckas didn't even pay for my cab back home. It didn't make any sense though, I thought, as I sat in back of the cab. I always thought that Terrance and Michael Stone set me up. But what if this nigga Kinko was playing me all along—using me as a pawn? I probably was his scape goat.

I got back home around ten that night. Danielle was still up. When I walked through them doors, she was sitting on the couch wit' the lights off. She got up and started to approach me. I flicked on the lights and noticed she had been crying.

"Is it true, Ricky? Is my cousin dead?" she asked, staring at me.

I bit down on my bottom lip, not wanting to tell her the truth. I tried to divert my eyes away from her, but she sternly said, "Look at me, Ricky, and tell me the fuckin' truth. Is she dead?"

I gazed into her eyes and reluctantly answered, "Yes."

Just like that, she burst into a hysterical cry and fell into my arms. "Why? Why, Ricky? Who killed her? Who killed my fuckin' cousin?"

I held her in my arms and lied. "I don't know, but I'll find out, baby. I promise. I'll find out."

I hated myself. I hated knowing the damn truth and not being able to will myself to tell her. I felt I had betrayed Danielle in so many fuckin' ways. I'd lied, cheated, and did so many things in the dark that I was buggin' the fuck out. She gave her heart and soul to me the day we first met, and what did I give her? Nothing but bitterness and grief. I wanted to open up to her and confess everything—my affair wit' Gwen, the killings, Des and my son, and even that I was falling back in love wit' my ex-girl. I shoulda done it that night, but I held my secrets inside me and pretended like everything was gonna be all-good—like my life could end happily-ever-after.

NINETEEN.

The very next night I was down at the club. I didn't see Kinko around, which was a good thing. I was built up wit' anger and bitterness against that nigga, wondering if he had snitched on me, and why. And Gwen's death had me stressed too. But what did I do to release my stress? I was fuckin' Des on my desk, trying to get my mind off of shit by being in some pussy.

"I love you, baby," Des whispered as she bounced that ass against my nuts, clutching my chest. Her pussy felt so wet and tight.

"I love you too, baby."

We both were butt ass-naked and not using a condom. We were in the heat of the moment.

"I'm gonna cum!" I shouted.

Afterward, Des got dressed and I did the same.

"I needed that," I said.

"You and me both, Ricky."

"Raheem at the babysitter?" I asked.

"Yeah." She then gave me this pleasant smile and started staring at me. "You really love him, don't you?"

"Yes. I mean. . . . it's funny for me, but I'm glad to be his father," I stated smiling from ear to ear.

"Thank you, Ricky," Des said.

"For what?" I asked.

"For not dissin' me and turning your back on us like most brothers would have done."

"Well, I'm not most brothers."

"I know. These past weeks you definitely looked out for us in so many ways, and I thank you so much for that. Raheem needs a father like you in his life."

I went up to Des, put my arms around her, kissed her on the lips, and said, "And I'm gonna stay in that boy's life and in your life, too. I wanna be wit' you Des fo' real. I wanna be in you and my son's life forever. Let's get married."

Des' eyes damn near popped outta her skull. "What?" she asked. "Are you serious? What about your woman and your baby she's having? I mean, you can't just dog her out like that."

"I'm not. I mean, I love Danielle. Well, I thought I did. But these past two months, I ain't been feeling for her like I've been feeling for you. We got chemistry, Des, and I love dat shit."

Des laughed and said, "My pussy must got you trippin'."

I smiled and said, "It's something."

"I gotta get back to work. We still on for tonight?" she asked.

"Of course. But think about us, Des. I want to take care of you."

"Ayyite, babe. Later." Des gave me a quick kiss on the lips.

Damn, a nigga buggin'. Danielle appeared in my mind, and I had to wonder what da fuck was going on wit' me. Was my life so crazy, deranged, and hectic that I gotta pro-

pose to one woman while I'm living wit' another who's
pregnant wit' my child?

It was going on midnight, and the night was calm and
peaceful. I was sitting at the bar wit' Manny, drinking some
rum and Coke, and watching Des do her thing on stage stirring these niggas in my club crazy.

"You okay, Rick?" Manny asked. "I'm sayin' you look
like something stressing you out. What is it?"

I shook my head, "Nothing, just some shit on my mind."

"Yo, I'm sorry about Gwen. I heard about it yesterday.
Dat shit is fucked up, yo. They know who did it?"

"Nah."

"I heard cops were questioning you about it. What's
going on wit' dat?" he asked, being in a nigga's business.

"Yo Manny, you wired for sound?" I asked, irritated by
all the fuckin' questions.

"Nah, Rick, I was just asking."

"Well, stop fuckin' asking!" I shouted.

"My bad, Rick. I was just curious, you know, Gwen was
my home girl and all . . ."

"Manny, for once, shut da fuck up!"

He looked at me and sighed, then focused his attention
on the customers at the bar. I ain't mean to snap on him like
dat, but the nigga didn't know when to shut his lips about
shit. He one of them niggas that keep going and fuckin'
going. I had enough to worry about without this nigga
being in my business and running off at the mouth.

My mind was somewhere else that night as I loitered
around the bar sipping on drink after drink. Des was about
to get off stage soon and I just wanted to leave. And when I
mean leave, I wanted to go far off somewhere and take Des,
Raheem, even Danielle, and move em' out of town. I was
tired of the city. It was too much for a nigga. My life was a
bestseller, and it only got better.

"Sugar," I called for the female bartender. She came up to

me wit' her voluptuous breasts mashed together in this revealing tight black shirt.

"What can I get you, Ricky?" she asked.

"Another rum and Coke, ayyite, honey?"

"Take it easy, Ricky. I know it's hard."

"Just bring me my drink, Sugar. Okay?" I snapped.

"Okay."

I wasn't in the mood. I looked over at Des and watched her rub her tits in some nigga's face. I got a bit jealous and quickly turned my head. Sugar brought my drink and set it in front of me. I glanced up at her and took two quick sips. I rested my elbows on the bar counter, closed my eyes, and thought about this nigga Kinko snitching. If it was true, then fuck him. It was on. I spent four years in hell because of that day I got caught. I didn't put it past him because Kinko was a grimy muthafucka.

I first heard the horrifying screams at twelve-twenty AM. The screams were followed by a loud nerve-rattling burst of rapid gunfire. It caught my attention promptly because when I looked over to my left, I saw two large hitmen dressed completely in black entering my club wit' AK-47s. They began to open fire on everybody.

Without hesitation, I hit the floor, taking cover as panic and chaos spread throughout the club. They were shooting everywhere, striking whoever got in their way. The screams were so loud and terrifying they almost drowned out the loud gunfire.

"Rick, here, take this," Manny shouted, tossing me a 9mm. He open fired back at the assailants. There were people everywhere. I didn't know where to shoot, but I knew I couldn't go out like a sucker. I stood up and returned fire wit' Manny by my side. The barrages of bullets were tearing my club apart. I saw bodies everywhere. It felt like I was in some kind of small war. I continued to fire my gun as I took cover behind the bar counter. Manny went off like a true soldier. I couldn't believe that this shit was happening. And then just like that, the shooting stopped and both men were gone.

"Fuck me," I shouted, looking around at all the dead bodies after the carnage and chaos had stopped. I still had the gun gripped in my hand. The ones left alive were crying, in shock, and trying to make sense of the situation.

"Rick, you okay?" Manny asked.

"Yeah, I'm good."

"Yo, what da fuck just happened?" Manny asked, staring at me.

"I don't know what da fuck happened just now."

But I knew what those two men were here for—retaliation against Kinko. Those were Ra-Ra's men. And they had come to send him a clear and bloody message that Kinko had fucked wit' the wrong man. I knew it. I fuckin' knew it. Ra-Ra hit us hard and strong.

I looked around my club and my shit was in shambles— blood, bodies, bullet holes. It would never be the same for me. I looked on the stage and that's when I saw Des sprawled out on her back.

"No!" I screamed and rushed to her aid.

I jumped up on the stage and grabbed Des into my arms. She wasn't moving.

"Des, get up baby," I said, hysterically, "c'mon, get up baby."

I shook her to get a reaction, but there was none. I didn't see blood at first. But then I saw her back, and it was covered wit' blood. I figured the bullet had exited through her back.

Manny came up to me. "She okay?"

"Get a fuckin' ambulance!" I screamed. He went for the phone.

I held her in my arms, knowing the truth. She didn't need an ambulance. She needed a morgue. I gripped her in my arms, tears streaming down my face.

I knew it. I fuckin' knew it. Kinko fucked wit' Ra-Ra and his men came in shooting my place up. And the fucked up thing, Kinko was nowhere in sight. I became furious wit' Kinko. Don't get me wrong, I wanted to rip Ra-Ra's heart out. I wanted to kill both those bastards. We did the crimes, so why did others have to suffer? Des was about to do her thang. She had a son. She had my son, and now she was lying dead in my arms. I shook her, wishing I could bring her back to life, but her eyes stayed shut, and her body remained motionless.

"She's gone," Manny said. "Yo, the cops are coming."

I looked up at Manny wit' my eyes stained wit' tears. The devil was in me. I had so much hatred in my heart that I needed to release this energy. I wanted to kill these mutha-fuckas.

I stood up. My hands were covered wit' blood.

"Yo, Rick, cops are on their way, man," Manny repeated.

I ignored him. I went into my office, opened my safe, and retrieved two .45s. I left the club out the back way before the cops even entered.

Life. It's a muthafucka. And to end someone's life is even more of a muthafucka.

I quickly jumped into my ride and sped off before the first cop car turned the corner. I picked up my cell phone and called Kinko.

"What up, Rick?" he asked.

"Yo, we got a fuckin' problem," I told him.

"What is it?"

"I need to meet wit' you right now," I said.

"Ayyite, where at?"

"Somewhere isolated, and come alone. Some shit went down tonight."

"I'll meet you by the J.F.K. Airport," he replied. "You know where."

I knew what spot he was talking about, so I agreed. Before Kinko hung up, he asked, "Everything good, son?"

I didn't answer him. I just hung up on him. I had both .45's placed on the passenger seat in the car. I was gonna kill Kinko tonight, gun him down and leave him for dead. He was an idiot. He couldn't let shit be, so now Des and other innocent victims had to lose their lives because he wanted to be fuckin' greedy and make unnecessary and dangerous moves against the wrong fuckin' man. So Kinko had to die. He was too dangerous to live.

My mind was racing as I drove down Farmers Boulevard. I thought about Mr. Jenkins and the advice he had given me over the years. I needed to call him. I wanted to confess to him and get shit off my mind. Plus, I needed a favor from him.

I picked up my cell phone again and dialed Mr. Jenkins' number. His cell phone rang four times before he picked up.

"Hello?"

"Mr. Jenkins?" I asked.

"Ricky, what's going on? Why are you calling me so early in the morning?"

"She's dead, Mr. Jenkins."

"Who's dead?"

"Des, my son's mother," I shouted.

"What happened?"

"Coward muthafuckas killed her for no reason, that's what happened. They shot up my place, and now . . ." I paused, breaking into tears, "shit gotta get done, Mr. Jenkins. Niggas gotta go."

"Ricky, you're not making any sense. Calm down and talk to me. Don't go out there and do anything stupid."

"It's too late for that. I lied to you. Remember when you

asked if I ever killed a man? Well, I did. I killed a man once. He disrespected me and I gunned him down."

I heard him sigh before saying, "Oh God, Ricky. What is going on with you?"

"I'm sorry I lied to you, but I figured you deserved the truth. I'm hurting, Mr. Jenkins. This shit is too much for me. I'm gonna kill these niggas."

"Ricky, meet me at my home," Mr. Jenkins suggested.

"Mr. Jenkins, don't care for me anymore. It's too fuckin' late for me. I thank you for all you done for me, but tonight belongs to the devil."

"Are you crazy, boy? Stop talking that nonsense. I can help you."

"Nah, Mr. Jenkins, I can't be helped. I can't help nobody. Everything I touch turns into shit."

"There's always a chance."

"Man, fuck a chance! Des died in my arms tonight. She died! First my father, then Des. My fuckin' mother abandoned me when I was young. Shit ain't right."

"Ricky, I'm getting dressed so I can meet you somewhere," he said.

"No, you stay away from me. I'm poison to everyone around me. I do no good. You're a good man, Mr. Jenkins. You don't need to be in my life. I'll just fuck yours up."

"Ricky, please, I'm begging you, as your friend, meet me somewhere and we'll talk."

"Ain't no more talking, Mr. Jenkins. I'm done wit' talking. I need a favor from you."

"Favor? Come to my home and we'll talk. I'll help you get through this madness."

I ignored his pleas to come to his home and returned wit', "My son, Mr. Jenkins. I want you to look after him for me. I want my son to be raised right. I don't want him growing up around the madness I grew up wit'. I want him to have you in his life. I want my son to be free from this shit. Please, Mr. Jenkins. He's a sweet kid. Take care of him for me. His name is Raheem Johnson and he lives out in Brooklyn, over on Flatbush Avenue. You can help him more than you can help me."

"I'll do what I can," Mr. Jenkins said.

"Promise me you'll look after him. Promise me that."

"I promise, Ricky."

"Thank you again, Mr. Jenkins, for everything you've done for me. But some men weren't meant to ever change. I'm sorry."

I hung up and sped off to the airport. It's fucked up how twisted and deadly this game could become. In this game, your best friend could become an enemy within the blink of an eye. Your family could be destroyed, innocence became lost, your freedom could be taken away from you so quickly, and your soul ripped away from you so easily. There's no integrity, no respect, and no dignity anymore—just greed and death.

I made it to the spot where Kinko suggested. It was a remote area mostly surrounded by marsh. The planes flew over on their way to the landing strip connecting to the airport. I was ready to accept my fate, even my death, for the choices and mistakes I'd made in this lifetime. I wasn't afraid to die. Fuck that. Maybe it was for the best that one of us departed this earth.

I pulled up and put my car in park. It was dark out there, and Kinko wasn't around yet. I got out of the car, concealed one of the .45s in the waistband of my jeans, and leaned against the car gazing around the area.

The loud roaring sound of what sounded like a 767 flew over my head. I looked up at the plane and wished that I could have been on a plane somewhere. I wanted to leave and travel far off to some island. But that was a fantasy. Niggas like me didn't have fairy tale endings. We didn't live happily-ever-after. We didn't live happy most of our lives. I lived in reality, where the truth was. In this game ninety percent of the time we either got locked away or carried away in a body bag. And I knew that my fate was no different. I knew I couldn't change the outcome. Tonight it was gonna be one of two things: I would die or Kinko would die.

Ten minutes after my arrival I saw headlights coming in my direction. I knew it was him, so I stood up and looked alert wit' my eyes never leaving his car.

His BMW approached, and my eyes squinted because his headlights were so bright. I put my hand up and over my eyes, trying to see if Kinko had come alone like I asked him to. My heart started to beat a little faster. I was kinda nervous about this meeting. I thought about how it was going to play out.

The car stopped and the lights went off, and that's when I noticed two more silhouettes sitting in the car wit' Kinko. Fuck him. I told him to come alone. Kinko stepped out first, and then Lil' Ra and Banks followed. They all stepped out of his BMW looking tight faced and scowling at me.

"Ricky, what's up, nigga? Why you call us way out here for?" Kinko asked, his actions were very suspicious, and I knew we both didn't trust each other.

"Shit is over, Kinko," I shouted. We were standing about thirty feet apart. "We got hit hard."

"Yeah, I know. Niggas shot up the club," he said, approaching me wit' Lil' Ra and Banks following right behind him.

"I told you not to fuck wit' Ra-Ra, nigga. You fucked up," I shouted. I had my hand near the gun just in case.

"Same ol' Ricky, always scared to make moves. That's why you'll never be big in dis here game. You're weak. Too weak, Ricky. I need strong and bout it niggas by my side, not you," he said, sneering at me. "Here you are worrying about Ra-Ra when I put a bullet in dat nigga's head two days ago." He chuckled.

"What?" I was confused.

"I shot up da club, nigga!" he said to me, and then added, "I wanted to get rid of your bitch ass!"

After hearing those chilling words and seeing the look on all of their faces, I took quick action. I gripped my .45 and opened fire. But I was outgunned and definitely outnumbered. I took cover behind my car and heard the bullets puncturing my Jaguar.

"You're right, Ricky!" Kinko screamed. "It's definitely over for you, nigga!"

I stood up and fired multiple shots back. I opened the passenger door and grabbed the second loaded gun.

"Fuck you, nigga," I yelled.

"Fuck you! I'm tired of your bitch ass!" Kinko yelled back.

I lay low behind my car, wondering why these niggas didn't just run up on me. They had the advantage. I gripped both .45s in my hand.

"Ricky, it ain't personal. It's just business," Kinko said. "You were never cut out for this game. I tried to put you down, but some niggas are just too fuckin' soft for this. We had a time, but you gotta die tonight, nigga."

I stayed crouched behind my car and heard the gunshots riddling the body of my car. I started to breathe heavy.

"C'mon nigga, make it easier on us. Don't let us have to chase you, nigga," Kinko threatened. "It's only gonna get worse."

"Fuck this," I muttered under my breath. I stood up fast and opened fire. Lil' Ra was just a few feet away when I saw him sneaking up on me, but a quick shot to his head dropped him. One down, two to go.

"Lil' Ra, Lil' Ra," I heard Kinko call out.

"Dat nigga dead!" I shouted. "Just like I'm about to do your bitch ass!"

"Fuck you, nigga," Kinko shouted, and then him and Banks open fire on me again.

"You a snake and a snitch, muthafucka!" I shouted. "You snitched me out!"

"Hey, a nigga had to do what he had to do," Kinko said. "It was either me or you. And it damn sure wasn't going to be me. But you only did four years, nigga. What you beefing for?"

We gotta die sometime, right, I thought. I had a good run. I started to think about Danielle and Des, and then I became fueled wit' rage thinking about how Des was killed.

Another plane flew over our heads. The loud roaring engines were deafening, but it gave me a distraction. *Fuck it.* I gripped both guns tightly, removed myself from behind my car, and opened fire on Kinko and Banks.

TWENTY.

I was weak, bleeding badly, and trying to navigate my way through the streets of Queens. I had blood all over my front seats, and I was struggling to keep my eyes open. One of the guns was resting on my lap, and it was empty. The two gunshot wounds I suffered were burning and hurting like hell. I got shot once in my lower abdomen and another bullet struck me in my shoulder. I fucked up. I thought Kinko was dead. I saw him and Banks fall before they struck me wit' two shots. They gotta be dead. They didn't deserve to live.

I was becoming delirious and more fatigued wit' every passing minute. *Why da fuck was I driving?* I saw the green become yellow, and the yellow become red, but I didn't stop. I blew right through the light. I heard the sound of a loud horn blowing at me, but I didn't stop. I had no idea where I was driving. I just wanted to escape the madness I'd been living in.

My life was over, so why stop? I continued to drive and barely noticed the blue and red light flashing in my rearview mirror. It had to be po-po, but I didn't stop. My mind told me, *try to escape*. But to where?

Des was dead, people's lives were ruined, so why stop? Danielle and the baby could do without me. I was poison to her, and it would be the best thing for them if I was outta their lives. Maybe she'd meet some guy who would treat her better. I was a complete fuck-up. I belonged to the streets, not her. The streets had my heart, and now these same streets were tearing me apart and breaking my heart. This king's reign was finally over. I felt my soul being ripped away from me. I had success, and never realized it till it was too late. Mr. Jenkins and Danielle, they were my wealth and my fortune. But I was too stupid to see it and let niggas like Kinko manipulate my mind into thinking that money was the key to happiness. But it wasn't.

The flashing police lights came closer, indicating for me to pull over. I didn't. I kept going. My grip around the steering wheel became weaker and my body started to feel numb. Breathing was becoming more difficult wit' each passing second.

Life was a muthafucka.

I closed my eyes for a quick second. When I opened them, I saw myself crashing into an oncoming car doing about forty-five MPH. Flatline.

EPILOGUE.

Mr. Jenkins stared out his bedroom window with his heart saddened. It was ten after midnight, and he couldn't sleep. He had watched the ten o'clock news and it was very disturbing to him. One of his students was dead. Ricky led the police in a five to six block chase in Queens, New York, and then crashed into an oncoming car. Ricky Johnson was pronounced dead on the scene. When Mr. Jenkins heard the news, he felt pain and hurt. He knew he had failed.

"Baby," his wife called out to him, rising up from her position. "Come to bed. It's getting late."

Mr. Jenkins continued to stare out his bedroom window with a few tears trickling down his face. "In a minute, Janet. I'm just thinking," he said to her.

Janet moved toward him, and then embraced him by putting her arms around her distraught husband. She knew and understood his relationship with Ricky. She met the boy a handful of times and liked him. But she understood too, that you can't help everybody.

"You tried with him, Richard, you did. You gave him love and respect. You were another father to him. You were there for him from the beginning. But don't blame yourself for his death. He chose his way."

"But it feels like I've lost another son. It feels like Jimmy all over again. We keep losing our young black men to drugs, prison, and violence. It's got to stop one day, baby. I thought I could help Ricky. Where did I go wrong?" he cried out.

Janet hugged her husband tighter and then said, "You can still help him, by not giving up, baby. You got to still go out there and lead and guide our young children. Don't let Ricky's death deter you from doing what's right in the world."

Mr. Jenkins turned to his wife and said, "You know he had a son. And before he died, he'd asked me to do him a favor."

"Like what?" she asked.

"He wanted you and me to raise his son. He wanted us to give him the type of home he never had growing up. The mother was killed in that club shooting the other night."

"You want to bring his boy into our lives?" she asked.

"Yes, Janet. I want to give this young man a fresh start at life. How do you feel about us adopting his child?

"I'm for it."

He smiled, then hugged and kissed his wife. "I love you, Janet."

"I love you too, Richard. You're a good husband, and a wonderful man. We can't help everybody, but you gave your best with that boy, and to me, you didn't fail with him. Failure is not trying to help him at all. Failure is watching him doing wrong and not saying or trying to guide him. You tried guiding him. You gave him direction, but he chose his own way. You're a winner. For years, I've watched you guide and teach young adults, Richard. You helped them with scholarships, their education, and leaving the streets alone. You've helped them with problems at home, and so many other things that you are far from a failure. If there were more men like you in the world, then there wouldn't probably be so many black men in jail or in the streets."

Richard smiled. His wife always was a pick-me-up. She was his queen. She made him a great king and a leader.

"I love you, Janet."

"I know, baby, I love you, too, now come to bed," she said.

Richard's heart was at ease for that night. Next week, he and his wife would begin the procedure in adopting Raheem Johnson. His wife was right, it wasn't over. Raising Raheem would be a new start for them both.

Danielle sat crying on her living room floor after she heard the news about her man's death. It was hard to believe and swallow. First her cousin Gwen, and then Ricky. For that brief second, she thought about taking her own life and her baby's. Ricky came into her life so suddenly, and she loved him so much in the seven, eight months they knew each other. She cried and asked, "Why me?"

Doctors told her that she was having a boy. Danielle thought she was alone in raising her son. She was scared and lost. She still had to finish school, and now without Ricky in her life, she thought about how she was going to be able to support herself, go to school, and raise her unborn son. She threw a quick tantrum in her apartment, throwing dishes and glasses against the wall, and tearing up furniture.

"WHY. . . . NO. . . . PLEASE, WHY ME? OHMIGOD . . . I HATE THIS . . . WHY . . . I HATE THIS!!" she shrieked.

She then collapsed on her floor, sobbing in tears. She stared at a picture of her and Ricky on the coffee table, and it brought more tears to her eyes and pain to her heart. Danielle lay on her floor for an hour, not caring to get up.

She wanted to lay there and slowly die. She heard the phone ring, but she didn't bother to pick up. Five minutes later, it rang again, but, again, she let it ring. The caller refused to give up, and the phone kept ringing back to back for the next half-hour.

Frustrated, Danielle picked up her phone and shouted, "Hello?"

"Danielle," Mr. Jenkins said. "It's Mr. Jenkins."

"Yes," Danielle replied, her voice a little calmer.

"How are you holding up?" he asked.

Danielle was quiet over the phone, her teary eyes stared at the picture of her and Ricky. "I'm . . . I'm okay Mr. Jenkins," she lied.

"Danielle, I know it's hard, but you are not alone in this. Please remember that. I'm always here for you and the baby. Ricky may be gone, but he lives on through his son. I know it's hard with school, money, and the baby, so if you need us, do not hesitate to call me or my wife. You understand?"

"Yes, I understand, Mr. Jenkins," she said. A faint smile came to her.

"My wife and I want you to come over for dinner this Sunday."

"Sunday?"

"Yes, you are family to us, Danielle, And we need to talk."

"Thank you. I will definitely make it."

"We're gonna take care of you, Danielle. You are not forgotten," he said.

They talked for forty minutes, and after the conversation ended, Danielle felt a whole lot better. She took a seat on her couch, picked up the picture of her and Ricky, and softly said, "I love you, Ricky."

She would never know the truth about Ricky and her

cousin, or his affair with Des. That would forever be in the dark. Ricky took his secrets to his grave.

A young black male with multiple gunshot wounds was rushed into the emergency room at Jamaica Hospital. Survival for him looked bleak. Nurses and doctors rushed him into the O.R., where they would begin to perform hours of surgery on him.

Two hours later, he was in stable condition, but still being closely monitored. He lay in his hospital room with about three I.V's in his arms. He was lucky; they removed one out of the two bullets that were embedded into his chest.

"He'll make it," the doctor told the shift nurse. "Does he have any family?"

"No one that I know of," she said.

Jamal Tyler, A.K.A Kinko, would survive tonight.

ABOUT THE AUTHOR.

Erick S. Gray, author of the urban sexomedy *BOOTYCALL,* has been writing well thought out plots to keep the reader interested with every turn of the page.

This entrepreneur is also the owner/founder of Triple G publishing and is making moves in other markets as well.

Born and raised in the south side of Jamaica, Queens, this 28 year-old young, gifted author has brought himself out on a high note with his first endeavor. He continues bringing you good stories as he shows in his collaboration with Mark Anthony and Anthony Whyte, *Streets of New York Volumes 1 and 2,* and his novels *Ghetto Heaven* and *Money, Power, Respect.* He is also the author of *Naughty Girls* and *It's Like Candy.*

Erick S. Gray is showing that young African-American males don't all fall into the same categories of drug dealer/thief/statistic. His future is filled with the promise of more intriguing and diverse stories for the masses to digest.

"Don't judge the book by its cover!"

NOW AVAILABLE FROM

Q-BORO
B O O K S

NYMPHO
$14.95
ISBN 1933967102

How will signing up to live a promiscuous double-life destroy everything that's at stake in the lives of two close couples? Take a journey into Leslie's secret world and prepare for a twisted, erotic experience.

FREAK IN THE SHEETS
$14.95
ISBN 1933967196

Ready to break out of the humdrum of their lives, Raquelle and Layla decide to put their knowledge of sexuality and business together and open up a freak school, teaching men and women how to please their lovers beyond belief while enjoying themselves in the process.

However, Raquelle and Layla must learn some important lessons when it comes to being a lady in the street and a freak in the sheets.

LIAR, LIAR
$14.95
ISBN 1933967110

Stormy calls off her wedding to Camden when she learns he's cheating with a male church member. However, after being convinced that Camden has been delivered from his demons, she proceeds with the wedding.

Will Stormy and Camden survive scandal, lies and deceit?

HEAVEN SENT
$14.95
ISBN 1933967188

Eve is a recovering drug addict who has no intentions of staying clean until she meets Reverend Washington, a newly widowed man with three children. Secrets are uncovered that threaten Eve's new life with her new family and has everyone asking if Eve was *Heaven Sent.*

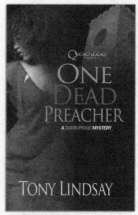

COMING SOON FROM
Q-BORO
BOOKS

MARCH 2008
1-933967-39-0